ALL THE NICE GIRLS

There comes a time in every bachelor naval
officer's life when he starts to lean a bit towards
the champagne and the confetti. He need only
lean a little way – but there's always a wench on
the spot to take him up on it.

This is a hard fact of life learnt by Lieutenant
Dagwood Jones, R.N., when H.M.S. *Seahorse*, the
Navy's latest submarine, arrives at a shipyard in
the fine old mercantile city of Oozemouth for a
long refit.

Dagwood is determined not to take a wife, but
the ladies of Oozemouth have other ideas – and
they are not alone. Controlling events with a fine
Greek hand is the genial but Machiavellian figure
of the Admiralty Liaison Officer in Oozemouth,
Commander Robert Bollinger Badger, D.S.C.,
R.N., otherwise known as The Artful Bodger.
Once The Artful Bodger begins to take an interest
in his affairs, Dagwood is damned – to matrimony.

All the Nice Girls

John Winton

Maritime Books

First published by
MICHAEL JOSEPH LTD
26 *Bloomsbury Street*
*London, W.C.*1
1964

© *copyright 1964 by John Winton*

Reprinted 2004 by
MARITIME BOOKS
Lodge Hill
Liskeard
Cornwall, PL14 4EL

I

'Not often we get a submarine up here,' said the Oozemouth River Pilot, conversationally. The rain streamed off the back of his cap.

'Not often we come up here,' replied Lieutenant Gavin Doyle, the Navigating Officer, brusquely. The rain had penetrated the towel round his neck and was now soaking under his oilskin and into his shirt and vest.

'Going to be here long?'

'About a year, I expect.'

'A year!' The River Pilot grimaced. 'Not often we get one for that long.'

'Not often we send one here for refit.'

'Refit? At Harvey McNichol and Drummond's?'

'That's right.' If there was one thing Gavin Doyle disliked more than navigating an industrial river in freezing rain, it was having to do it with a chatty Pilot. Still, Gavin consoled himself, this was the last time. This time tomorrow he would be on leave in London and then good-bye rain, good-bye watch-keeping, good-bye *Seahorse*. A roseate vision of inviting arms, seductively curved lips and warm comfortable bosoms fleeted across Gavin's mind.

The rain increased in a vicious gust, driving horizontally into the faces of the men on the submarine's bridge. Gavin and the River Pilot ducked and remained with their heads bowed, letting the water run off their noses.

Behind them, the Captain still stood bolt upright. He had a megaphone at his face, held reversed so that the wide end covered his face and he could look out through the narrow end into rain which would otherwise have blinded him. It was a resourceful little trick and it was typical of the man. The Captain had a reputation as one of the wiliest officers in the Submarine Service; he had been selected to go to America for nuclear submarine training and he was leaving the ship that night. This was now for him a moment of farewell. He was handling his ship, H.M.S. *Seahorse,* for the last time, bringing her into refit at the end of her commission, and reflecting as he did so how curious it was that the ends of commissions in H.M. Ships, like babies' births and remote cousins' weddings, always took place in disgusting weather.

The rain eased for short periods, before lashing the submarine's bridge again with fresh violence. During one of the lulls, the Captain was able to lower his megaphone.

'Mr Gillespie,' he said, 'I take it that's the Great Iron Bridge I can see up there?'

'Aye, that's it.' There was a note of pride in the River Pilot's voice. The Great Iron Bridge was the City of Oozemouth's main landmark and the symbol of her civic pride. Bristol might have the Clifton Bridge, London her Tower, Liverpool her Liver Birds which flap their wings when a virgin passes by – Oozemouth had the Great Iron Bridge, a hundred years old and a monument to its creator, the incomparable Brunel.

'What's that white post fine on the port bow, looking like a spar buoy?' The Captain retreated behind his megaphone again.

'That's the beacon for Harvey McNichol and Drummond, Captain. You'll leave that to port and then turn hard to port for the entrance. You'll need to watch the tide just at the entrance, Captain. The current's always ebbing past the entrance, even when the tide's flooding. It's just slack water now, but you'll find it ebbing past the entrance.'

An easterly wind whipped the dun brown waters of the estuary, raising a short swell which was flattened and speckled by the sweeping rain. Even on a fine summer's day the shoreline of Oozemouth was an unlovely prospect; on a dark February morning with visibility interrupted by drenching squalls the waterfront had taken on that appearance of aggressive squalor common to all industrial rivers. The waterfront was both the city's blight and its strength. Although it chilled an onlooker's heart to realise that man had actually laboured to create such an appearance, the city's prosperity still largely depended upon those seven miles of docks, wharves, building slips, puddled roads, tangled railway sidings and heaps of coal tumbled haphazardly together just as they had grown under a skyline of cranes, elevators and tall chimneys.

Behind the Captain, Wilfred Garnham, the First Lieutenant, stooped and shook the rain off the rim of his oilskin hood. For him too, this was a moment of farewell, of nostalgia. This was his last hour on *Seahorse's* bridge as First Lieutenant. He would be leaving the ship that night to join the training course for future submarine captains. The next time he stood on a submarine bridge in an executive capacity he hoped it would be as captain. In any case, there was no alternative; if he failed the course, he would never go to sea in a submarine again except as a spectator.

The fourth, and last, occupant of the bridge was the Leading Signalman. He was also leaving the ship that day and was glad of it. The Signalman was a bitter man, like all of his calling. (No branch of the Navy develops a more embittered view of life or a more cynical temperament than the Communications Branch.) The Leading Signalman had long ago formed his own final opinion of Oozemouth and its river.

'Like a wet afternoon in a bloody Welsh graveyard,' he told himself. 'With no cigarettes.'

The submarine rounded the beacon and headed towards the biggest cranes and the highest and dirtiest buildings on the waterfront, where an enormous sign read: 'HARVEY McNICHOL & DRUMMOND (SHIPBUILDING &

ENGINEERING) CO. LTD.'. Two very much smaller notices, one on either side of the basin entrance, read: 'DEAD SLOW.'

'I hope that's not an omen for the refit,' said the Captain, when he saw them.

As the River Pilot had warned, it was a tricky approach. The Captain had to strike a nice balance between wind and tide to avoid hitting the downstream knuckle of the opening. The Captain was particularly anxious not to make a mistake. After handling the ship for eighteen months without colliding with anything, it would be a pity if he damaged her now. The Captain drove his submarine as cautiously as a man driving his car to the garage to sell it.

His caution was almost in itself an error and there was one moment of suspense when the Captain ordered full astern (while the dockside magically cleared of spectators) before the submarine slid quietly through the entrance and into the calm of the basin where she was secured by wires from the dockside. Behind her, the caisson started to move across the opening and seal her off from the tidal estuary. As the first wire was winched in, the Captain felt a great weight drop from his shoulders.

The Leading Signalman's opportunity was now at hand. It was his duty to report to the Captain the movements of the propellers while the ship was manoeuvring. For two years the Signalman had stood on the bridge, in summer and winter, rain or fine, through all the comedies and tragedies of entering and leaving harbour, and had solemnly recited his own interpretations of the water washing to and fro at the stern. It had always been the Signalman's secret conviction that nobody had taken notice of anything he had ever said. The Signalman had often promised himself that one day he would put his conviction to the test. That day had now come to pass.

'Port and starboard screws dropped right off, sir,' he reported, in his most neutral, official tone of voice.

8

'Very good,' said the Captain, mechanically.

The Signalman choked on a gasp of glee and hugged himself exultantly. '*Got'im!*'

'Signalman,' said the Captain.

'Sir.'

'I know you've been *bursting* to say something like that the whole commission. Let me assure you, I do notice what you say even though I may sometimes forget to acknowledge it. Thank you for your assistance during the last eighteen months.'

The Signalman blushed remorsefully and mumbled to himself.

A man in a brown overcoat and a bowler hat had climbed on board from a small rowing boat. 'Good morning, Captain. Will you stop your shafts now, please? We'll take the ship from here.'

'Here you are, Signalman,' said the Captain. 'Here's your chance to shine. There's the voicepipe. Tell the control room, finished with main motors and steering.'

Still blushing, the Signalman passed the order, whereupon a great surging cheer came up the voicepipe.

The Captain grinned. 'No sentimental nonsense about the end of *this* commission, anyway,' he said.

The man in the bowler hat climbed on top of the bridge and began to wave his arms, shout and blow short blasts on a whistle. In obedience to the bowler-hatted man's signals the wires rose and dipped as the submarine was warped into the centre of the basin. The Captain looked on with the superfluous, unemployed feeling of a captain whose ship is being handled by others.

The dockside of Harvey McNichol & Drummond had a devastated, almost lunar, appearance. Close to the jetty's edge there were several corrugated iron sheds which looked as though they had been hastily assembled to meet some long-past emergency and never pulled down again. Underneath the cranes and between the railway tracks lay the debris of

9

years – baulks of timber, strangely contorted pieces of rusting metal, lengths of corroded anchor chain and a stack of rusty acetylene bottles. A small locomotive, apparently abandoned, was hissing and blowing steam between its wheels. Groups of workmen gathered listlessly to watch *Seahorse* come alongside. The dockyard looked like the camp of several hundred displaced persons who had squatters' rights in a junk yard.

As *Seahorse* reached a position in the centre of the basin, a hooter blew over the rooftops. The sound had no significance for the Captain but it had a remarkable effect upon Harvey McNichol & Drummond. The man in the bowler hat pocketed his whistle, nodded to the Captain, climbed into his boat and pulled for the dockside. The men who had been handling the wires on the winches dropped the bights and doubled away. Simultaneously, from every doorway, every alley, every nook and crevice of the yard, men poured out and began to run round a corner and out of sight. More men leaped down from cranes and from the backs of lorries to join the throng. Within a minute the side of the basin was a moving mass of men. Within another minute the same dockside was deserted, frozen still, as though under an enchantment. The Captain, Wilfred and Gavin looked about them in bewilderment.

'Now what?' said the Captain.

'That was the nine o'clock hooter, Captain,' said the River Pilot.

'What about it?'

'They stop work, Captain. It's the tea-break.'

'But they can't leave us here!'

'They have, Captain.'

It was quite true. The Captain looked disbelievingly along the jetty. The only sign of movement came from a group of three men who had been sheltering from the rain under an overhanging shed roof. Two of the men wore grey raincoats and trilby hats. The third wore a blue naval raincoat and, above a wide grin, the uniform cap and gold braid of a

Commander. The Captain hailed him.

'Hello Bodger!'

'Hello Broody,' said the grinning Commander. 'How's yourself?'

'Bloody awful. Look Bodger, what's happening here?'

'You'll have to stay where you are for the moment.'

'Why?'

'It's the tea-break, old man.'

'So what?'

'So they won't work during the tea-break. There's a no overtime ban on!'

'We can do the rest ourselves, can't we?'

The two civilians beside The Bodger each took a sharp step backwards, as though Broody had made an indecent suggestion.

'Can't do that, old boy. The unions!'

'Well, can we at least put the Pilot ashore?'

'Yes, that's all right.'

'I'm very grateful to you, Bodger.'

'Don't mention it.'

'What time will they be back?'

'A quarter past nine.'

'Have we just got to stay here doing nothing while they have their tea?' said Broody, incredulously.

'I'm afraid so.'

'You're not serious, Bodger.'

'I am. Think yourself lucky this isn't the annual holiday. You'd have been stuck where you are for a fortnight!'

'Good God!'

'See you in fifteen minutes' time, Broody.'

Not trusting himself to say another word, Broody left the bridge and climbed down into the control room, where he met interrogative looks from the control room watch below.

'Cox'n.'

'Sir?'

'Enter in the log : Secured by four wires in the middle of Harvey McNichol and Drummond Main Basin while the British Workman has his tea-break.'

'Aye aye sir.'

2

In the wardroom, *Seahorse's* two technical officers had over-heard the outcries from bridge and control room and were awaiting the Captain's arrival with the liveliest anticipation.

Ollie Frith, the Engineer Officer, was a burly man, pre-maturely bald, who had the sort of beaming *bonhomie* normally associated with the landlords of successful hotels. He had been promoted from a submarine artificer and had served in submarines, as rating and officer, for more than fifteen years. Ollie's uniform was always the oldest in the wardroom, his buttons the greenest and his gold lace the most tattered. If a pair of mouldering sea-going shoes were discovered hidden behind a pipe two minutes before an Admiral was expected they always belonged to Ollie. His cap could always be distinguished from a long row of others outside the depot-ship wardroom by its khaki-coloured cap cover. Ollie had a tendency to entertain the wives of senior officers with his most Rabelaisian anecdotes and Broody had sometimes suspected that he drank too much, though he had carefully avoided putting his suspicions to the test. Ollie might not have been thought a very prepossessing member of a submarine wardroom but he had one quality, one supreme gift, worth more than gold or rubies. If Ollie announced that the ship would be ready for sea by a certain time then the ship was ready. Against all probability, in the face of the blackest of outlooks, the most acute shortage of spare gear or the most pressing demands of time, if Ollie said he would be ready, it was so. Broody could go to the Submarine Staff Office and confidently announce, amidst general disbelief, that he would be ready. Similarly, on the rare occasions when Ollie admitted that he could not finish in time, Broody had learned that it was fruitless to debate the point. No matter how much the workforce was augmented, no matter what the pressure from above to get the submarine to sea, if Ollie said he would not be ready then it was so; as Broody said, it was like having someone who could always tell you whether a horse would win or not.

Dagwood Jones, the Electrical Officer, had an altogether different personality. He was a small, dark-haired, ferret-faced young man whom a degree at Cambridge had left unusually erudite for a naval officer. He often gave Broody the impression that he was only present in *Seahorse's* ward-room in order to raise it from the social level of an enclosed fish-and-chip shop. Dagwood was even more tactless with senior officers than was Ollie with their wives. Broody had even considered banning Dagwood from the wardroom when Admirals were present; his heart still bore the scar of the occasion when Dagwood had informed an audience of three Admirals, one of them the Director of Torpedo Research, that the best torpedo the Navy had was still the original Whitehead, designed at the turn of the century.

The Steward poured the Captain a large precautionary cup of hot black coffee while he unwrapped his wet clothes. Ollie and Dagwood could tell, by the expression of repressed volcanic activity on his face, that Broody was raising steam for an explosion.

'Actually,' he said mildly, at last, 'this just illustrates some-thing I was going to tell you about anyway. You've heard these stories about the British Workman. Here, you're in one of his strongholds, the ship-building industry. The medieval ship-building industry. In the industrial relations sense, you're now in the dark ages. I know, because I once joined a boat in this yard on commissioning. That was during the war but I'm told things haven't changed very much. This place is run on feudal lines. A skilled man can work here for forty years and still get his cards on a Friday night just as if he was a casual hop-picker. And that goes for everybody. Unless you had the good fortune to be born a Harvey, a McNichol or a Drummond or had the good sense to marry a Harvey, a McNichol or a Drummond you're about as secure in your job in this place as one of Haroun Al Raschid's viziers. Once you come through the dockyard gate you're back in the Middle Ages. You'll see men doing extremely skilful work by Gothic lighting in dark caverns built before the Crimean War using tools designed when Leonardo da Vinci was a lad. By the way, guess who I saw waiting on the jetty just now? The Artful Bodger himself!'

'The Bodger!' cried Dagwood. 'What's he doing here?'

'Come to visit the scene of his former triumphs, I expect,' said Ollie.

'Perhaps he's taken over Harvey McNichol and Drummond's?'

Broody laughed. 'I wouldn't put it past him. Anyway, we'll get the whole story when the British Workman's finished his tea and *condescends* to let us get alongside.'

At a quarter past nine the hooter blew again, the yard was repopulated, the man in the bowler hat resumed his whistle and his stance on the bridge, and *Seahorse* was warped in. On the dockside a race of stocky, gnome-like men, all dressed in buff fearnought jackets and shapeless cloth caps and all addressed as 'Wack,' sprang up as though they had been sown in the concrete and began to swarm around *Seahorse's* wires, jabbering amongst themselves in their own private chattering dialect. ' . . . Ey Wack, gie'us a hand, Wack . . . Shove us that line, Wack . . . Ey *Wacker,* wheer d'ye want yer breasts, Wack?'

When Broody descended from the bridge for the second time that morning and for the last time that commission, the two civilians and The Bodger were already sitting in the wardroom, the former wearing expressions of slightly abashed shyness on finding themselves in unfamiliar surroundings

15

and the latter looking about him with an air of close, proprietary interest.

'The old place hasn't changed a bit, Broody,' said The Bodger.

'Glad to hear it,' said Broody. 'I half expected you to shout out loud that I'd let the boat go to rack and ruin. But if you'll pardon my curiosity, Bodger, what on earth are you doing here? Not that I'm not delighted to see you of course . . .'

The Bodger chuckled. 'You're now looking at the Admiralty Liaison Officer for the City of Oozemouth. How about that!'

'Hell's teeth,' said Broody.

'Quite so. Mind you I've only been here a couple of weeks. My wife and I thought we could just do with a quiet year or two ashore, so when I was offered the job I took it. I don't know how long I'll last in it, of course.'

Commander Robert Bollinger Badger, D.S.C., R.N., known universally as The Artful Bodger, was a man of some presence. He had a shock of black hair, now going grey at the sides, and a ruddy jovial face. The Bodger had had a varied service career, the vicissitudes of his life being largely caused by his knack of speaking honestly to the wrong person. Nevertheless, The Bodger had always been followed by miraculous luck, he had a large number of friends who came unexpectedly to his assistance, and an unsuspected (except by those who knew him) talent for turning circumstances to his own profit (a talent which the malicious might have called low cunning, but which he himself described as 'kicking for touch when under pressure'). He was rightly called The Artful Bodger and he was indestructible. Whatever crises blew up in his life, whatever cataclysms shook his world, sooner or later The Bodger bobbed up again, hopefully, as though he expected at any minute to be offered a drink. He too was a submariner and had indeed been *Seahorse's* first captain, taking her to sea for the first six months of her commission until he was (by an unlikely series of circumstances) promoted and relieved by Broody.

'Broody, let me introduce Mr Tybalt, one of the overseers here.'

Mr Tybalt rose and shook Broody's hand. He was a dark man with a decisive lantern jaw, hollow but sun-tanned cheeks, and shrewd blue eyes with tiny crows' feet at their corners. He was wearing an excellently-made dark grey suit, a Bengal-stripe shirt and an R.N.V.R. tie. He looked like a consumptive but successful wild fowler. 'I'm what's laughingly called the Admiralty Constructor Overseer here,' he said. 'This is Mr Day, Ship Manager for *Seahorse* on the firm's side of the fence. Known as Happy.'

Happy Day wrung Broody's hand warmly. He was a fat, round, red-cheeked man with white hair cropped close to his head. 'Very pleased to meet you, Commander,' he said.

'*Well*,' said Broody. 'That was a fine welcome you gave us this morning!'

Mr Tybalt showed the mettle of his pasture at once. 'What did you expect,' he replied, sharply, 'cherubim and seraphim?'

'Well no, not exactly,' said Broody, a little taken aback. 'It was just a little humiliating to be left out there in the middle of the basin while everyone else pushed off. It gave us the feeling nobody loved us.'

Happy Day hastened to reassure Broody on behalf of his firm. 'You're very welcome here, Commander, you can be sure of that. We only had three weeks' warning that you were coming here for refit.'

'I wish you'd given *us* the tip,' said Gavin, the Navigating Officer. 'We didn't know we were coming here until we got our sailing signal. We thought we were going to Chatham.'

'The Chief Stoker's brought all his tropical uniform with him, sir,' said Dagwood. 'He heard a buzz we were going to Singapore.'

'Now that you are here,' said Mr Tybalt, 'Mr Day and I have worked out a very rough skeleton programme for your

refit. I've brought some copies with me for you to look at.'
Mr Tybalt distributed some sheets of typed paper. 'You must
understand that this was all rather sprung on us and we are
a bit inexperienced at it. This will be the first submarine
refit we've done in this yard for a very long time. Mr Day
can explain this better than I can.'

Happy Day was only too glad to have a chance to justify
his firm. 'This won't be the first submarine we've handled,
not by a long chalk,' he said, eagerly. 'We used to build them
here, as you know. We built twenty or thirty during the war.
But we got no more orders at all once the war ended. So we
broke up our submarine working gangs, got rid of our draw-
ings and generally finished with our submarine facilities. We
use the submarine dock for tugs and dredgers now. But we're
glad to have one back again, Commander. A lot of my staff
have volunteered to go back to the submarine section . . .'

'They get more money for working in submarines, don't
they, Happy?' Mr Tybalt enquired innocently.

'Now Frank, you know it's not that! Though I'll not deny
we're glad of the work. The job's come up suddenly, that's
true, but it'll not make a ha'porth of difference to your refit
in the long run, Commander, I can assure you of that.'

'I'm sure it won't,' said Broody.

'When you think of it,' said The Bodger, 'it does seem a
little strange them sending you here out of the blue like this.
I suppose Their Lordships don't want to have all their eggs
in a few baskets. It's too easy to let a few yards have all the
business. They get better at it, they can train up their staff,
buy special machinery and so on. But what if anything
happens to those firms or you have to double your output
suddenly in wartime, where are you? Besides, it's a good thing
to spread it around a bit. Keeps them all on their toes.'

'Very probably,' said Mr Tybalt. 'To get back to the programme, the firm accept responsibility for the custody of the
submarine from this afternoon. I imagine most of your ship's
company won't be staying long?'

Wilfred, the First Lieutenant, nodded. 'Most of them are catching the seven o'clock train south tonight, sir.'

'And that will leave you with a hard core, to finish destoring, stand by during the refit, and make up the nucleus of the next commission?'

'That's right, sir.'

Broody and The Bodger began to look at Mr Tybalt with a good deal more respect. The man seemed to have a much better grip of the situation than they had expected. For someone who had never refitted a submarine before and who had suddenly had one thrust upon him, Mr Tybalt was doing very well.

As though he had read their thoughts, Mr Tybalt said: 'You're probably wondering how I come to be so well up in all this, having just said the whole thing caught us by surprise. The answer is that I rang up a chum of mine who's doing this same job at Birkenhead and he gave me all the dope.'

'*Ah,*' said The Bodger. 'That's better than cherubim and seraphim, anyway.'

'Will you be at the refit conference tomorrow?' Mr Tybalt asked The Bodger. He sounded as though he were anxious to meet The Bodger with the gloves off.

'I don't know,' The Bodger said, doubtfully. 'It's nothing to do with me really. I . . .'

'That's a point, Bodger,' said Broody. 'I hope to get the midnight train tonight. Would you like to look out for me at the refit conference?'

'I'd be delighted, Broody! Refit conferences are normally better than the Crazy Gang! I wouldn't miss it for worlds!'

'I hope we shan't disappoint you,' said Mr Tybalt. 'Who will be standing by the refit?'

'The Engineer Officer and the Electrical Officer.'

'Either of you married?'

'I am,' said Ollie.

'I'm not,' said Dagwood. 'And I hope to stay that way.'

19

'I hope you succeed,' said Mr Tybalt dryly. 'Though I ought to warn you the local talent's pretty thick on the ground in these parts.'

'Oh,' said Gavin. As the wardroom's acknowledged lady-killer, he appeared to be disappointed that he was leaving so soon.

Mr Tybalt returned to his programme. 'I've fixed two lighters to take away your surplus oil fuel this afternoon and there are a couple of railway trucks for your stores to go back to Portsmouth. When you've finished loading them, just put a padlock on them and give the keys to me. You've been allocated three offices for your refit crew and two stores for your spare gear. I've also arranged accommodation for three officers for tonight. Is that enough?'

'More than enough, sir,' said Wilfred. 'Gavin and I are off tonight and so's the Captain. That only leaves two.'

'That's all right then. I've got you rooms at the Northern Steam Hotel which is about two hundred yards from the main gate. It's not what you'd call elegant but it'll do until you find something more permanent. How about the sailors?'

'Don't worry about them,' The Bodger said. 'In my experience of sailors you can set them down anywhere and inside half an hour they're fat and laughing with their feet under the table and their own front door keys!'

'That's fine then. Now if you don't mind, I'd like to go through the refit programme with you, in case Mr Day and I have forgotten anything.'

Although he had been given so little time to prepare, Mr Tybalt had already settled dates by which the main items of machinery would have been removed from the submarine and had obtained provisional estimates from the firm on when they would be ready to put them back. He had fixed dates for representatives to attend trials and had arranged for the carriage of torpedoes and the supply of fuel. He had even looked up tidal data on suitable days for sea trials. Mr Tybalt's master plan contained a complete blue-print for the refit, from the initial stripping of portable fittings to the final coat of paint and clean. The Bodger, Broody and the other officers were deeply impressed.

'I congratulate you,' The Bodger said. 'You ought to have been a staff officer.'

Mr Tybalt flushed. 'I'd call that a left-handed compliment. This is how we'd *like* to do it. It's a tight programme and there's absolutely no leeway anywhere. One strike could put the whole thing out. But Mr Day will look after that, eh Happy?'

'It's not up to me, I can tell you,' said Happy Day, bitterly. 'It's up to the bloody Unions.'

A workman pulled the wardroom curtain aside and seemed disconcerted to see the meeting inside.

'What's up, lad?' Mr Day asked.

'I were going to start stripping wardroom, Mr Day.'

'You can do that. We're on our way.'

3

The work of de-storing the ship was already well in hand. The submarine was being systematically gutted. Gangs of sailors carried piles of crockery, boxes of books, bedding, curtains, clocks, barometers and tools out of the submarine and loaded them into the railway trucks. The firm's joiners had already begun to strip out the furnishings and fittings in the living spaces. The interior of the ship, which had reflected and shaped *Seahorse's* personality for two years, was being dismantled piecemeal. It was as though the ship had taken a massive emetic before undergoing a major surgical operation.

Outside the submarine, a widening band of green weed along the hull water-line showed the effects of the work being done by the Chief Stoker and his party of stokers who were pumping all remaining surplus liquids into lighters. This too was a necessary operation before a refit (though it corresponded not so much to an emetic as to an enema).

As every stowage space, locker and corner of the submarine was cleared, articles began to come to light which had long been thought irretrievably lost. Gavin was embarrassed by the return of a sextant box which had been missing for more than a year and which he had testified, over his signature, had been lost overboard one particularly dark and stormy night off Ushant. Ollie discovered an electric hand drill which he swore fiercely had been dropped down an inaccessible bilge one particularly dark and stormy night off Ushant. The Coxswain came across a case of tinned meat which he had long since written off as spoiled by the ship's rolling one particularly dark and stormy night off Ushant. The Chef recovered his favourite knife-sharpener – lost on commissioning day. The Captain was handed his wife's photograph, extracted from behind his cabin desk; the loss of the photograph had caused Broody more anguish and brought him under graver suspicion than any other single event of the commission. A hundred different articles emerged whose loss had been mourned over, denied, or carefully concealed. By six o'clock that evening *Seahorse* was only a wraith of the submarine she had been; she had been reduced to a shell, cold, already filthy, and inhospitable.

Wilfred, Gavin, and most of the ship's company left by the seven o'clock train, some to courses, some to join other submarines immediately and some to embarkation leave; with them went the last of *Seahorse's* corporate spirit. Ollie and Dagwood carried their bags over to the Northern Steam Hotel. Broody, who was not travelling until midnight, joined them for supper.

Mr Tybalt had not over-estimated the Northern Steam Hotel's attractions. Broody and his two remaining officers gloomily drank pints of beer in a bare bar with a tiled floor. Between rounds the barmaid sluiced the floor, and their shoes, with a wet mop. There were no other customers. Afterwards, they ate supper of tomato soup, fried cod and chips, and bread and butter in a barrack-like dining-room next to the bar. They sat at a centre table and were served by a waitress who brought their food as though their presence was a conspiracy to prevent her going home. Four commercial travellers, one in each corner of the room, eyed Broody and his small party covertly from behind their evening newspapers. A moribund fire flickered in a miniature grate. There was no coffee, only tea.

'This is the way it always ends,' Broody observed, moodily. 'Not with a bang but a whimper.' He sipped his tea despairingly, and shuddered. He put the cup down. 'It's no use. I can't drink it. I *cannot* drink tea after dark.'

'It's a sure sign that you're in a barbarian land, sir,' said Dagwood. 'When they give you your evening meal about three hours after lunch.'

'There speaks the bloody Londoner,' said Ollie scornfully. 'West of the White City the dark continent begins.'

'. . . The anthropophagi and the men with heads under their armpits,' added Dagwood.

Broody noticed that two of the commercial travellers were rustling their newspapers. Their glances, if cool before, were now actively hostile.

'Of course,' he said, in a loud resounding shout, 'the custom of High Tea goes back to the days when the Picts and the Scots were being attacked by the Roman Legions. They had to cook their evening meal before it got dark so the legionaries couldn't see the camp fires!'

The newspapers were rustling in all four corners of the dining-room. Dagwood noticed them.

'Julius Caesar said that all the country north of a line drawn between Start Point and Flamborough Head was inhabited by barbarians whom neither gods nor men could favour,' he said (making the quotation up as he went along). 'Start Point to Flamborough Head,' he repeated dogmatically.

'I reckon Hadrian had the right idea,' said Ollie, twisting the knife.

'He even went as far as dividing Yorkshire into three parts, like Gaul,' Dagwood went on. 'Even now they're still called the North, East and West Ridings.'

The newspapers had stopped rustling. Dagwood's voice rang out in an ominously silent room.

'Hey steady Dagwood,' Ollie murmured cautiously. 'We'll be having a racial riot on our hands.'

At that, the four commercial travellers rose as one man, folded their newspapers and made for the door. One of them half-paused by Broody's table and then walked out. They heard the phrase floating back through the doorway, faint but clear.

'Bloody foreigners.'

'Exit: pursued by a bear,' said Dagwood. 'Well, do we stay in the Waldorf-Astoria here, or do we try the bright lights of Oozemouth, sir?'

'I can't think which would be worse,' Broody said, despondently.

'If the rest of Oozemouth's like this bloody place we might as well stay where we are,' said Ollie.

Their dilemma was solved by the appearance of The Bodger. He seemed to bring with him a breath of hope, of renewed optimism. Their eyes brightened at the sight of him.

'Sorry to leave you all like that,' he said, breezily. 'My wife and I had to go to a dreadful cocktail party at the Swedish Consulate and I've only just managed to get away. What are you all doing now?'

'Nothing, except quietly dying in our socks,' replied Broody.

'I know a quiet little pub down by the river. How about a few glasses?'

The Bodger drove rapidly and unhesitatingly through several side streets, crossed a bridge over a railway, passed a stretch of waste ground littered with bottles and the rusting bodies of old cars, and turned along a road which ran by the river. The others began to wonder to what sort of pub The Bodger was taking them. Dagwood rubbed the mist off the car window and stared out.

'Proper Fagin country,' he muttered.

'This is about the best pub in the whole of Oozemouth,' The Bodger explained. 'I nearly always go there at lunch-time.'

The Bodger sniffed and drove faster, as though his destination was already extending welcoming wisps of warmth and whisky. Dagwood was just thinking of Mole guiding Rat towards Mole End when The Bodger turned sharply right, just as Mole had suddenly dived down his hole, into a small cul-de-sac.

At the far end, about fifty yards back from the street, they could see two brightly-lit windows and a lighted sign: 'The Smoking Dutchman.'

'Here we are!' cried The Bodger. He leapt from the car and galloped towards the door. The others followed him through the doorway and became aware of the warmth of an immense log fire, rows of gleaming glasses, the nutty smell of beer, the landlord's green velvet waistcoat and the landlord's voice saying, 'Good evening, Commander!'

Dagwood would have been hard put to it to define what he meant by a real, warm-hearted pub, but he knew one when he saw it. 'The Smoking Dutchman' had it – that magic quality which transformed a public house from a mere structure containing beer and spirits into a rendezvous, a club and a refuge. 'The Smokers' was a delicious self-contained world. It was a place to take troubles to and forget them. Once through the door, Broody and his officers forgot the driving rain in the streets outside, the horrors of the Northern Steam Hotel and the whole appalling grey city of Oozemouth.

The floor was made of scrubbed red bricks, laid on end, with a large white sheepskin rug in the middle of the room. The fireplace took up the whole of one wall and there were two wooden seats in the corners on either side of the fire. The chimney-piece was stacked with assorted bric-à-brac which had accumulated there over the years. There was a square clock in a varnished case; a blue china pot containing coloured wooden tapers; a curious potato which someone had given button eyes and matchstick lips; a stuffed owl in a glass cupola; a collecting box and a tray of paper flags; a round Victorian glass paperweight; a miniature cactus in a pot; and a carved conch shell with a picture of the Great Iron Bridge painted inside it. Above this debris was a watercolour, probably by a customer, of Oozemouth Harbour and above that again a printed notice: 'We have an arrangement with

the Bank. We don't cash cheques and they don't serve beer.'
The walls were panelled in dark wood but the panelling was almost completely hidden by two oil paintings of full-rigged East Indiamen, a dart-board, dog-eared election placards, notices of past by-elections, posters for race meetings and boxing matches, playbills for the local cinemas, an advertisement for an amateur performance of 'Private Lives,' and a calendar of a nude blonde stretched out on a red rug, on which someone had scrawled 'Daphne, after closing time.'

The bar itself was set at convenient elbow height and was made of slabs of black marble so cunningly dovetailed that it required a regular customer of many years' close acquaintance to detect the joints. A brass footrail ran the length of the bar and upon it The Bodger was already conserving shoe leather and chatting to the landlord.

'Guv, some friends of mine,' he was saying. 'They're from *Seahorse,* the submarine that came in here today.'

Guv nodded. 'Good to have the Navy back again,' he said. 'We've missed you, and no mistake. On VJ night the Navy drank two hundred quids' worth of beer in this bar. Always used to have the Navy in this bar.' Guv pointed to a long row of ships' crests above the mirror at the back of the bar. 'Mind you, they broke thirty quids' worth of glasses the same night. But it seemed like the very next day they were gone and we've never seen 'em since.' Guv shook his head. 'Those were the days and no mistake.'

'Never mind, you've got us now,' said Broody.

'That's true, sir. What'll it be?'

'How about it, men? Best bitter?'

'Seeing what a dirty evening it is, sir, how about four of Daphne's, just to start off with?'

'Of course!' cried The Bodger. 'Four of Daphne's.'

'Hello, love,' said Daphne, appearing behind the bar.

Daphne was the kind of barmaid a man would trek many leagues across a waterless desert to rest his eyes on. She might have sat for Rubens. Her buttocks were poems ('Like tea-

27

cosies' The Bodger once said). Her figure might have inspired the Song of Solomon. ('Thy navel is like a round goblet, which wanteth not liquor; thy belly is like a heap of wheat set about with lilies.') The slope of her bosom, marginally contained by a black dress scalloped deep and low in front, was as refreshing to the eye as a foaming waterfall in the Sahara. The most hardened mild-and-bitter drinkers were sometimes moved to ask for a glass of lager because it was kept on the bottom shelf below the bar and Daphne had to bend down to get it.

Daphne came round from behind the bar and gave The Bodger a comprehensive kiss. The black dress creaked against The Bodger's chest.

'It's me birthday, love,' she said.

The Bodger, who had dropped back a step during the embrace, blushed and said: 'It seems a pity it only comes once a year.'

'And then only for me regular customers, love. You just wait a minute and I'll mix you all something to warm ye. Won't be a minute.'

Dagwood and Ollie watched this small comedy with interest.

'It's what I've always thought, sir,' said Dagwood, guile-lessly. 'If you want a good run ashore, always follow the married men and the padre!'

'Just watch it, young Dagwood,' said The Bodger, sternly. 'There's many a good man married a barmaid, let me tell you. They make splendid wives.'

'Ah, there I disagree, sir,' said Guv. 'A real barmaid'll never make you a good wife unless you let her keep a bar. Customers are always asking me when I'm going to marry Daphne and I always say no wife of mine will serve behind a bar. Daphne's a *proper* barmaid, you understand, it's born in t'blood with her and she'll never be happy anywhere else. Besides, she is married. She was away for two years and then she comes back sudden one day and asks for her job back.

Said she couldn't stand it. Said she missed the company.'

'What was that, Guv?' Daphne asked, returning to the bar carrying a tray with four steaming tankards on it. 'What were you saying?'

Dagwood leapt in with both feet. 'We were debating whether this house prefers a white woman on black sheets to a black woman on white sheets.'

Daphne set down the tray. 'If ye haven't made up yer mind yet, lad,' she retorted, 'yer never will.' She looked Dagwood up and down. 'I'll take ye on, love. Winner take all!'

Dagwood scowled, while the others all bellowed with laughter. Daphne possessed that unabashed knock-down kind of repartee which always disconcerted him. He had met it before in fishmongers' wives, bus conductresses and some times in school teachers.

'Never mind, love,' Daphne said, kindly. 'Here's your drink.'

Dagwood took one sip and felt the warmth tingle through his veins. He took another and his eyes watered. His breath came sharply and his belly seemed one large glowing pit.

'Gosh, what's in this?'

'D'you like it, love?'

'I probably will, when I can taste it, but what's in it?'

'It's a strong ale and rum and a bit of whisky and bit of nutmeg and spices, all heated wi' red-hot pokers.'

'I can see I'm going to have difficulty in keeping out of this place during the refit,' Dagwood said.

'Are ye spoken for, love?'

'Am I what?'

'Oh 'ark at 'im, are ye *married?*'

'Good gracious, no!'

'It's not only drink will be your trouble here then,' said Daphne.

'You've got to have something to do in the long northern nights, Dagwood,' said The Bodger.

'I can assure you, sir,' said Dagwood earnestly, 'I haven't

29

the least intention of getting married.'

'Nobody ever has,' said The Bodger. 'Nobody ever intends to catch German measles, but they do.'

'I'm sorry, sir, but I just can't see myself married to a naval wife.'

'Naval Wife!' shouted Broody. 'Dagwood, my poor innocent youth, you don't know what a Naval Wife is! They're a dying breed. Isn't that so, Bodger?'

The Bodger nodded. 'The war had a lot to do with it,' he said knowingly. 'Nowadays people tend to marry nurses or school teachers, or Wrens. And a good thing too. They're normally healthy wenches with a strong sense of the ridiculous. Freshens up the strain a bit. In the old days every wife you met looked as though she'd stepped straight out of the blood-stock catalogue at Newmarket. My father told me that when he was out in Malta during the thirties there was one girl in the Fishing Fleet who was actually known as The Thousand Guineas. I tell you, boy . . .' The Bodger took a long draught of Daphne's special, coughed, and went on, expanding to his subject ' . . . the Naval Wife of the old days was a pretty formidable proposition. She made a career of it. Coffee mornings with the other wives were a sacred rite. They used to sit around drinking their Java juice as though they were serving in the temple of Priapus. Every cocktail party, every summer ball, every invitation to dinner with the Captain was just one more step towards an Admiralty House address and a rather smart little flag with red balls on it. When the old Naval Wife went to a party she could give you the seniority of every officer present, to the nearest day. And she could give you the cost of every wife's clothes, to the nearest penny. Yes, there are two mammals I'm glad I didn't meet in their hey-day: one is the sabre-toothed tiger and the other is the Naval Wife!'

'However,' said Broody, 'In spite of that, there comes a time in every man's life when he starts to *lean* a little bit towards the old champagne and confetti and there's always a wench there to take him up on it. Dagwood, me old hearty, I reckon you're ripe!'

'Besides, there's always a critical time for marriage.' Ollie said. 'I remember someone telling me during training about a Gaussian curve . . .'

'A what?'

'A Gaussian curve of probability. You can plot a series of points on an exponential curve which will tell you the point that an event or a series of events is most likely to take place. A pile of sand is a good example . . .'

The Bodger was mystified. 'What's a pile of sand got to do with young Dagwood here getting married?'

'If you allow sand to drop on to a flat level surface it will heap up into a smooth pile. If you could somehow cut cleanly through the middle of that pile the cross-section would show a perfect Gaussian curve because the sand has heaped itself in the most probable way, that's to say more of it in the middle and less to the sides.'

'I'll be damned!'

'If you selected a million school children at random, gave them an intelligence test and plotted the results, they should give a Gaussian curve. Promotion chances in the service are supposed to be worked out in the same way . . .'

'That they're not!' said The Bodger, with conviction. 'Promotion in the Navy is done by cutting a pack of cards, thinking of a number, doubling it, and when the music stops the last man to sit down is made a Commander. I happen to know!'

'Anyway sir, there's supposed to be a theory that your chances of getting married before you're thirty follow the curve. How old are you, Dagwood?'

'Twenty-six,' said Dagwood, reluctantly.

'Slap bang in the middle of the curve!'

'You have been warned, Dagwood,' said Broody.

Dagwood cast about in his mind for a change of subject. 'What's the form about this refit conference tomorrow, sir?'

he asked desperately.

It was a lucky shot. The Bodger had very strong views on refit conferences.

'If either of you think that your refit conference tomorrow is going to be a private contest between yourselves and the yard, you've got another think coming. You'll be amazed at the little men who are coming from miles around, all converging on Oozemouth at this very minute, just to attend your refit conference. There'll be dozens of them, all having their say and all having quite a lot of power. You and I are the *last* people to be consulted. We're only the poor bastards who have to take the thing to sea once it's all over. The only time we *might* get a word in edgeways is when they discuss the list of defects and decide some of the things they're going to do. Even this is a farce, because you can take it from me it's all been decided already, long before we came on the scene. But if you want something done, I'll give you a little hint. Your chances of getting anything done are directly proportional to the cost of doing it. If it's big enough and expensive enough you'll get everything you want. They'll give you a sonar set which can hear a herring having the squitters in the Gulf of Mexico. They'll force a radar set on you which can pick up a seagull at a hundred miles and tell you what colour eyes it's got. They'll positively *press* on you a torpedo fire control system which does everything but cheer when you get a hit. They'll give you all that. *But . . . Ask* them to reposition a valve so that you can open it without giving yourself a hernia, ask them to put a seat in the sailors' heads that people who haven't got isosceles triangle-shaped backsides can sit on and they'll politely tell you to go away and boil your socks. So be warned. If you want anything, make it big. You mark my words tomorrow.'

The Bodger and Broody had the rare capacity of stimulating each other's conversation. They were both, after another round of Daphne's specials, in top form. They entertained the whole bar with their views on such subjects as the passing of the days of the Navy's greatness, the present technique of Grandmother's Footsteps whereby nothing ever happened in the Navy except when one's back was turned, and the Navy's grapevine, the envy of Reuter's, by which no naval officer could do anything, from mouse-trapping to murder, in Baluchistan or in Bath, without his contemporaries hearing the details by noon the next day.

While they talked, they drank. Broody drank more that night than Ollie or Dagwood had ever seen him drink before. It was as though he were washing away the old commission and preparing for the new. He would wake in the morning with a foul head and a clear conscience.

At closing time, they took Broody and his baggage to the station. Ollie and Dagwood carried his bags while Broody himself did a soft-shoe shuffle up the platform and collapsed into a sleeper, humming 'I Heard My Goldfish Yodelling.' Ollie wrote his destination on a label and put it into his top jacket pocket while Dagwood tipped the attendant to look after him. It was their ultimate act for the passing of *Seahorse*. When Broody left, the last remnant of the commission left with him.

4

Driving into Harvey McNichol & Drummond's yard the next morning to attend *Seahorse's* refit conference, The Bodger felt pleased with all the world. He was delighted to be back once more in submarine circles, even though only as a substitute for Broody. The Bodger was looking forward to the refit conference and was determined to fight as hard on Broody's behalf as though *Seahorse* were still his own command.

The Bodger's good humour survived the surly yard policemen, who argued for some time before admitting him without a pass. He smiled indulgently at the workmen, all apparently possessed of a strong death-wish, who strolled casually in the path of his car. Even when a grey chauffeur-driven Rolls turned sharply in front of him, forcing him to brake and skid sideways, The Bodger was still able to smile pleasantly.

Not so the passenger of the Rolls. A side window was furiously wound down.

'Are you *blind!*'

The Bodger became aware of a large leonine face and a black bowler hat. He caught a glimpse of heavy, lowering yellow eyebrows, a pink carnation, and a thick gloved hand.

'Are you blind, I say?' repeated the domineering, arrogant voice.

'No,' said The Bodger, politely.

'God damn your impertinent eyes, sir! I say you must be blind! Didn't you see my car?'

'I did. I also assumed that the driver knew the rule of

the road and would allow through traffic to pass first.'

'I'll drive my car where I damned well like in this yard!'

'As you wish,' said The Bodger. 'It's no concern of mine if you choose to kill yourself on the road. But it would be a pity if you killed someone else at the same time.'

So saying, The Bodger reversed, turned round and drove off.

Apart from that minor contretemps, preparations for the refit conference were very much as The Bodger had forecast. The conference was held in Harvey McNichol & Drummond's main boardroom and was attended by fifty-seven people. Dagwood counted them. Every department in Harvey McNichol & Drummond's was represented, together with the firm's main sub-contractors. Admiral Submarines was represented several times. So also were Admiralty research establishments dealing with sonar and radar, and several sections from the Admiralty at Bath, and there were other representatives whom Dagwood was unable to identify.

Assuming an average salary of fifteen hundred pounds a year, Dagwood calculated that there was approaching a hundred thousand pounds' worth of talent on view.

'Lot of high-priced help here today, sir,' he said to Mr Tybalt.

'You should be flattered. You've got all the King's horses and all the King's men.' Mr Tybalt looked at the row of Harvey McNichol & Drummond faces opposite him. 'That's the First Fifteen there. You've even got Sir Rollo.'

The conference fell swiftly into shape. Everyone present knew his place in the battle formation. The seating plan was evident. The yard men and their supporters sat on one side of the table. The Admiralty sat on the other. An Admiralty Overseer sitting among the ranks of Harvey McNichol & Drummond's would have been about as incredible as Horatius taking up arms for the ranks of Tusculum. The Chairman sat halfway down one side of the table with Mr Day on his right and on either side of them the managers of departments, all wearing those expressions of permanent pessimism which are inbred amongst shipyard managers. Opposite the Chairman sat Mr Tybalt and on either side of him sat the Admiralty Overseers, each Admiralty man facing his counterpart in the firm. Thus Mr Swales, The Principal Electrical Overseer, directly confronted his personal opponent Mr Burlap, Harvey McNichol & Drummond's electrical ship manager. Mr Vietch, the Admiralty Engineer Overseer, glared straight into the eyes of Mr McGillvray, the engineering ship manager. Behind the main combatants were drawn up secondary and tertiary lines of assistants, personal secretaries, satellites, seconds, henchmen and auxiliaries, ready to give information, matches, murmured words of solace or smelling salts at moment's notice. The lists were drawn up. The battle was pitched. At the far end of the table sat the reason for the assembly, the prize over whose bodies the battle would be lost and won – Dagwood, Ollie and The Bodger.

The Bodger had attended several refit conferences during his career but he had never before seen a refitting shipyard present such a united front. Harvey McNichol & Drummond's van was as solid as a Roman testudo and as uncompromising as an army with banners. The Bodger was suspicious of such a show of strength. In particular he mistrusted the Chairman. The Bodger had the normal naval officer's ignorance of civilian firms; he knew very little of the managerial caste in industry; but he could recognise a little tin god when he saw one. He could also recognise, with some inward qualms, the man who had been the occupant of the grey Rolls that morning.

Major Sir Rollo Falcon Hennessy-Gilbert, M.C., T.D., Bart., formerly of the Irish Guards but now Justice of the Peace, Chairman of Oozemouth Conservative Association, President of Oozemouth Chamber of Commerce, Captain of Oozemouth Racquets Club, Commodore of the Royal Oozemouth Yacht Club, Master of the Beaufortshire Forest Hounds, President of Oozemouth Harriers R.F.C., and

Governor of St Edward's Grammar School, Oozemouth, was also chairman and managing director of Harvey McNichol & Drummond (S. & E.) Co. Ltd. Furthermore, he was a nephew of old Lady Drummond, a nonagenarian who still owned a proportion of the company's shares and who lived some miles outside Oozemouth in a Victorian castle surrounded by thickets and gigantic rhododendrons which secluded her in mystery worthy of the Oracle at Delphi. (Old Lady Drummond's employees, none of whom had ever seen her, often speculated on her seclusion. The apprentices believed it was because she was being held ransom by a gang of international crooks; the yard managers contended that she had never really recovered from the shock of the Abdication; while Mr Tybalt maintained that she was merely sobering up after the news that Mafeking was relieved). In her absence, her nephew ruled Harvey McNichol & Drummond with the absolute power of a Mogul emperor. Mr Tybalt, who had the most frequent dealings with Sir Rollo for the Admiralty, had found him an unpredictable and dangerous man. While waiting to enter Sir Rollo's presence Mr Tybalt had often felt that he was about to discuss an Admiralty contract with Surajah Dowlah and that he should first have safeguarded himself by bringing with him Happy Day and Sid Burlap, as hostages, in chains.

The proceedings were opened by Sir Rollo himself. 'Gentlemen,' he said ponderously. His red-rimmed eyes under their overhanging eyebrows travelled sardonically along the row of Admiralty men opposite him. 'We meet in very happy circumstances. Once more we have one of the Sovereign's submarines in Harvey McNichol & Drummond's yard. May I, on behalf of the firm, welcome Commander . . . Commander . . .'

'*Badger*,' said The Bodger, in a resonant voice.

Sir Rollo paused and looked along the table. His eyes met The Bodger's in a glare of ferocious recognition.

' . . . Commander Badger and his officers to this shipyard.' Sir Rollo spoke for some time. He spoke of the 'dawning of a new era on Oozeside,' of 'adding one more jewel to Oozemouth's crown of lustre' and, without warmth, of 'extending the warm hand of friendship towards Commander Badger and his officers.' Most of Sir Rollo's audience had heard him make substantially the same speech many times before. The shipyard men listened, or appeared to listen, with expressionless faces (as long as the old bastard gave nothing away, he could talk on as long as he liked). Mr Tybalt listened with more attention. His ears were cocked for the tell-tale phrases in Sir Rollo's peroration. Mr Tybalt knew from experience that the sting would be in the tail. If Sir Rollo ended 'the great resources of this great shipyard must be fully utilised to give this Sovereign's ship a fresh start in life,' then Mr Tybalt knew he could relax. His job was a sinecure. *Seahorse* would get a good refit – or Harvey McNichol & Drummond heads would roll. But if Sir Rollo ended 'every endeavour therefore must, and will, be made to make this job an undertaking worthy of Harvey McNichol and Drummond craftsmen,' then Mr Tybalt knew that, so far as Sir Rollo was concerned, H.M.S. *Seahorse* for all practical purposes did not exist and he, Mr Tybalt, was faced with a long exhausting struggle to get the ship out of the yard bearing any resemblance at all to an operational submarine.

Dagwood lost the thread of Sir Rollo's speech around the second reference to a welcome being extended to Commander Badger and his officers. As Sir Rollo's voice rose and fell, Dagwood studied Sir Rollo's private secretary who was sitting immediately behind him. She had a notebook on her lap and glasses on her nose. Occasionally she made a note in her book and then reaffixed her eyes upon the small of Sir Rollo's back Dagwood noted the contours of the figure underneath the short grey bolero coat and silk blouse and just as he was deciding that behind the spectacles and beneath the notebook there might be more than met the innocent eye, the girl turned her head. Dagwood half-smiled. The girl looked at him. Dagwood's half-smile faded. Her look had plainly said: 'The bus leaves at noon – be under it.'

Dagwood turned his attention to the boardroom. It was a long gloomy chamber, a mausoleum in honour of the men who had ruled Harvey McNichol & Drummond's and of the ships they had built; the room was lined with portraits, all very large, very dark and, at the time they were painted, very expensive. Each picture was fitted with a tiny light above it but none of the lights were switched on and Dagwood could not make out more than the pale blurs of the faces in the sombre backgrounds. By straining his eyes he could just read the small gilt plaques on two of the nearest pictures: 'Harvey McNichol 1813-1865' and 'George Drummond, 1841-1902.' Glass cabinets were placed on tables along the room containing examples of the ships the firm had built. Dagwood could see a clipper, an early paddle steamer with a tall brass funnel, a dreadnought, a First World War monitor, a destroyer of the '30s, a 'River Class' submarine, and a range of passenger ships. Dagwood felt a sudden sympathy with the firm; they had a long and famous tradition of ship-building. They had a right to be proud of themselves. It was just that the faces Dagwood could see representing the firm now seemed somehow unworthy; Dagwood had the suspicion that none of them would have satisfied 'Harvey McNichol, 1813-1865' nor 'George Drummond, 1841-1902.'

Dagwood came to as Sir Rollo was winding up his address.

' . . . every endeavour therefore must, and will, be made to make this job an undertaking worthy of Harvey McNichol and Drummond's craftsmen!'

There was a simultaneous expulsion of breath, all round the conference room. The Bodger, Dagwood and Ollie were the only people oblivious of the atmosphere. Harvey McNichol & Drummond men sat back in their chairs; they had been given their instructions. Mr Tybalt and his team braced themselves. They too, had received the signal. Mr Tybalt compressed his lips and thrust out his jaw.

There followed a weary discussion on contracts, penalty

clauses, delivery dates, costing, overtime bans, and union negotiations. It was all double Dutch to The Bodger. He attempted to follow the arguments but they were mostly beyond him. He could see that Mr Tybalt was obviously battling strenuously on their behalf but felt powerless to help him; it was like watching a man fight a lion behind a sheet of thick glass. It was not until the conference passed to the lists of defects to be made good that the ship's officers sat up in their chairs and felt that at last they could begin to make a real contribution.

But even here they were superfluous. The refit was to cost what sounded to The Bodger a fantastic sum of money but the defect lists covering the work were dealt with in about forty minutes. Mr Day read out the defect numbers and Harvey McNichol & Drummond men nodded or shook their heads to signify whether or not they would undertake the work. The Bodger was reminded of a high-speed auction, where the proceedings were unintelligible to all save the cognoscenti. Whenever the Harvey McNichol & Drummond men shook their heads, Mr Day and Mr Tybalt exchanged glances of complicity. The reading of the defect list was obviously only a formality; like the marriage ceremony, it authorised in public form an agreement which had been consummated in private some time before. When the conference reached the last and least important list of defects, an exasperated Bodger decided to take a firmer stand.

The list of less important defects, known as the White Defect List, was a list of requests for shelves to be rearranged, for an extra drawer to be fitted, for an awkward step to be removed, or for a cover to be made for a piece of equipment which was always being drenched with sea water. They were almost all small items, designed to make living in the submarine more comfortable for the ship's company and they were always very dear to a submarine captain's heart. It was a very pusillanimous submarine captain who did not put up a fight for his White Defect List. The Bodger was sure that on his deathbed Broody would have whispered: 'Let not my poor White Defect List starve.'

When he discovered that most of the White List was not going to be undertaken, The Bodger let out a roar of indignation which made the whole conference start and look sideways at the end of the table. To tell the truth, they had quite forgotten that the ship's officers were present.

'Am I to understand,' The Bodger demanded, 'that almost the *whole* of this list is not approved? Without any discussion whatsoever?'

'Commander,' Mr Day began, 'it's a question of . . .'

'Might I remind you gentlemen,' The Bodger breathed heavily down his nose, while Dagwood, remembering the danger signals, grasped firmly the seat of his chair, 'that this refit has two purposes? The first is the repair and maintenance of the hull and machinery. I don't profess to know all the technical ramifications of that. There are too many people here who know much more about it than I do. But the second purpose of the refit is to make this ship a better fighting unit and that means making it more convenient for people who've got to fight in it, bearing in mind the experiences of the first commission. And this is something I *do* know about! I was the first Captain to take this very submarine to sea so I know what I'm talking about. Take the first item on the list. Item number one. To fit a screen over the forrard bunk in the sailors' mess. Now I happen to know who sleeps in that bunk. It's one of the asdic watchkeepers. You're going to put a simply splendid asdic set in the boat during this refit. I've just heard you say so. But that asdic set has got to be worked by a sailor and what sort of watchkeeper is that sailor going to be if every time he goes off watch he finds his bunk soaked in condensation? The ship's company were sometimes at sea in that submarine for six weeks at a stretch. How many of you know exactly what that means?'

The conference considered. It was not an aspect of the

refit which had ever occurred to them before.

The Bodger glowered down the table. 'Stand up the man here who's spent six weeks at sea in a submarine? Any of you?'

The conference sat small in their chairs and looked straight in front of them.

'Mr Day, have you got a price quoted for this screen?'

'Why yes, Commander, thirty pounds.'

'*Thirty pounds,*' hissed The Bodger contemptuously, as though Mr Day had quoted thirty pieces of silver. 'And how much is the new asdic set going to cost?'

'Well Commander,' Mr Day glanced uncomfortably at Sir Rollo, 'this is really a matter for the Admiralty to decide . . . they tell *us* what they want done . . . In any case the exact cost is not final . . .'

'But it will be several thousands of pounds?'

'Well, that isn't . . .'

'Won't it?'

'Yes, Commander.'

Sir Rollo frowned. 'Somebody show me,' he said.

Mr Day pointed out the item.

'Do it.'

'Sir Rollo, this isn't included in the price we've quoted . . .'

'*Then do it for nothing man!*'

The Bodger saw that he had scored a major forensic triumph. He hastened to follow it up. 'Now take the next item. To fit a cover over the junction box at the end of the Captain's bunk. Do you know why the last captain put that in? It's not because he doesn't like looking at junction boxes. This again is something I know from personal experience. When I slept in that bunk I found that every time I turned over, my big toe caught in the junction box, there was a blinding great blue flash and the gyro compass stopped! Now how about that one!'

'But this is ridiculous,' said Mr Swales, the Principal Electrical Overseer, peevishly. 'This defect list is a standard one for all ships of the class. We can't make exceptions for one ship . . .'

'I like the way you talk about "all ships of the class",' The Bodger said grimly. 'We've only got one of the class at the moment. We're still waiting for the others.'

Dagwood had not noticed Mr Swales before he drew attention to himself, but once he had looked at him closely Dagwood knew that he had seen Mr Swales many many times before. Mr Swales, pale-faced, spectacled, bald-headed, sat behind a thousand Admiralty office desks, insisting on the correct forms in quintuplicate. Mr Swales's voice, querulous and dogmatic, spoke over a thousand Admiralty telephones complaining that at least three months' notice was required before any action could be taken. Mr Swales's spidery signature endorsed a hundred thousand demand notes returned to their despairing senders because the item was not held in stock. In fact, Dagwood knew Mr Swales very well indeed.

'It may be true that we're using a standard list for all ships of the class,' said Dagwood. 'But we're not refitting *all* ships of the class. We're refitting *this* one. If we don't make allowances for the individual case of this ship, then most of what's been said has about as much bearing on H.M.S. *Seahorse* as the eleven thousand monographs written on General Wallenstein since the Thirty Years' War.'

Mr Swales had opened his mouth to answer when he saw the note Mr Tybalt had pushed in front of him.

'Whose side are you on?' the note asked.

Mr Swales sat back, flushed and biting his lips, and said no more. Had Dagwood studied Mr Swales's face a second time he would have realised that General Wallenstein had made him an enemy.

Mr Swales was not alone in his dislike of General Wallenstein. Sir Rollo regarded Dagwood's speech as an impertinent intrusion. In spite of Sir Rollo's hostility, The Bodger's rhetoric might have won the battle for Broody's White Defect

List. But after General Wallenstein, the day was irretrievably lost.

'These remaining items will have to be discussed later,' said Sir Rollo curtly.

After that there was no more to be done except for Sir Rollo to close the meeting, which he did with another speech, a short one, which ended, 'I repeat, gentlemen, every endeavour therefore must, and will, be made to make this job an undertaking worthy of Harvey McNichol and Drummond craftsmen.'

Mr Tybalt came out of the refit conference wearing the determined look of a man confronted by a soaring mountain which, no matter what the cost, had to be climbed.

5

When Dagwood went down to look at *Seahorse* the next morning, he was astonished by the work which had already been done on her. Someone had obviously risen very early that morning and wrenched half her casing away. Long bald patches of the pressure hull were now showing and pipes normally decently covered were exposed to the light, giving the submarine an extraordinarily naked, helpless appearance. A travelling crane was preparing to lift yet another section. Ollie was arguing with a watchman sitting in a little hut by the gangway.

'I never thought I'd see the day,' Ollie said to Dagwood. 'They won't let me down my own submarine.' Ollie turned back to the watchman. 'Look here, this gentleman is the Electrical Officer of this submarine. *He'll* vouch for me.'

'Can't help it, sir. You got to have a pass.'

'But this is our submarine! We live here!'

'Got to have a pass, sir.'

'Oh all right.'

The section of casing was ready to be lifted off. When it was gone, most of the pressure hull aft of the fin would be exposed.

Dagwood was impressed. 'They're certainly getting on with it,' he said. 'At this rate we shouldn't have any difficulty in getting out of here on time.'

But Ollie was not so impressionable. 'It's easy enough to rip things out. Anybody can do that. It's putting them back, that's what counts. That's the bitter bit. Let's go back to the office and see if we can get some passes to satisfy old Interpol here.'

'Not my fault, sir,' said the watchman doggedly. 'Got to have a pass.'

'All right, all right.'

The Chief Stoker was waiting in the office. He had a list of names and several forms.

'Landlady money, sir,' he said to Ollie.

'Have you all got digs?'

'We've got the digs all right, sir. No trouble at all. Now we need some money to pay the landladies. Suspicious lot round these parts, sir.'

The ship's company had indeed had no trouble at all in getting digs. *Seahorse's* sailors settled in Oozemouth as though they had been born there. The Chief E.R.A. went to live with a married cousin living in the city. The Chief Stoker was a Murphy and there was a thriving, spawning clan of Murphys in Oozemouth. The Electrical Artificer and the Petty Officer Electrician made the acquaintance of two widows in the lounge bar of the Hotel Metropole and were offered, and accepted, permanent accommodation. Leading Seaman Miles, the senior torpedoman, and Leading Seaman Gorbles, the senior asdic rating, investigated an advertisement in a tobacconist's shop and found themselves under the care of two unmarried but well-preserved sisters. Able Seaman Quickly and Stoker Gotobed pulled off the most spectacular feat of all, being found digs by the policeman who took them in charge at closing time (that perspicacious officer, who would clearly go far in the Force, tempered justice with financial appreciation by taking the two sailors to his mother-in-law, who was looking for lodgers). For those who could not find lodgings on their own account, there was always the Landlady Book.

'The Landlady Book!' Dagwood was charmed with the idea. A book of landladies was as delightful a notion as a medieval book of beasts.

The Landlady Book combined the functions of medieval bestiary, Michelin guide, Citizens' Advice Bureau and agony column. During the years Harvey McNichol & Drummond had been building ships for the Navy, many thousands of sailors had come to Oozemouth, stayed while their ships were completed, and left again. But they had bequeathed a record of their experiences to their successors. They had very quickly found out which landladies favoured sailors, which were the best cooks, served the largest helpings, were most generous over the rent, and had the prettiest daughters. The Landlady Book held within its covers a Landlady Lore, a legend of landladies, which had been added to, kept up to date over the years, and passed on from ship to ship. Dagwood could see by the earliest dates in the book that the original landladies must have been dead for many years and that the daughters ascribed to them must by now be grandmothers, and probably landladies, themselves. Some of the prices and terms of hiring had an oddly archaic flavour. 'Mrs Davies,' Dagwood read, '7 days board and lodging with meat sandwiches at mid-day, 17/6d.' Also Mrs Thoroughgood who 'would polish shoes and tender to other small needs for no increment of the weekly charge of One Sovereign.' Amongst the more modern entries Dagwood noted 'Mrs Hawkins. Grub good, Telly, but no sandwiches. House haunted. Would suit Chief Stoker interested in spirits.' Dagwood wondered what incredible psychic phenomenon had manifested itself at Mrs Hawkins'. Then there was Mrs Bragg: 'Husband away, no telly, record player,' Mrs Stott: 'Blonde daughter, would like to go steady with respectable sailor with good intentions. Good grub,' and Miss Emblem-Smith: 'Prayers after meals, would suit Padre.'

Dagwood read the later entries carefully. He himself needed digs. He could stand no more of the Northern Steam Hotel. He noted down a few addresses and decided to look at some during the lunch hour.

First there was the question of what to wear when calling

on landladies. It was a nice point. If Dagwood wore his best dark grey drinking suit, submariner's tie, and polished black shoes he ran the risk of having a guinea a week added to the rent before he had a chance to see the room. If he went to the other extreme and wore the clothes he normally wore at sea in the submarine, he was likely to be dismissed as a dangerous layabout before he had set foot over the threshold. Dagwood decided on a Harris tweed coat, cavalry twill trousers, a woollen tie, and brown Italian leather shoes. That ensemble, Dagwood hoped, would strike the neatest balance between affluence and poverty.

'I want to look like an up-and-coming bank clerk on his way to change his library book,' he told Ollie.

'You're wasting your time,' said Ollie realistically. 'They can tell who you are with half an eye open.'

'Anyway, here goes.' Dagwood looked at the list. 'Mrs Gladstone, 41 Forsyth Street.' The Landlady Book did not commit itself to any further information on Mrs Gladstone.

Forsyth Street was less than a mile from the shipyard and had once been the centre of the fashionable district of Oozemouth, where the doctor drove his brougham, where the policeman came only to call on Cook and where the piano legs were fitted with frills. The houses in Forsyth Street had once been family mansions, built of brick or Portland stone by prosperous Victorians and intended to last for a dynasty.

But when Dagwood walked along Forsyth Street to call upon Mrs Gladstone times had changed. The social pendulum had swung away and left Forsyth Street behind. Most of the houses had been converted into makeshift and inconvenient flats, with kitchens in what had once been maid's rooms and lavatories in the airing cupboards. One house was wholly occupied by insurance companies who advertised their names in black and gold lettering along the front of the house. Two of the basements contained Chinese restaurants and a third a barber's shop. The largest house in the street had been converted into a school for deaf children and across the road, in the house to which old Lady Drummond had come as a bride, the Harvey McNichol & Drummond Social & Billiards Club had its headquarters.

The lace curtains at No. 41 waved as Dagwood walked up to the front door. Dagwood noted Mrs Gladstone's curtains quivering: first at the top floor, then at the second floor, the first floor, and finally the ground floor, marking Mrs Gladstone's progress towards the front door. By the time she reached the front door, Mrs Gladstone had scrutinised Dagwood from four different angles and would now be able, Dagwood could wager, to describe him to the police.

'Yes?'

Mrs Gladstone was a professional landlady. Even Dagwood, novice at the game though he was, could see that. She had iron-grey hair, iron-grey eyes set in an iron-grey complexion, and she wore an iron-grey dress. When her iron-grey lips split in a mechanical smile of welcome Dagwood saw that she had iron-grey teeth. Mrs Gladstone was a terrible, an implacable figure, an apparition from a child's nightmare, a distillation of all the repressive governesses, nannies and arithmetic teachers who ever lived. Mrs Gladstone was the sort of woman who inspired men to revolutions, if only to create a new world where there could be no more Mrs Gladstones; and yet, paradoxically, Dagwood could quite well have imagined Mrs Gladstone herself knitting at the foot of the guillotine. Dagwood realised that he might have made a mistake and attempted to withdraw, but Mrs Gladstone had already summed him up.

'You've come about the room,' she stated.

'That's right but . . .'

'It's three guineas a week. Four if you stay the weekend. You'll want to see it.'

'Er, well . . .'

'Come in.'

Silent-footed as an Apache in her iron-grey felt slippers, Mrs Gladstone led the way into the hall. Dagwood's own footsteps rang echoingly on a floor of black and white tiled squares. He looked around him. On every side lay evidence that Mrs Gladstone's guests lived in what amounted to a police state. 'Close This Door QUIETLY' said a notice on the front door. A long mirror hung by the front door in such a position that anyone entering or leaving the house automatically looked in it. Dagwood was chilled to the heart by the words 'Rent Day is FRIDAY' pasted along the top of the mirror. Remember you must die, the words reminded Dagwood, all flesh is mortal but death and rent endure. Opposite the mirror were an angular mahogany hall-stand ('Guests Are Responsible For Their Own Clothing At ALL Times'); a telephone with a coin-box ('Do NOT Ask For Change'); and a brass gong with a padded drumstick in a stand ('Guests Are Expected To Be Punctual For ALL Meals'). Dagwood could no more imagine anyone ignoring Mrs Gladstone's summons, beaten out on that brass gong, than he could have imagined them missing the Last Trump.

'This way, please.'

Mrs Gladstone proceeded towards the stairs ('Keep Right At ALL Times In Case Of Fire'). Dagwood followed. Half-way up the stairs Dagwood came upon a poignant sign that someone, at some time in the past, had tried to gain asylum from the Gladstone regime by one superb, cathartic act of rage and desperation. 'Do NOT Throw Geometrical Instruments Over These Bannisters' said the notice.

'Laundry goes on Mondays,' Mrs Gladstone was saying, conversationally. 'Exact money to be put in an envelope to go with the soiled clothing.'

'I see,' said Dagwood. 'But I really . . .'

'Hot running water is provided in all rooms. Baths are sixpence extra. Each bath.'

'I see.'

They had reached the first floor landing. Here the walls were a dull mustard yellow (in contrast to the glacial blue of the hall). A life-size gun-metal bust of Napoleon stood on a pedestal and near it hung a print of 'The Monarch of the Glen.' On the other side was a picture so dark and obscure that Dagwood had to step close to it before he could see that it was an engraving of an emaciated Elijah standing at the mouth of a cave and staring, with understandable anxiety, at the flight of some ravens in the distance.

Mrs Gladstone began to mount the stairs again to the second floor landing, her legs rhythmically pumping.

'All guests eat the same meals. Special dishes are charged for.'

The last sentence was said in a tone of such menace that Dagwood had a vivid mental picture of a polyglot community of Moslems, vegetarians and head-hunters, all eagerly eating Mrs Gladstone's regimented dishes rather than cause Mrs Gladstone inconvenience.

The first floor carpet was replaced by linoleum on the second floor which itself gave way to bare boards on the third floor. The only fittings on the second floor landing were a titanic wicker laundry basket and a framed picture of an etiolated hollyhock. On the third floor there was nothing to be seen at all except two doors, both varnished a sombre vault-like brown.

'All new guests are on the third floor,' Mrs Gladstone said.

'Oh?'

'Mr Benjamin has been with me ten years and he's still only on the second floor,' Mrs Gladstone added, with some satisfaction.

It had not occurred to Dagwood that there might be protocol in a boarding house. Plainly all Mrs Gladstone's guests had to accumulate many years' seniority of faultless lodging before they were promoted from the limbo of the third floor to the carpeted elysium of the first floor.

Mrs Gladstone took a key from her apron. 'There's five shillings deposit on the key,' she said, pushing the door open.

The room was as functional as a lavatory and as welcoming

as a monastic cell. The furniture was of the most utilitarian kind – an iron bed with brass knobs on the posts, a wardrobe, a small table and a chair, a wash-basin, a gas-fire, and a gas-meter with the inevitable exhortation 'Do NOT Use Foreign Coins In This Meter.' The floor was bare except for a strip of felt by the bed. The window admitted a view of No. 42 Forsyth Street, opposite.

Dagwood was not surprised by the room. After the preliminaries leading up to it, he had expected nothing else.

'Such a friendly room,' said Mrs Gladstone.

'Yes,' said Dagwood.

There was a pause. Dagwood knew that the next move in the comedy was up to him. He had been carried thus far by Mrs Gladstone's deadly precision. If he hesitated now, he would be bound in Mrs Gladstone's steel web for as long as he remained in Oozemouth. This was a crisis. Dagwood rose bravely to meet it.

'I won't take it,' he blurted out breathlessly, and waited apprehensively, half-expecting Mrs Gladstone to disappear in a puff of many-coloured smoke and reappear as a malignant witch at last uncovered in her true form.

But Mrs Gladstone merely nodded. There *were* people who refused her rooms, just as there *were* people who refused the last rites. Both categories were equally damned.

Mrs Gladstone led the way down again, down to the linoleum level, past Napoleon, Elijah and the Monarch of the Glen to the carpet line, down past the hall-stand and the mirror to the front door. The door swung open. Daylight streamed in. Dagwood walked out, only then conscious that sweat had been running between his shoulder-blades and down the backs of his legs. Mrs Gladstone had not asked Dagwood's name nor what he did for a living. He had been admitted, assayed, found wanting and, like a bent coin, rejected.

'Great Zot!' said Dagwood, aloud. 'You're well out of that, young Dagwood.'

Dagwood took out his notebook, crossed out the dread name of Gladstone, and then, feeling completely unnerved, went to 'The Smokers' for a drink.

6

'I don't know why you bother with digs, love,' said Daphne, when she heard about Mrs Gladstone. 'A young ram like you would be far better off on his own.'

'You mean get a flat or something?'

'Of course, love.'

Dagwood considered the idea. Never in his life had he looked after himself. Home, Cambridge and the Navy had always provided him with food and lodging and all the comforts of life. Like the lilies of the field, like almost every bachelor officer in the Navy, Dagwood had never cooked for himself.

'Oh I don't think I could.'

'Yer a big softie, love.'

Dagwood did not question the statement. 'D'you really think I could get a flat?'

Seeing that Dagwood was slowly catching on to the idea, Daphne called to Guv: 'Wasn't there someone in last night talking about Bill Watson's barn, Guv? Didn't they say he'd converted it into a flat?'

'That's right. Just looking for a tenant. Just finished it. Hasn't even put it in the evening paper yet.'

'There you are, love,' said Daphne triumphantly. 'Now you go and have a lewk at it and don't come back here and say ye haven't taken it because ye don't know how to lewk out for yourself.'

'Oh very well,' said Dagwood resignedly. 'How do I get there?'

Mr Watson's farm lay on the outskirts of Oozemouth,

54

eight miles from the shipyard and almost on the border of the neighbouring county of Beaufortshire. The farm was in a district which could still be classified as countryside but the processes were already at work which one day would swallow the farm and the nearby village and include it in the town. Oozemouth was already shooting out long suckers which in a few years' time would encircle the farm and engulf it. On the way out there in the bus Dagwood noticed places where this process had already been completed, where grey stone country houses, each with a surviving strip of vegetable garden and a small orchard, were surrounded by lines of new red brick villas whose gardens were still no more than churned-up plots of raw earth.

Dagwood could get no answer from the front door of the farmhouse. He made his way round to the back and, glancing through a window, caught sight of a girl, stripped to the waist, washing herself in the kitchen sink. The girl looked up at that moment. She and Dagwood stared at each other.

'Be with you in a minute!'

The girl snatched up a towel while Dagwood retreated to the back door. She was wearing a heavy oiled-wool sweater when she opened the door. Repressing the tiny urge of sexuality at the knowledge that she was almost certainly wearing nothing underneath the sweater, Dagwood raised his hat.

'Is Mr Watson at home?'

'He isn't at the moment,' the girl said. 'But can I help you? I'm Mrs Watson.'

The girl blushed. Dagwood blushed in sympathy.

'I've come about the barn you're converting into a flat,' Dagwood said, his blush deepening into a ripe peony colour.

'Gosh, how did you come to hear about it so soon? We've only just finished it.'

'Somebody in 'The Smokers' told me about it.'

'Gosh, how the word gets around! It's not quite finished yet, but would you like to see it?'

'Yes, please, Mrs Watson.'

'My name's Molly, actually.'

'Molly.'

Molly took a key from behind the kitchen door and led the way across the yard, past a line of sheds and a well.

'That looks a very old well,' Dagwood said.

'Oh yes, they say it's about a thousand years old. The pump doesn't work now. Nobody's been able to get any water from it for years.'

They were joined by a sheepdog puppy, which began to bark and jump at Dagwood's heels.

'What's his name?'

'Shep. Don't mind him, he doesn't mean any harm. It's just his nature to do that.'

Molly walked up a cinder path to the barn.

'Here we are.'

The Tithe Barn was constructed like a Roman granary, and was probably almost as old, with solid stone walls and thick buttresses. A slate roof had been added and windows cut in the walls. Inside, the barn was split into two compartments, the first a large, high-roofed living-room and the second a much smaller section containing the kitchen and the bathroom. The bedroom was above the kitchen and bathroom and was approached by a set of wooden steps from the living-room. The living-room was lighted by four windows, two looking north towards the yard and the farmhouse and two looking south over the orchard and a field. There was also a long skylight in the roof. Molly showed Dagwood the electric cooker, the kitchen sink and the bath, the immersion heater in a cupboard, and the coal shed outside the back door. There was a brown stove in one corner of the living-room, two old armchairs and a sofa, a dining table set against the wall, and four chairs. The inside walls had just been whitewashed and there were several faded carpets covering most of the stone floor. It was crude, and probably very cold in winter time, but for one person looking after himself it appeared to be almost ideal.

'I'll take it,' said Dagwood impulsively.

Molly was more practical. 'It's four pounds a week,' she said cautiously. 'That includes water and rates but not electricity.'

'That's all right.'

'When would you like to move in?'

'Now.'

'Oh, but there are lots of things we've got to do first! We have to get the electricity man to read the meter . . .'

'What for?'

'You want to start off with a clean sheet, don't you? You don't want to have to pay for the electricity we've already used this quarter.'

'Oh, I see. Yes. Oh yes, you'd better get the electricity man.'

Molly was slowly realising that Dagwood was even more inexperienced as a tenant than she herself was as a landlady. 'You'll need some coal,' she said. 'Shall I order some for you?'

'Yes please, if you would.'

'What sort of coal do you want?'

Dagwood was nonplussed. To him coal was coal, and there an end.

'Is there more than one kind?'

Molly giggled. 'There's lots of kinds. You leave it to me. I'll get you some. Now how about food? We can supply you with milk and eggs from the farm here.'

'That would be splendid,' said Dagwood, vaguely.

'How much milk do you want a day?' Molly asked mischievously, waiting to see what Dagwood would say.

'A quart?' Dagwood suggested, experimentally.

Molly burst out laughing.

'Is that a lot?'

'Well, it's rather a lot for one person! Tell you what, we'll say a pint a day to start with and see how you get on. How about a daily woman? The wife of one of our men can come in two days a week and do for you, if you'd like that?'

57

'Now that's a good idea,' said Dagwood. 'I shall probably need a bit of professional help.' Dagwood was gradually becoming aware that there was more to taking a residence, even a Tithe Barn, than merely walking in with the landlady and saying you'll have it.

'Will you bring your own linen?'

'Eh?'

Molly repressed a smile. 'Sheets, etcetera.'

'Oh of course yes, sheets . . . I've got to go home anyway and pick up my car. I'll get sheets and things while I'm there. I'll manage the sheets. You leave that to me.'

'That's all right then. Shall we say you'll take it from next Saturday?'

'O.K. I probably won't arrive until Sunday.'

'Oh, by the way, I'd better have your name.'

'Jones. Lieutenant Dagwood Jones, Royal Navy.'

'Gosh, this'll be the first time we've had a naval officer in this village! We'll expect you on Sunday then, Lieutenant Jones?'

'Not Lieutenant Jones. Dagwood.'

'All right, Dagwood,' said Molly, smiling.

Dagwood returned to Oozemouth glowing all over with a sense of accomplishment. 'Good lad,' said Daphne, when she heard of Dagwood's decision. 'You'll have the time of your life.'

Daphne's opinion was not shared by Dagwood's mother when Dagwood went down to Buckinghamshire to see her and collect some sheets.

Dagwood's mother had been known to the family as Dame for as long as Dagwood could remember. She had been left a widow when Dagwood's father, a banker, had died exactly a year after he retired to the large cottage where Dame now lived with her black labrador Sammy. She had married late in life, when she was nearly forty and she had married, in her family's opinion, rather below her. The Earl, her grandfather, had at last silenced all family opposition by saying, or rather shouting at the top of his voice, 'If this banker fellow *Jones* doesn't marry Rosemary, who the devil will?' Dame was a vague lady who still had only the haziest idea of what her son did for a living. She knew that he was in the Navy but she had an almost Elizabethan attitude towards the status of naval officers; she looked upon them as superior artisans, above a head coachman but definitely below a butler. She could see Dagwood (a nickname he had irremovably acquired at the age of six months, his baptismal name being Hugh) in ruff, pinked doublet and sword, hailing 'Sink me the ship, Master Gunner, split her in twain!' from the poop-deck, but her imagination baulked at the idea of Dagwood actually labouring in the waists, as the Master Gunner. The concept of Dagwood as an Electrical Officer defeated her entirely; she knew as much of electricity as she did of linear B. She lived in mortal terror of her own electric kettle. Dagwood often wondered how he had ever come to join the Navy (the Interview Board had asked him that very question and he had been unable to frame an intelligent reply).

Unknown to Dagwood, his father and Dame had given a great deal of thought to the choice of a career for him. They had dismissed the Army: the boy was too intelligent for that. Yet he was probably not intelligent enough for the Law or Accountancy. He was too honest for the City or the Church and too squeamish for Medicine. They had not considered the R.A.F. at all; they would as soon have thought of apprenticing the lad as a garage mechanic. It had to be the Navy, but Dame had been uneasily conscious that none of her family, not Lionel, the baron who carried the Coeur de Lion's standard before the walls of Acre, nor Louis, the comte who carried the china commode before the Sun King at Versailles, and least of all Charles, Bishop, Gonfalioner and Captain General of the Holy Church of the Emperor Charles V who could drink forty bottles of Bordeaux wine (one for each day in Lent) at a sitting, would have approved.

'Hello dear,' said Dame, giving Dagwood a kiss and a look which reminded him that he must get a haircut. 'Have you come from Oozemouth?' It might have been thought an unnecessary question, considering that Dagwood had telephoned specifically to say that he was coming, but Dame had a great respect for travellers. She felt an almost medieval concern for journeys. She herself went down to the village to do her shopping carrying a loaded stick and holding Sammy back on a slip-leash, as though she expected at any minute to be set upon by a gang of starving soldiers returning from the Wars of the Roses.

'Yes, Dame,' Dagwood answered absently.

'Did you say that you were going to live in a flat, dear?'

'That's right. It's a tithe barn actually.'

'It doesn't sound very comfortable, Dagwood. Are you sure it isn't very damp?'

'Oh it's fully furnished and everything, Dame. It's got a great big stove in it.'

Dame remembered another important point. 'I do hope you're going to get enough to eat. Who's doing the cooking?'

'I am.'

'Oh dear,' said Dame, anxiously.

'It shouldn't be all that difficult,' Dagwood said, with more confidence than he felt. He had enough imagination to be able to visualise the quite probable results of his first efforts – the smoke, the vicious sizzling noise, and possibly Molly's alarmed face hovering outside the window, wondering whether her Tithe Barn was safe. 'I've never been one for very much breakfast, as you know. So coffee and toast and marmalade is enough for that. I get lunch free at the yard. So the only real meal to worry about is supper. I expect I'll have steak or scrambled eggs for that. If I get fed up I can always go down to the local and have beer and sandwiches. It should be all right, Dame, don't worry.'

Dame was still not convinced. 'It doesn't sound very nourishing,' she said.

'If you're really worried Dame, you can help by lending me some extra crockery and things. I've got a list here. A spare electric fire if you've got it. And *sheets*, they're very important.'

'I still think you'd be better off in digs, with someone to look after you. How about darning and mending . . .'

'Dame, don't *worry*. Everything will be all right.'

With Dame's last pieces of advice still in his ears, his car packed with most of his worldly belongings, and the boot filled with food carefully selected by Dame, Dagwood drove up to Oozemouth. With a house, a car, and an independent future, Dagwood felt himself to be a man of substance, a citizen of consequence in the neighbourhood. All I need now is a wife, thought Dagwood carelessly, and began to laugh so much that he nearly ran over one of Molly's hens, jay-walking in the yard.

7

'Frank, tell me your honest opinion,' said The Bodger. 'How do you think this refit of *Seahorse's* is going?'

Frank Tybalt pulled down the corners of his mouth in an expression of indecision. He seemed reluctant to come forward with his honest opinion.

'It could be better, I'll tell you that,' he said.

'That's what I rather thought.'

'It's much too early to tell just yet,' said Frank Tybalt carefully. 'I'm never particularly worried at the start of these things. It's the middle and the end that count. My honest opinion is that we're in for a hard struggle.'

'You mean Sir Rollo?'

Frank Tybalt nodded. 'For some reason or other, he's not interested in *Seahorse*, in fact I would go further and say he's definitely agin' her.'

The Bodger looked guilty. 'I had a minor punch-up with Sir Rollo on the morning of the refit conference, you know . . .'

'I heard about it. That may have had a small bearing on it but Sir Rollo has always been anti-Navy. It's a well-known thing . . .'

'You don't mean he's actually going to stop jobs on *Seahorse* being properly done?' cried The Bodger.

Frank Tybalt shook his head. 'Oh nothing as tangible as that. He couldn't do it anyway. We wouldn't let him get away with it. No, it's much more subtle. It's all a question of priorities. Supposing the yard have only a certain number of one kind of workmen on a given day. Now, they can put them on *Seahorse* or they can work in that Norwegian tanker, say. I'm only taking a very general case here. So you find those workmen working in the Norwegian tanker . . . With a perfectly good excuse, mind you. Say you have two lathe operators, one good and the other not so good. You'll find that you've got the less good one and the good one is working on a job for another ship. There's nothing concrete, nothing you can put your finger on. Nobody has actually said, Let's do *Seahorse* dirt. It's just an attitude of mind, a sort of atmosphere which percolates down from the top. You'll find they all use *Seahorse* as an excuse to work off departmental scores. There are times, Bodger, when the shipbuilding side of this firm is barely on speaking terms with the engineering side. Sometimes you'd hardly believe they were supposed to be working for the same firm. The battle and the intrigue goes to and fro and your wretched vessel is in the middle of it like an Aunt Sally . . .'

'Frank, you make it sound like one of those medieval courts!'

'Nicolo Machiavelli would have felt really at home in this place,' Frank Tybalt said, bitterly. 'He'd probably be on the board of directors by now.'

The Bodger stared into the remaining inch of beer in his tankard. 'What we really need is some way of changing Sir Rollo's attitude?'

'That's it in a nutshell, Bodger. If Sir Rollo suddenly started to bear down on *Seahorse's* refit, the word would soon get around.'

'I wonder if a naval son-in-law would help?'

'I should think it might have a very good . . . *Bodger,* you're not suggesting that . . .'

'I'm not suggesting anything,' said The Bodger, urbanely. 'I'm told that Miss Hennessy-Gilbert is a real dish . . .'

'Bodger, you black-hearted old . . .'

'Be honest with yourself, Frank. You'd be prepared to go to a lot of trouble to make *Seahorse's* path plain, wouldn't you?'

'I would,' Frank Tybalt admitted.

'Then just leave it with me for a bit. I don't guarantee a thing. It's just that I have a theory that matters will often turn out the way you want them to, provided you're prepared to give them a discreet nudge. Are you having the other half?'

Frank Tybalt surrendered his tankard to Daphne with the helpless feeling of a man who has set forces in train more powerful than he had bargained for. Looking at The Bodger's bland expression, Frank Tybalt felt like the man who has rubbed the lamp, expressed his wish to the genie, and must now abide by the consequences.

In spite of Mr Tybalt's dark fears, *Seahorse's* refit appeared, outwardly at least, to be progressing very satisfactorily. The ship's company had settled into the shipyard as effortlessly as they had settled into the city. The Chief E.R.A., the Electrical Artificer and the other senior technical ratings swiftly worked up that miraculous liaison with their counterparts in the firm which was, and always would be, the envy of the wardroom. Able Seaman Quickly, who had been the Coxswain's storekeeper and tanky, took it upon himself to refurnish *Seahorse's* office accommodation. For the first fortnight of the refit gangs of men who announced themselves as summoned by, and friends of, Able Seaman Quickly, brought new chairs, new desks, an extra telephone extension, jugs, kettle, cushions and miscellaneous office equipment. Stoker Gotobed had few talents but one of them was the ability to make fluids pump or flood in any direction or in any quantity he chose. The plumbing in the office block was notoriously unreliable. Generations of occupants had cursed its vagaries. The office plumbing flooded, froze, or dried up, according to the weather and its own whims. But Gotobed, with a hammer and a couple of spanners, struck the living rock like Moses and water gushed forth; similarly, with a screwdriver and jubilee clips, he reclaimed a vast area of the office block from its liability to periodical flooding.

In *Seahorse* herself the refit was progressing, in Broody's phrase, through a series of Grandmother's Footsteps. Nothing ever appeared to be happening on board but day by day the ship lost the tight, braced look she had worn when she arrived. Her stays had been thoroughly loosened. Dagwood had often read magnificent pieces of descriptive writing by authors of sea yarns on the chilling lifelessness of a ship in dockyard hands. The writers put themselves to considerable trouble to compose striking similes: they wrote of the soul which had fled the ship, of the life blood only throbbing feebly through her ravaged veins, of the dead hand of the dockyard, and of the ship's bedraggled appearance, recalling an alley-cat which had lost interest. Dagwood had admired these writers' industry, but now saw, through *Seahorse,* that they were all mistaken. The ship was not dead. Her soul, if she had ever possessed one, was still on board. She had only exchanged one form of life for another. She was sloughing off her old skin and growing a fresh one. She was not dead but merely submitting to a gigantic and ear-shattering manicure.

Dagwood's own department was making faster progress than any. The main batteries had been removed, the wireless office and the sonar room were unrecognisable: consoles had been ripped out piecemeal, ranks of valve panels had been dismantled and hundreds of cables hung in tangles like abandoned nerve ganglia. In what had once been the radar office Dagwood came across a workman stripping wiring leads. The man was tearing out lengths of wire and tossing them into a bucket. Dagwood stood and watched him for some time.

'Is there anything wrong with those leads?' he asked at last.

'Couldn't tell you, sir,' said the man, shortly.

'Are those circuits going to be rewired?'

'Couldn't say, sir.'

'But if there's nothing wrong with them couldn't they be taped off and left where they are?'

'I'm only doing what the gaffer tells me, sir,' said the man resentfully.

'But surely . . .'

'I only work here, sir.'

Dagwood went to see Mr Swales. He did not expect a great deal of co-operation from Mr Swales but he was not prepared for the rock-hard stubbornness, the mulish obstinacy, which Mr Swales displayed. Mr Swales flatly refused to take any action whatsoever.

'This is an Admiralty contract,' Mr Swales said, 'and it's going to be carried out according to Admiralty instructions. The Admiralty want those leads taken out. They're taken out. If *you* want it done any differently you've got to show me the Admiralty letter authorising it. Show me the letter reference, that's all I say . . .'

'I see your point about the Admiralty reference, Mr Swales . . .'

'Just show me the reference . . .'

'Yes, yes, I *quite* see that, but if there's nothing wrong with those leads and if nothing's going to be done to them while they're out, then why not just leave them in? They're not in anybody's way . . .'

'The Admiralty has laid down that those leads are to be taken out,' Mr Swales said in a taut, restrained voice, 'and they always are taken out. And they always will be, unless you can show me some authorisation . . .'

'I know this is only a small point, Mr Swales, but it's a matter of *principle*. Enough of these small points can delay our completion date . . .'

'I am not interested in your completion date, Lieutenant.'

That was final. That was what The Bodger would have called the Knock-Down Answer. Once that had been said, there could be no further discussion.

Dagwood left Mr Swales's office without another word and, bubbling over with rage, went to see Mr Tybalt. This was a drastic step to take (and Dagwood was not at all sure he was entitled to take it) but his argument with Mr Swales was so fundamental that Dagwood felt that he must have his own position clarified. This issue went far beyond the mere question of whether or not several hundred three-foot lengths of co-axial cable should be removed from H.M.S. *Seahorse*. It was a point on which the whole basis of the refit rested.

Mr Tybalt heard Dagwood out. Then he got up from his desk and went over to the window.

'Come over here a minute, Dagwood,' he said.

Dagwood joined Mr Tybalt at the window.

'What do you see?'

Mr Tybalt's office looked out upon a kind of canyon, cut through the shipyard. The Admiralty offices formed one side of the canyon and the boilermakers' shop formed the other. Through the floor of the canyon ran a narrow road and a single track railway line. A corrugated iron roof jutted out just below Mr Tybalt's window, sheltering rows of racks in which scores of Harvey McNichol & Drummond workmen stabled their bicycles during the working day.

'It's not very inspiring,' Dagwood admitted.

'Mr Swales's office is directly below this one,' said Mr Tybalt. 'He hasn't even got this view, such as it is. His office has a prospect of the back of that bicycle shed. Do you know how long Cyril Swales has been there?'

'I've no idea, sir.'

'Eleven years. Eleven years of trying to make this shipyard build things that will stand up to Admiralty specifications. Nobody who hasn't had intimate dealings with a British shipbuilding firm can really understand what that means. Those people down there are wrangling, and arguing, and striking, and gradually pricing themselves out of their own bread and butter. We're fast getting to the stage where the Royal Navy will be the only people who can *afford* to send work to British shipyards. Mr Swales and I and people like us live in this bedlam and try and produce what the Admiralty want out at the end of it all.'

'But Mr Swales didn't even *listen* . . .'

'You may or may not be right in this particular case. It's not Mr Swales's job to decide that and it's not mine. Mr Swales does his job, you can be quite sure of that. Not only does he do it today, he'll do it tomorrow and next week and next year. He's been doing it for eleven years in this ship-yard and is quite capable of doing it for another eleven.'

Mr Tybalt returned to his desk and clasped his hands in front of his chin.

'Every now and then we get actual naval officers working with us. They're interested in what they call the operational side of things. I use the word advisedly. They want to make their ship live and work and fight efficiently. At the same time they want it to be comfortable to live in. They want an armoured glove which fits them like silk. Commander Badger made this point quite convincingly at the refit conference. It's an admirable objective. But it's not *our* objective. *Our* objective is to see that when the Admiralty specify steel of a certain kind, then that steel is used, and when they specify a test pressure of so many pounds to the square inch, that test is applied and sustained, or when they specify an insulation of so many megohms, that value is achieved. I'm sorry to talk so pompously, I can see by your face that I haven't succeeded in making my point. Just take my word for it, Dagwood, we are trying to get the best refit we can for you out of this firm. And if you don't like Cyril Swales's attitude,' said Mr Tybalt, grinning, 'why, you'll just have to lump it. Won't you?'

'Yes, sir,' said Dagwood, not believing a word of it. Later, when he mentioned the Great Swales Controversy to The Bodger, expecting sympathy, he did not receive it. On the contrary, The Bodger was horrified.

'It's my own fault,' said The Bodger. 'I should have warned you. Dagwood, you, as a ship's officer, mustn't have anything to do with the workmen. I don't say you won't get to know them, because of course you will, and a bit of chiyacking about what a bloody awful team Oozemouth United have got

68

is probably a good thing. But if you see a workman doing something wrong or even if he just looks as though he's loafing, you must never, never, *never* interfere. If you're unhappy about what's going on you must go and see the Admiralty Overseers about it. They deal with the firm. Not you. No ship's officer carries the least bit of weight in a private yard. You're only there in an advisory capacity. It's the Overseer's responsibility to see that everything is up to scratch. Not yours.'

'Why do they call themselves 'Overseers,' sir? They sound like Simon Legree or someone.'

'Anyone less like Simon Legree than the average Admiralty Overseer would be hard to imagine, as you know,' The Bodger replied. 'They're normally funny-looking little men in scruffy suits. They have a civil servant's attitude to life and they fuss around and get in your way. At least, that's how everyone in the Navy tends to think of them. But you've got to see these fellows' point of view, Dagwood. They're being pushed from three directions all the time. On one side they've got the Admiralty pestering them for reports, raising hell when a ship is delayed and blaming them when things go wrong. Then they've got the firm telling them that unless the Admiralty stop changing their minds about what they want fitted in the ship and, furthermore, unless they *send* the stuff once they have made up their minds, the ship will never make its completion date. And on top of all that they've got the laughing, chaffing ship's officers, who wait until everything's finally in place and buttoned up and then come along and point out that nobody will be able to get in and work it if it's left where it is and while they're on the subject could they have the ship panelled out in green and not blue. So it's not easy for the Overseers and you've got to see their point of view. They're worth cultivating, these chappies. It's just as important to get on well with them as with the firm. More important, in fact. Tact, Dagwood. Tact is the thing. Tactfulness is more than godliness in a shipyard.'

'I don't see why we need Overseers anyway, sir. We're quite capable of looking after the refit ourselves.'

'Quite right,' said The Bodger, 'but this is not the only place where stuff for the Amiralty is being made nor are you the only Admiralty contract even here. You forget that the Admiralty are a suspicious bunch. There probably hasn't been a more suspicious bunch of coves since the Court of the Star Chamber. They think everyone's trying to see them off, and nine times out of ten they're dead right. So they have a great team of men all over the country whose job it is to look after the Admiralty's interests. I don't think you've any idea of the sheer scale of the thing, Dagwood. There isn't *anything*, no matter how small nor how cheap, bought or made for the Admiralty where a little man doesn't come along first and inspect it and put his chop on it to show that it's been passed for Admiralty consumption. They have quite a difficult job too. It's not easy to come along to a firm that's been beavering away for years and tell them that what they're doing is no good. Tact again, you see. Tact makes the world go round, Dagwood. The business world anyway. By the way, I hear you've been lashing yourself up to a little love-nest in the country?'

Dagwood flushed. 'I wouldn't exactly call it that, sir.'

'What would you call it then?'

'Well, it's a flat really. It's actually a converted Tithe Barn.'

'Sounds just the job. Can you cook?'

'Sort of.'

'The next thing is, you'll be giving discreet little dinners. For two.'

'Oh, I doubt that sir.'

'Don't be too sure. You'll meet some girl or other, I can guarantee,' said The Bodger, casually.

The Bodger's words were prophetic. Hurrying round the corner of the main Harvey McNichol & Drummond office block the next morning, Dagwood did indeed meet a girl. He met her in the classic manner – head on.

The girl spun round with the impact and fell to the ground.

'You clumsy great *oaf!*' she said to Dagwood.

'I'm most terribly sorry. I really am. Let me help you up.'

The girl's eyes snapped at him. 'That's the least you can do, you great elephant!'

The girl took Dagwood's hand and pulled herself up. Dagwood recognised her as Sir Rollo's private secretary. Without her spectacles and in the plain light of day Dagwood could see that she was a very pretty girl. Dagwood felt a sudden urge of panic that he might have injured her.

'God, look at that stocking! And the heel of my shoe's come off! Oh *you* . . .' The girl gritted her teeth.

'Let me . . . Let me help you into the hall porter's office?'

'Thank you,' the girl said coldly.

She held Dagwood's arm and hopped and limped into the hall. Her grip was firm and light. Dagwood felt a strange but pleasurable prickling between his shoulder blades.

'Thank you. Now please go.'

'But can't I do anything? Fetch something?'

'I shall be quite all right, thank you.'

'Hadn't we better patch you up before the Great Bogle wonders where you are?'

'The Great . . .' The girl stared at Dagwood. 'If you mean my father, Sir Rollo,' she said icily, 'I'm sure he'll understand. Now . . . do . . . please . . . GO!'

Dagwood obeyed. He raced up the stairs to his own office, burst through the door and shot into his chair.

'What's the matter, Daggers?' Ollie asked.

'Tact, *tact*, TACT!' Dagwood shouted at the wall.

8

'Dagwood,' said The Bodger, over the telephone, 'Have you ever met Rob Roy?'

'No sir, I didn't even know he was still alive.'

'He's very much alive. My wife and I had dinner with him the other night. He was in cracking form but he sounded a little wistful that more people didn't call on him. It's the anniversary of his V.C. this week so I think it might be an idea if one of you called on him and made your number with him.'

'Right, I'll do that, sir.'

'He's in the telephone book. I should give him a ring first.'

'Right, sir.'

Dagwood put down the telephone. 'Ollie, where's that bit of bumf that arrived the other day, all about Rob Roy's V.C.?'

'In your "In" tray.'

It was the custom of the Submarine Service to publish on the anniversary of every submarine Victoria Cross a Special Order of the Day describing the exploit and its chief participant. Rob Roy's Special Order was short but it might have been the raw material for a 'Boy's Own Paper' serial. Dagwood read how the submarine E.41, Lieutenant-Commander Robert Iain MacGregor in command, dived at noon on 20th March, 1916, penetrated the inner defences of Kiel Harbour and immobilised the heavy cruiser 'Hohenzollern' with two torpedo hits just before dusk. Retreating under cover of darkness, E.41 surfaced to recharge her batteries but was surprised and nearly run down by another German cruiser which she hit with one torpedo, fired from the surface. E.41 finally drew clear after engaging with gunfire an armed German trawler – for all of which exploits her Commanding Officer, Lieutenant Robert Iain MacGregor, R.N., was awarded the Victoria Cross.

'Man,' said Dagwood admiringly, 'this Rob Roy character must have been quite a lad!'

'He's not dead, you know,' said Ollie. 'He turns up to the odd Reunion.'

'I know he's not dead. He lives around these parts. That was The Bodger on the telephone just now suggesting that one of us go and call on him. Shall I do it?'

'Certainly. He'll probably be thrilled to bits. I don't expect he gets many chances to pound people's ears about the good old days. You'll be a godsend to him. You never know,' said Ollie slyly, 'he may have a daughter.'

'Do me a favour Ollie and just drop dead. Let's have a look at the directory.'

Dagwood rapidly riffled through the pages. '. . . This must be him. Rear-Admiral R. I. MacGregor, King's Monachorum. Telephone number King's Monachorum 27.'

The telephone was answered by a cool, feminine voice. 'Hello?'

'I wonder if I could speak to the Admiral, please?'

'I'm afraid the Admiral's busy at the moment. May I take a message? I am his daughter.'

'His *daughter?*'

'Yes.' The voice grew several degrees less cordial. 'Is that so strange?'

'He's *got* a daughter?'

'I am his daughter,' said the voice frostily; Dagwood could almost feel the rime forming on the receiver.

'I'm sorry to be so rude . . . I'm in the Navy here . . . In Oozemouth . . . I wondered if I could call . .'

'*Who's that?*' Another voice, roaring like a Force Nine gale, drowned Dagwood out. It could only be the Admiral himself, speaking from another extension.

'Who's that? What's he saying, Patricia?'

'I think he'd like to call on us, Daddy . . .'

'*Splendid!* Who is he?'

'He's . . .'

'*What?*'

Dagwood thought it time he rejoined the conversation. 'My name is Lieutenant Jones, sir, I . . .'

'Good morning, Jones!'

'Good morning, sir. I'm refitting a submarine here and I . . .'

'*Submariner,* eh?'

'Yes, sir.'

'You must come and see us. Come on Saturday. Come for lunch!'

'I'd be delighted, sir . . .'

'Good. We'll expect you. Good-bye!'

'Good-bye, sir . . .'

'Daddy, hadn't we better explain how to get here?'

'Nonsense! He's got a tongue in his head, hasn't he? Good-bye, Jones!'

'Good-bye, sir, I . . .'

The line went dead.

'All fixed up?' said Ollie.

'Well, I gather so.'

'I suppose the voice I could hear plainly from here was the Admiral himself?'

'Right. He's invited me to lunch on Saturday. Now where the devil *is* King's Monachorum?'

Dagwood took down the AA Handbook from the shelf which also contained the Navy List, Bradshaw's, Whitaker's, Pears Cyclopaedia, Wisden's, Timeform and other volumes without which no submarine refitting office would have been completely furnished.

'It's not here. It must be a pretty obscure sort of place.'

The AA Handbook should have warned Dagwood. By a

quarter past twelve on Saturday he was lost. A succession of knowledgeable-looking locals had listened to the name Admiral MacGregor and had directed him unerringly to two deserted farmyards, one clump of impenetrable bramble bushes at the end of a stony lane, and an abandoned quarry. At last Dagwood met met a woman on a bicycle who looked like the local midwife.

'Rear-Admiral MacGregor? How ever did you get up here? You'll have to turn and go back the way you've come until you reach a signpost. One way says 'King's Monachorum' and the other says 'Tilsey Caldicote.' Don't take the King's Monachorum one. Take the other one and keep going until you reach a long copper beech hedge on your right with a white gate in it. That's where the Admiral lives.'

'Thank you very much,' Dagwood said gratefully, recognising in the copper beech hedge and the white gate landmarks he had already passed and repassed many times.

When Dagwood got out of his car to open the gate he saw a notice in the hedge.

'Don't Drive. Walk.'

Obediently, Dagwood parked his car on the grass verge and began to walk.

The Admiral's house lay a full hundred and fifty yards back from the road and was approached by a gravel drive which had clearly been laid down by a madman or a somnambulist for it meandered towards the house in a series of sweeping bends and zigzags. Daffodils grew in clumps in the grass which was still unmown and unkempt after the winter. A double row of lime trees bordered the grass on each side.

A window in the front of the house opened and the gale blew out of it.

'What's your height, Jones?'

'Five foot ten, sir,' Dagwood shouted, quick as a flash.

'Thought so.'

The window shut. Dagwood continued his walk with the

uncomfortable feeling that his every movement was being watched and, furthermore, predicted. After a little while it occurred to him that his walk was being considerably lengthened by the eccentricities of the drive. It would be far quicker to leave the drive and walk straight towards the house on the grass. Dagwood stepped off the drive.

'Don't walk on the grass! Stay on the drive!'

Dagwood returned to the drive. He was a philosophical young man and believed that every man was king on his own land; if the voice from the window had ordered him to walk the remainder of the distance on his hands he would have done his best to comply.

Patricia was waiting for him at the front door.

'Good morning, Mr Jones. I'm sorry you had all those instructions. It was just Daddy practising.'

'Oh yes?' Dagwood said, lamely. Perhaps it was his imagination but he thought he could hear a sound from inside the house. It was a familiar sound, very faint, the faintest of whispers, but it struck a responsive chord in Dagwood's memory. Like a name that was on the tip of his tongue, Dagwood could remember it well but could not quite recapture it.

'Do come in. I'm Patricia. The Admiral's daughter,' she added.

'How do you do?'

When he tried to describe Patricia MacGregor to Ollie, Dagwood could only think of the Snow Maiden. She made him think at once of that tragic pale princess who could never fall in love because of the ice splinter buried in her heart. She was tall for a woman, as tall as Dagwood himself, and she had long blonde hair to her shoulders, hair which was brushed but not waved or styled in any way. Her eyes were large and blue and appeared not to be focusing upon Dagwood at all but on some point behind him. She was wearing a grey cardigan and a tweed skirt and she had a single string of pearls round her neck. Dagwood looked down and noted the inevitable brown brogue shoes and lisle stockings. Dagwood put her age at about twenty-nine or thirty and she looked as though she had spent all her life in this house, walking and dreaming of the man who would one day come to claim her. She looked as though she had already waited so long that she would not recognise him when he arrived; Dagwood had a suspicion that when Prince Charming came to call Patricia MacGregor would send him round to the tradesman's entrance.

'Are you going to come in?'

'Oh, of course, yes.'

The Force Nine gale blew once more, explosively down the Hall.

'*Jones!*'

Dagwood hurried into the drawing-room and shook hands with his host. He became aware of a russet-coloured dressing-gown and a pair of bright blue eyes.

'Sherry or whisky, Jones?'

'Sherry please, sir.'

'I hope you didn't mind my firing six fish into you as you passed that last lot of daffodils?'

'Not at all, sir,' Dagwood murmured politely, adding the remark to the sum of other inexplicable features of this house. He studied the Admiral closely while he was pouring the sherry. Dagwood was very conscious that he was in the presence of a man who was the paragon of his generation, who was still held up as the mirror of perfection amongst submarine captains. Working in tiny boats with elementary torpedo firing gear and a short dived endurance, this stooping figure in the faded dressing-gown and the ragged bedroom slippers had laid down principles of offensive submarine warfare which were still taught in the service. But time had taken its revenge. Dagwood was looking at the ruin of a once powerful and magnificent face. The eyes were still there, and the mouth, but the rest had decayed . . .

Dagwood was startled by the jangling of a bell above the

door. Patricia leaped to the window.

'It's the postman, Daddy!'

'Action stations! Attack team close up! Jump about a bit, young Jones, you can be my range and bearing recorder!'

Dagwood set down his drink carefully on a table, determined not to allow himself to be further surprised. His ears had not deceived him after all. The familiar sound which had puzzled him at the front door had been the authentic slither of a periscope moving through its gland. In an alcove at the far end of the room a periscope was rising from the floor. It was not a type Dagwood had ever seen before but it was the genuine article and the Admiral was handling it as though it were an extension of himself.

'It's the postman all right! What's his height?'

Patricia consulted a long board which hung against one of the bookcases. It appeared to Dagwood to be a list of names. He could just read the heading – 'Jane's Fighting Hawkers, Costers & Vendors.'

'Five feet eight inches, Daddy.'

'Set five feet eight inches!'

'*Set!*'

'Range on five feet eight inches is . . . *that!*'

'Thirty-two, sir.'

'Speak up!'

'*Thirty-two*, sir!' bawled Dagwood.

'Very good. Bearing is . . . that!'

'Green three five, sir!'

'Very good. I am forty degrees on his starboard bow. Down periscope.'

The Admiral glared at a stop-watch he had taken from the top pocket of his dressing-gown. 'I'll give him five seconds. By that time he should have reached the third lime tree. He'll have to turn to starboard then whether he likes it or not.'

'That's cheating, Daddy!'

'No it's not, my dear. It comes under the heading of local knowledge. Up periscope.'

The Admiral seized the handles as they rose towards him, unfolded them, and put his eyes to apertures in one fluid graceful movement.

'No he hasn't by God! He's fooled me! He's cut across the grass! I'm now five degrees on his *port* bow!'

Dagwood could quite understand why the 'Hohenzollern' had been doomed. Such was the Admiral's driving personality that it was difficult for Dagwood to remember that the enemy was only the postman, a public servant, dodging from daffodil to daffodil with the afternoon mail.

'... Range, boy, range!' roared the Admiral.

'Th-three nine, sir!'

'Bearing is ... *that!*'

'Green three, sir.'

The postman evaded. The Admiral followed. The postman jinked. The Admiral tracked him. It was an exciting attack and the postman only received the salvo as he made his final dash towards the front door where he rapped the knocker twice and, catching sight of Dagwood through the window, waved cheerily as he turned away.

'Good sort, that postman,' the Admiral said, approvingly. 'Used to be a submarine leading stoker. Not like those bloody dustmen. Bolshie lot of buggers. The paper boy is the best. Enters into the spirit of the thing. He'll make a good submariner when he grows up.'

The Admiral caught Dagwood's look. 'You must forgive an old man's foibles. This looks odd to you but it gives me a lot of innocent pleasure.'

'I don't think it's odd at all, sir,' Dagwood replied, loyally. 'May I just take a look at your "Jane's" for a moment, sir?'

'Patricia, show Jones our masterpiece.'

'Jane's Fighting Hawkers, Costers & Vendors' was an extraordinary document. It was a list of everybody who had ever called at the Admiral's house, together with their height, gait, periodicities of visits and any relevant information. Most of the entries were commonplace: 'Joe Glubb, green-grocer,

5'7", stiff walk (arthritis), calls about tea-time every Tuesday & Friday', but some of the other descriptions might have caused some heart-burning if they had ever been published amongst the Admiral's neighbours. The Vicar, for instance, would have been taken aback to find himself described as '6'0", walks like a nancy-boy, calls at lunch time on Sat. before 8th Sun. after Trinity.' The Lord Lieutenant of the county, a retired Major-General whom the Admiral detested, was dismissed as: 'Pompous five foot nothing, walks as though he had 2 hairs in his arse tied together, calls when he wants to borrow binoculars for Cheltenham.' Altogether 'Jane's Fighting Hawkers, Costers & Vendors' was a curious document. Dagwood found it hard to comment adequately upon it.

'I must say it's an interesting list, sir,' he said.

'D'you like it? Patricia and I get a lot of fun writing it up.'

'There's one more to go in now,' Patricia said. She took the list from Dagwood, wrote swiftly in it and handed it back to him. Dagwood read: 'Lieut. Jones, R.N. 5'10", quick walk but liable to erratic alterations of course. Reason for visit – duty.'

Dagwood revised his earlier opinion of Patricia MacGregor. When Prince Charming arrived, Patricia would not only direct him to the tradesman's entrance but would log his height, gait and excuse for visiting. Dagwood could even visualise the entry: 'Prince Charming, tall, dark and handsome, walks as though he owns the place, left a glass slipper in the coal shed.'

'What do you think of my periscope, eh, Jones?'

'I was a bit staggered to see it, sir . . .'

'It came from a German U-boat. They were breaking up a lot of boats just after the war and I asked the Admiral Submarines at the time to let me have one of the periscopes. I was his captain when he was a sprog sub-lieutenant . . .' A malicious gleam entered the Admiral's eye '. . . . so he could hardly refuse me. They sent me the periscope, the press, the wires, the pump and all the piping. I got our local builder to fix up the well and Mr Maggs our plumber did the piping . . .'

'Do you use ordinary telemotor oil in the system, sir?' Dagwood asked.

'No, it's anti-freeze!' The Admiral chuckled. He was obviously delighted by the question; it was not one which would have occurred to the majority of his visitors. It reminded him, pleasurably, that his present visitor spoke his own language. 'I tried ordinary oil from the car at first but it made a mess of the deck. I'll show you round . . .'

Dagwood had once been taken round a model train layout belonging to a retired spice merchant who was a neighbour of Dame's at home. He recognised the same fanaticism as the Admiral showed him the brick well in the drawing-room floor, the hoist wires concealed in conduits in the walls and the ceilings, the press hidden behind the bookcase and the pump stowed away in a niche under the window seat. The periscope was controlled by a lever fashioned out of a Rolls Royce Flying Lady which projected from the wall by the fireplace.

'Patricia normally looks after that,' said the Admiral.

The Admiral raised and lowered the periscope several times.

'Have a look through it, Jones!'

Dagwood was not an expert on periscopes but he knew enough about them to appreciate that the Admiral's periscope was in superb condition. There were no specks or flaws in the top face and there was not a suspicion of damp mist in the glass. The ranging mechanism moved like silk. Dagwood swung the periscope, expecting the tell-tale shudder of an imperfect bearing, but the instrument slid round without a tremor.

'It seems in very good nick, sir,' he said.

'It's as good as the day it was made. You can say what you like about Jerry but his glassware is still the best in the world. Always has been. I've always believed that the Germans made the best periscopes in the world. I also think they made

the best submariners too, though I suppose I shouldn't say
that. It must be something in their national temperament.
Scratch a German and you find a submariner. Even their
language suits submarines perfectly. I remember meeting Max
Horton just after the war. It was the last time I saw him.
He told me he'd just come back from Londonderry where
some of the captured U-boats were lying. He told me about
the German submarine crews. He said they were sullen, they
were scruffy and smelly. He said they were the bolshiest-
looking lot of ruffians he had ever seen and some of them had
hair as long as a girl's *but* . . .' – the Admiral shook
an emphatic finger at Dagwood – '. . . this is the point. They
didn't carry themselves like beaten men! They were all ready
to carry on the war with the Russians! Remember, this was
at a time when the U-boat Command had lost seven hundred
boats out of a total of eleven hundred and half their officers
and men were pressed men from the Luftwaffe! It hardly
bears thinking about, Jones.'

'No, sir,' said Dagwood, seriously.

The Admiral leaned forward to emphasise another point.
'I was telling our local Member the other night, the stupid
little man doesn't believe me, I said you will *never* stop the
Germans messing about with submarines. You might as well
try and stop the people of this country playing cricket. If you
stop them building real ones they'll build model ones. And
if you take your eye off him for a moment Jerry will have a
first-class, fully-trained U-boat fleet again before you can say
Jack Robinson. That's why I'm not worried about a Russian
fleet of so many hundred submarines. There's more to a
submarine fleet than building submarines. The history of
Russian submarines has been one long disaster. But if those
submarines are designed by Germans and if their crews are
German-trained and have a sprinkling of Germans amongst
'em, *then* I'm ready to listen . . .'

'Would you like lunch now?' Patricia asked.

'Take your glass in with you, Jones,' said the Admiral.

They moved next door to the dining-room. Dagwood was struck by the room's size. The table could have seated twenty people, but only three places were laid. The Admiral sat at the head of the table with Dagwood and Patricia on either side of him.

'We don't do much entertaining since my wife died,' the Admiral explained.

The long shining plane of polished table, the tiny patch of silver, cutlery and glass at one end, the portraits along the walls, the high oak sideboard with its knobs and ornamentally-carved drawers, all reminded Dagwood vividly of nights when he had dined in large wardrooms where most of the members lived ashore and only the duty officers dined in. There was the same sense of continuity, the sense that the figures seated at table were the tangible representatives of a far greater company, invisible, yet whose spirits still permeated the room.

Without any warning, the Admiral bent his head and said grace. 'No padre, thank God,' he barked.

Patricia served them with vegetable soup. The Admiral shook his napkin from its folds and swept it across his lap. Dagwood followed suit although, he admitted to himself, with far less panache.

'Help yourself to sherry, Jones,' said the Admiral hospitably.

'Thank you, sir.'

The Admiral crushed a piece of toast with his fist. 'How's our nuclear programme coming along, Jones?'

'I don't really know, sir. It's all on a need-to-know basis and I don't expect I know any more about it than the average member of the public can get from the newspapers.'

'Are Harvey McNichol & Drummond going to get a contract for a nuclear submarine?'

'There again I don't know, sir. Nobody's mentioned it.'

'Knowing them,' said the Admiral, 'I don't suppose it has occurred to them. If I was their managing director, what's his name again?'

'Sir Rollo, sir?'

'That's the fellow. If I was him I would be on the telephone every day and submitting a tender once a week.'

'I haven't heard anything about it, sir.'

'I wonder what sort of man will command these submarines, when we get 'em,' the Admiral said. 'When I pressed the button in the old days I only sank some terrified little coaster. Sometimes the fish came·back and nearly sank me! But when these fellows press the button they're going to destroy the equivalent of half the population of London! They're going to have more power in their little fingers than Nelson and all his captains had in their entire fleets. I trust they don't get a sudden rush of blood to the head one day. If you let one of those off by mistake you can't turn round and tell Admiral Submarines you're very sorry and you promise not to do it again, eh? Can't laugh one of those off, eh Jones?'

'No sir, you can't,' said Dagwood.

The Admiral finished his soup in half a dozen quick mouthfuls. 'Our local schoolmaster was telling me an interesting thing. It seems that when a Roman general had a triumph and rode through the streets of Rome in his chariot he always had a slave standing beside him who whispered in his ear to remind him that he was only mortal and not a god. In case the whole thing went to his head, I suppose. The Romans had as good an idea of the psychology of power as we have. Better, in some ways. But who's going to stand behind these nuclear boys and whisper in *their* ears, eh Jones?'

'*That's* a point, sir,' said Dagwood.

The Admiral wiped his mouth with his napkin. 'Met a fellow once, called himself a novelist. R.N.V.R. during the war. Said he was in corvettes. He had the infernal impudence to tell me that all submariners were either power maniacs, sadists or nautical romantics. Damned impudence!'

There was no doubt that the Admiral did himself well. After the soup, Patricia brought in grilled trout with white wine sauce, followed by beef olives tightly rolled in bay leaves sprinkled with mint, new potatoes and artichokes, Welsh rarebit with bitter sauce, and frozen chocolate mousse with grated nutmeg. By the time Dagwood started on his Caerphilly and his Ryvita biscuits and the Admiral passed round his madeira, Dagwood was beginning to feel quite groggy with food and drink.

Dagwood was puzzled by the absence of servants. There seemed to be nobody in the house except themselves. Patricia fetched the food from a hatch by the sideboard and took the plates away again afterwards. When Dagwood attempted to help, the Admiral said, 'Sit down Jones, it's better if one person does it and Patricia knows where everything is.' It was as though the house were solely dedicated to keeping alive the Admiral's dying spirit, with Patricia the acolyte tending the flame. Dagwood was awed by the girl's fortitude; he wondered at the qualities of patience and self-denial which kept her here to look after her father instead of running off to marry a groom, or getting a housekeeper's job in Ross & Cromarty, or emigrating to Australia, or doing any of the things Dagwood imagined girls in her position did. Patricia seemed to sense that Dagwood was wondering about her.

'Tell us what you do in the dockyard, Mr Jones,' she said.

'Oh, I'm just standing by while the firm refit the submarine.'

'How's that rogue Tybalt?' asked the Admiral. 'Been battering at you with his theories about what's wrong with the Navy, has he?'

'Not yet, sir.'

'He will. He's a good fellow but some of his staff are a bit dubious, eh?'

Dagwood thought of Mr Swales. 'I have had a bit of trouble with one or two of them, sir.'

'It's a good thing you don't always agree with the civil servants, Jones. Tybalt's not a civil servant of course, but the rest of that crew are. There are two forces that get things done in the Navy and one of them is the friction between civilians and serving officers. Friction leads to frustration and frustration is a powerful source of energy. Some of those civil servants hold a good deal of responsibility and handle large sums of money. Who do they think they are, they say of us in the Navy, they look down on the civil servants yet they can't see further than their present appointments and they won't give us the facts we need. The Navy, on the other side, deal with actual men and conditions. Who do they think they are, we say of the civil servants, sitting in their damned little offices and telling us what to do? They ought to come down and actually see what goes on for a change. Both sides swear at each other and the remarkable thing is, something *happens!*'

It was a good point. Dagwood acknowledged it. 'But what's the other force in the Navy, sir?'

'Ah, I thought you'd ask that! It's the struggle against chaos, Jones. The Navy is always on the brink of chaos. I served for forty years and I never took over a job that wasn't in a state of chaos. I worked for two years to put it right and the man who came after me always thought *he'd* taken over the job in a state of chaos. The Navy runs in a state of suspended dissolution. Always has. Always will.'

It was now very plain to Dagwood that he had gravely misjudged the Admiral. All that business with the postman dodging and jinking across the lawn had been very misleading. The Admiral was not, as Dagwood had first thought him, just another retired flag officer quietly going bonkers in the country. He was still very much alive and sensitive to the changes taking place in the world and the Navy.

As if to prove that he was not yet a doddering old fool, the Admiral suddenly switched his attack on to Dagwood himself.

'You're a technical officer, aren't you, Jones?'

'An electrical officer, sir.'

'That's a pity.'

Dagwood reddened. 'I don't think so, sir.'

'Of course it's a pity! The Navy's a damn fine life for a

young man, whatever his particular expertise is, but there's only one job in the whole Navy that makes the whole lot worthwhile and that's to command your own ship. It doesn't matter how old or how small she is, once you've commanded her the Admiralty won't owe you a penny. There's no other job like it and once you've done it every other job, no matter how responsible or interesting, seems flat and stale. I know.'

Dagwood was not disconcerted by the attack. He relished it. Beneath the Admiral's dogmatic assertions and massive blockbuster arguments, assembled piece by invulnerable piece, Dagwood perceived the charm of manner for which Rob Roy was still remembered in the service.

'If you didn't have technical officers, sir, the most you could command nowadays would be a dumb lighter.'

'Of course! And that's my answer!'

The Admiral, too, was enjoying himself; it was seldom someone came to see him who spoke his own language (albeit a primitive dialect of it). The Admiral began to talk of his early days in the Navy. ' . . . Submarines were just starting when I joined. When they asked me why I wanted to join the Navy I said I wanted to be a submariner. In those days I might just as well have said I wanted to practise robbery with violence! I was nearly failed out of hand! Submariners were supposed to be pirates you see, and there was a suggestion that they should be hung from the yard-arm if they were captured in time of war . . .'

The Admiral remembered the days in E-boats in the Dardanelles. ' . . . Sometimes we were not sure we could dive and when we did dive we were not at all sure we would ever come up again. Everything was new and raw. It was like living in the early days of the wild West. All the fun's gone out of it now.'

He talked of the grotesque, steam-driven K-boats. ' . . . They were meant to be a submarine which could work with the fleet, like a submersible destroyer. It was a contradiction in terms. The submariner is the cat who walks by himself. Any destroyer captain worth the name will never stop to have dealings with a submarine in war-time. He'll sink it first and ask questions afterwards. And quite right, too.'

He spoke of the huge M-boats, one of them fitted with an aircraft in a hangar and another with a battleship's gun. '. . . I never commanded one myself but they used to tell me that gun was very useful. Not as a gun, of course. As an extra hydroplane. Even if you had a bad trim, the gun helped you get down!'

It was very late in the afternoon before Dagwood said good-bye.

'Glad you came, Jones. You must come again. Come in the evening next time. We'll have a real talk. Is that the baker's van, Patricia?'

Dagwood left them in the early stages of the attack.

9

On Sundays Dagwood went to morning service at the Church of St Giles, Little Binton. Little Binton was almost twelve miles from the Watsons' farm and Dagwood might have thought it an unreasonable distance to travel to a church service, were it not for the Vicar of St Giles.

The Reverend Godfrey Potter, M.A., had been padre to submarine flotillas for twenty years until the end of the war when he retired from the Navy to become a country parson. Despite the ancient superstition which forbade padres to go to sea in a submarine or even go on board one except by express invitation of the Captain, the Reverend Godfrey had come to be recognised as padre to the Submarine Service. Perhaps there was some quality in the boats and the men who went to sea in them which fascinated him but he still spoke wistfully of his days on the China station, in Malta, in Scotland, and wherever submarines were gathered, as the happiest of his life and he was always extravagantly delighted when any submariner called on him. He himself was a short, thickset man, almost bald except for a ring of ginger hair round his scalp. His figure suggested that he wore a suit of armour under his vestments and indeed he might have been a throwback to one of those formidable, warlike bishops of the Middle Ages who were quite capable of enforcing Holy Writ with a spiked iron ball on a length of chain.

Although the Reverend Godfrey had left his mark on the Navy the service had also stamped him. His sermons had not changed since the days when he had pitched his voice to carry to the last rank of a thousand sailors formed up on the quarterdeck. The regular St Giles congregation of four elders, seventeen elderly ladies and Dagwood were quite accustomed to their pastor's admonishments from the pulpit on the moral dangers of consorting with loose women and indulging in strong liquors. On the first Sunday he attended, Dagwood had been gripped with emotion when, to the text James 3 : 10 – 'Out of same mouth proceedeth blessing and cursing. My brethren these things ought not so to be,' he and the seventeen elderly ladies had been harangued on the subject of swearing on the messdeck.

Indications of the Reverend Godfrey's long association with the Navy abounded in his church, not only in the ship's bell used as a stand-by font and the Sea Cadets' colours laid up behind the choir stalls, but also in his Standing Orders which Dagwood saw pinned to the vestry door.

'Vicar's Standing Orders,' Dagwood read. 'Short title V.S.Os.'

'Fifteen minutes before the start of the service, the Verger will report to the Curate : 'Church ready for service.'

'This report will be taken to mean :

    1 Hymn sheets and hassocks issued.
    2 Altar candles burning brightly.
    3 Emergency candles tested and correct.
    4 Hymnboard reading hymns for the day.
    5 Crypt bilges dry.
    6 Trim on the font.
    7 Lectern voicepipe cocks checked open.

'Ten minutes before the start of the service, the Organist will report to the Curate : 'Organ and choir ready for service.'

'This will be taken to mean :

Organist and choir closed up and correct.
Main organ ready Group Up.
Blower running on all bass and treble pipes.
Choir stalls secured for service.

'Five minutes before the start of the service, the Curate will report to me:

All hands on board.
Main door shut and clipped.

'On receipt of these reports, and being in all respects ready for service I will take up position in rear of the convoy and give the order: – 'Let go forward, let go aft, start the voluntary!'

'The service will then begin.'

That, thought Dagwood, should cover it.

It was not until he had shaken hands with the Reverend Godfrey after the service and was on his way back to his car that Dagwood thought again of Patricia MacGregor. He had summed her up as the Snow Maiden but he had done nothing to try and thaw her. He had barely spoken to her. Dagwood made up his mind to change that. Patricia MacGregor was something of a challenge. He stopped at the farm to ask Molly if he could use their telephone.

'Of course you can, Dagwood,' Molly said. 'Any time you want to, just come across. Are you getting on all right over there? We never hear anything so we assume everything's all right.'

'I brought up a lot of stuff from home,' said Dagwood, 'so I'm pretty well fixed now.'

'Well, just say if you need anything. The telephone's in the hall.'

Patricia answered it herself.

' . . . I just thought I'd ring up and say how much I enjoyed lunch yesterday,' Dagwood said to her.

'That's all right. We were very glad to see you. You must come again.'

'I'd like to very much, but in the meantime how would you like to come and have a meal with me?'

'You mean at your digs?'

'No, no, I've got a flat.'

'Oh.'

'At least it's not exactly a flat. It's actually a tithe barn.'

'You mean, come and have dinner with you at your tithe barn?'

'Yes,' said Dagwood. Put like that, it did sound an unlikely sort of proposition.

'That sounds lovely.' When would you like me to come?'

'What day suits you?'

'I don't do very much here . . .'

'I'll bet you don't,' Dagwood said to himself.

' . . . Any day would suit me.'

'How about Wednesday then?'

'Yes, I think that's all right.'

'Would you like me to come and collect you?'

'No, I'll drive myself over in the car. Where do you live?'

'At Watson's farm. It's . . .'

'I know where that is. *That* tithe barn. Have they made it into a flat? I'd love to see that.'

'Well, Wednesday evening then. About seven thirty.'

'Lovely.'

Dagwood put down the receiver with a feeling of disappointment. She had been polite, but nothing more. There had been no sign at all that the iceberg was beginning to melt. Dagwood had a sudden premonition that perhaps this particular iceberg would require more heat than he was able to generate.

However, there were artificial aids. Daphne appreciated the problem at once and produced two bottles of dark Burgundy. The wine was a glowing red, hot and rich like the blood of martyrs.

'There you are, love,' she said. 'Two pints o'that and she'll roll over and show you the promised land.'

'I don't know what you mean, Daphne.'

'You know what I mean, love.'

The butcher in the village also had an accurate grasp of the situation. 'For two, sir?' he said, when Dagwood came into his shop on Wednesday evening.

'Yes, please.'

'Steak, sir?' said the butcher, giving his knife a preliminary sharpen.

'Wait a minute!' Dagwood remembered something he had read in a women's magazine. Steak by itself was mortally dull. How about shush kebab? 'Just give me one piece of steak. And a piece of liver. And kidney and some sausage. Two bits of bacon and can you chop the whole lot into small pieces?'

'What's this, sir, Irish stew?'

'Shush kebab. I'd better have a couple of skewers too.'

'I've only got metal ones, sir. Now if you'll take my advice, there's a hazel bush in the hedge just at the back of your barn there. You cut a couple of straight pieces from that, whittle of the bark, sharpen the ends and you'll have two fine skewers. Makes the meat taste a lot better, sir.'

'What a splendid idea!'

'That'll impress her, sir.' The butcher winked.

With shush kebab, the grocer warmly recommended rice. 'Dead easy to cook, sir, and just put in some frozen peas and bits of cooked ham chopped into cubes. Add a bit of saffron to colour it and there you are.'

'Right,' said Dagwood. 'I'll do that.'

One more logistical requirement was supplied by Chubb. Chubb was a gipsy and a moucher. He had no job, but lived, literally, off the land. If it suited him, he dug a ditch, sharpened a saw or ground a lawn-mower blade. If it did not suit him, he did nothing. He made a very comfortable living throughout the year selling daffodils, fern plants, honeysuckle, watercress, mushrooms and blackberries in season to housewives. He also had understandings with some shopkeepers, supplying moss to the florist, bulrushes to the tailor and heather to the butcher. Chubb always knew before anyone else where the best plants grew, where every bird nested, and where the largest fish fed. He could also supply rabbits, hares and chickens, if he felt like it. Chubb was answerable to no man and gave Dagwood to understand that it was he, Chubb, who was doing him, Dagwood, a favour in providing primroses and daffodils to decorate the barn. Molly distrusted Chubb, but Dagwood, who did not have the country-born suspicion of gipsies, recognised that he was probably the most valuable acquaintance he had made in Oozemouth.

The last requirement to melt the iceberg was heat, actual physical heat. Dagwood remembered how cold the Admiral's house had been once they moved out of the drawing-room. Dagwood stoked up his stove until the back thrummed and glowed with heat and he had to take off his sweater as he skewered the pieces of meat, laid the table and looked out the tapes for the tape-recorder.

When Dagwood was ready, the whole tithe barn was warm; the corks had been drawn and the wine was taking deep breaths in the kitchen; the table was lit by three candles in a holder Dame had presented; and the tape-recorder was ready to play soft music. Dagwood had two hours and ten minutes of 'Eine Kleine Smooch Musik' on tape, an amount he estimated should be sufficient to complete the count-down. Looking round him, Dagwood considered that for a first night he had not made at all a bad job of it.

Patricia arrived at precisely half past seven. Dagwood was both pleased and chilled by this fact. He was pleased that she had thought it worthwhile to arrive on time but he was chilled by the sheer cold efficiency of it. He had no doubt that if he had asked her to arrive at twenty-nine and a half minutes past the hour she would have done just that.

'What a nice room,' Patricia said, as Dagwood took her coat. 'And *lovely* and warm!'

Dagwood's arrangements went off with precision. The candles cast an intimate light over the minestrone soup (from a packet) which was palatable though lumpy but, as Dagwood pointed out, minestrone was supposed to be lumpy. Patricia complimented Dagwood on his shush kebab. Dagwood did not spill anything, nor did the candles drip. The tape-recorder ground manfully away at its task of setting the mood. Logistics-wise, Dagwood told himself, we're hot.

But on the personal level the evening did not prosper so well. Like many another logistics wizard before him, Dagwood was in danger of being defeated by personalities. The food, the wine, the music, the girl, all were there but the mixture did not coagulate. They talked in general terms of Oozemouth and the people in it. Patricia asked Dagwood politely if he was enjoying Oozemouth. Dagwood replied politely that he was having the time of his life. They talked of her father.

'Daddy's still mad about submarines,' Patricia said.

'It's something that gets under your skin if you don't watch it,' said Dagwood, already wondering if he should use the eternal stand-by of submariners when entertaining women – the story of how he escaped from six hundred feet during the war bringing the injured Captain and all the confidential books up on his back. There were many variations in the story but all were of the generic type derisively referred to as – 'there was I, upside down at a hundred feet, and nothing in me glass' stories.

'About a year ago a lot of submarines were running aground,' said Patricia. 'Every day there seemed to be something in the newspapers about it. I had to get the doctor to come and see Daddy because I thought he was going to have a stroke. Daddy runs the Submarine Old Comrades' Association in Oozemouth. There are a lot of old boys living round about who used to be submariners and they all knew Daddy in the old days.'

'Does he go to the Reunion?'

'Oh yes, of course he does, when he gets his diary at the beginning of the year it's the first thing he writes in it. He goes every year. I don't know what he does while he's away but it always takes him a week to get there and back.'

Dagwood told Patricia of *Seahorse's* commission. He told her of the sudden crazes for strange clothes while the submarine was at sea, of the stokers' fashion for sombreros and moustaches and the torpedomen's six-shooters and sheriff's stars. He told her of the riot which broke out in the petty officers' mess when the Electrical Artificer, a man of erudition, had looked at the Sunday roast meat and vegetables and remarked to the Coxswain, who was suspected of being a secret bible-puncher, 'Hebrews thirteen, eight, Coxswain.' The Coxswain had looked up the verse and seen that it was 'Jesus Christ, the same yesterday, and today, and for ever.' Dagwood told Patricia of the minutiae of life on board, of the uckers games, the football matches, the brass plaque 'The Smallest Room' screwed on the door of the wardroom heads, the ketchup specially issued to submarines (Dagwood had never met it anywhere else) which had the evocatory label 'Take Lots Of It With Everything.' He told her of the day The Bodger thought he had appendicitis and was nearly operated on by the Coxswain and the First Lieutenant, of the day the Electrician's pet monkey electrocuted itself in the motor room, and of the day they held a Festival of Nine Lessons and Carols in the fore-ends of the submarine.

Patricia listened with polite attention but Dagwood knew that he was being boring. He realised it early but the knowledge only served to make him worse. Nobody can be as boring as an Englishman entertaining a woman; only an Englishman would have the effrontery to burden her with the trivia of his daily life. Dagwood endeavoured to become more intimate.

'But how about you, what do you do with yourself, living out there?'

'I do the cooking and the shopping and look after Daddy.'

'But how about dances and things?'

'We go to the Hunt Ball every year. Daddy enjoys it.'

'But don't you?'

She looked at him as though he had prodded her. Then she shrugged. 'They're quite nice. You meet all your friends.'

'Any particular friend?'

She looked straight at him and said, 'No.'

Dagwood decided that the time had come to cut the dialectics and get to grips. 'Come here,' he said.

They kissed emotionlessly. Patricia submitted as though Dagwood were pinning a lifeboat flag on her lapel.

'I wish I was a man and could just order someone to kiss me,' she said.

Dagwood's heart gave a jump. A hit, a palpable hit. Was this the first crack, the first tiny rivulet starting on the glacier face which would in due course send the entire mass sliding abandonedly downwards?

'You seem very calm about it, anyway.'

'Oh, I knew you'd do that sooner or later.'

'Oh did you?' Dagwood muttered grimly. He shook his head like a fighter in trouble on the ropes, took one last draught from his glass, and went to work. He kissed her mouth, her neck, her eyes and her forehead. He kissed her tentatively. He kissed her interrogatively. He kissed her tenderly. He kissed her roughly, harshly. He caressed her with his fingertips and explored the inside of her mouth with his tongue. He tried short affectionate pecks, interspersed with appreciative sighs, then leaning back as if to look over his handiwork. He tried long full kisses on the mouth, kisses so sustained that Dagwood himself was at last forced to disengage for fear of suffocating. He built up combinations of kisses, like a skilful but desperate in-fighter. He kissed her cheek in Morse code – kiss kiss long pause, long kiss pause until he had spelt out U.B.I.T.C.H.

Patricia responded correctly but as emotionlessly as though she were running the gauntlet of a street full of flag-sellers. After half an hour, when Dagwood had even succeeded in rousing himself, Patricia said: 'What do you want from me?'

Dagwood paused, arrested in full stride. The girl was full of his shush kebab and his burgundy. She was lying, full length but half nude, on his hearthrug. She asked him what he wanted from her.

It was an unanswerable question. Dagwood got up, brushed off the knees of his trousers.

'How about some coffee?' he said.

IO

The girl he had knocked down outside the main office block continued to occupy Dagwood's mind. True, their two previous meetings had not been propitious. But still . . . but still, Dagwood sensed subconsciously that the final words had not been said, on either side. Dagwood decided he should try and make amends. There was no harm in proffering the olive branch, even if he subsequently had it wrapped round his neck. Dagwood straightened his tie, smoothed down his hair, and polished his shoes by rubbing them up and down against the opposite trouser leg.

'What job are you applying for?' Ollie enquired.

Dagwood turned on him. 'Just because you go round looking like a tramp, that's no reason why everyone else should!'

'Pardon me,' said Ollie, not in the least abashed.

Dagwood was astonished to recognise his own nervousness as he descended the stairs towards Sir Rollo's office. He was even more astonished to find, seated in the small office which served as an antechamber for the throne room in which Sir Rollo sat in awful majesty, a quite middle-aged woman with grey hair tied in a ragged bun.

'Yes?'

Dagwood hesitated. 'I really wanted to see Sir Rollo's private secretary.'

'That's me.'

'Oh, but wasn't there a *girl* doing the job?'

The woman bristled. 'I have been Sir Rollo's private secretary for fifteen years.'

'You weren't doing it last week,' Dagwood insisted.

'I had 'flu last week. Sir Rollo's daughter did temporary work in my absence.'

'And she's gone now?'

'Yes.'

'She's not hurt, is she?' Dagwood asked, anxiously.

'Hurt?' The woman looked baffled. 'Why should she be hurt, may I ask? She was only here on a temporary basis . . .'

'I'm sorry. You misunderstood me.' Dagwood was conscious, from the curious look the woman gave him, that he had already said far, far too much. 'Never mind, I may look in later . . .' he ended, vaguely, and backed towards the door, opened it and slid outside, leaving Sir Rollo's private secretary gazing after him with a look of amazement.

'Did you get the job?' said Ollie.

'Oh for God's sake, Ollie, let's drop the subject. Anything wildly exciting happening today?'

'They finished taking the soft patch off last night and they're taking out the main engines this morning. That's worth looking at, if you've never seen it done before.'

The major items of the submarine's machinery, such as the main diesel engines and the main electric motors, were too large to be moved through any of the submarine's hatches. The problem of first installing them had been solved by putting them in place before the hull was complete, in effect by building the submarine round them. Once in place, they could only be taken out by burning away a long rectangular section of the pressure hull above the engine room. This removable section of the pressure hull was called officially the closing plate, but it was always known colloquially in the Submarine Service as the Soft Patch, or the Sunshine Roof.

Dagwood had never seen a submarine's closing plate off before and he was immediately struck by the size of the compartment which had contained the main engines. Now that all the machinery had been removed, the space looked as big as a ballroom.

'You could have a dinner dance and social in there,' he

said to Sam Sollarwood, the foreman of electrical fitters, who was standing on the dockside watching the awkward mass of the second main diesel engine being slung upwards.

'Aye, it makes you wonder where all the space goes to, when you see it like that,' said Sam Sollarwood.

Sam Sollarwood was one of the yard personalities whom Dagwood was beginning to be able to pick out. The great tide of figures which eddied about the yard at certain times of the day was beginning to have here and there an individual face. Harvey McNichol & Drummond's, being a feudal society, had the feudal rigidity of dress and headgear – particularly headgear. An ordinary workman might wear a grubby cloth cap or a grimy beret, but no man in any position of authority would ever have dreamed of setting foot inside the yard without his caste headdress. The caste rules were unwritten but as inflexible as the laws of the Medes and the Persians: by tradition, charge hands and above wore brown cloth caps; foremen and above wore light grey cloth caps with long peaks; managers and above wore brown trilbies; while directors, above whom there was nobody but God, wore black bowlers.

Dagwood and Ollie thought it a very good system; at least they always knew the sort of man they were talking to, even if they did not know his name. They decided to join the scheme. Ollie wore a conservative brown Gieves trilby but Dagwood sported a green deerstalker, covered with fishing flies, which had once belonged to his father. The deerstalker's debut in the yard aroused a great deal of comment. Workmen turned and gaped, as though Dagwood were wearing a diamond tiara. The apprentices who played football beside the plate shop in the lunch hour stopped their game to jeer and catcall. The typists on their way to and from the main office block tittered and dug each other in the ribs. But gradually the deerstalker came to be tolerated and, furthermore, associated with Dagwood. It was his trademark. Everyone knew who he was because of his hat. Anyone who wanted

Dagwood would never enquire after the Electrical Officer of H.M.S. *Seahorse* but would simply ask: ' 'Ave ya seen t'lad wi't Sherlock 'Olmes 'at 'ereabout?'

Sam Sollarwood therefore recognised Dagwood without even looking at his face, and prepared for a chat. Like all the foremen Dagwood had ever met, Sam Sollarwood was always ready for a gossip. Dagwood made a good audience. He had never heard the standard yard jokes nor the perennial yard grouses. Dagwood did not mind listening because he found that there was a practical advantage in gossiping with the foremen. It taught him much about the yard and its people; it also, Dagwood suspected, gave him a much more accurate picture of the real progress of *Seahorse's* refit than the stilted phrases of the progress meetings called by the yard managers.

It was Sam Sollarwood who told Dagwood the truth about George, the shambling figure in dirty brown overalls and grey cloth cap whom Dagwood saw about the yard every day and whom everybody seemed to know. Dagwood had noticed that nobody passed George by without a word. Even Sir Rollo said good day to him. It was plain that, so far as Harvey McNichol & Drummond were concerned, George was a member of the aristocracy.

'Who *is* that fellow?' Dagwood asked Sam Sollarwood one morning, after George had just passed them, acknowledging salutes to right and left. By his white hair and staggering gait, Dagwood judged that George must be at least eighty, possibly even ninety.

'Aye, that's Young George,' said Sam Sollarwood, in a tone of respect.

'*Young* George!'

'Aye. Old George, his father, had the job afore him.'

'What job is that?'

'Chain grubber.'

'What on earth's a chain grubber?'

'He looks up at ship when she's being built and says, "Aye," and then goes away and fixes chains for t'launching. Y'see, when we launch a ship from this yard, the river's too narrow to just let it go. We have to check it wi'chains. But . . . How *many* chains? If you put too many, happen ship'll not go at all. If you put too few, happen' ship'll go clear over to Maxwells'.' Sam chuckled. 'That nearly happened once. Bout five year ago when we launched *Empress of Ethiopia*. Sir Rollo had an idea, y'see. Progress, he said, that's the thing. We must progress. We must keep up wi' modern methods. *George's* methods are out-a-date, he said. So they had some *experts* down here.' Sam snorted contemptuously. 'Lot of young puppies wi' slide rules crawling about place. They measured owt and worked out owt and told Sir Rollo how many chains he'd need. Sir Rollo says fine, just do that. Come launching day, great crowd arrives, Lady Muck swings bottle, away goes 'Empress' and keeps *on* goin'! Tugs only just get a hold of her afore she runs right up on t' Maxwells' slip! *George* was back on t'job very next day. Aye, that would have been a reet laugh, if she'd run up Maxwells' slip!'

Maxwells' were Harvey McNichol & Drummond's closest and fiercest rivals. Their yard lay directly opposite, on the other side of the river. For more than two hundred years the two firms had eyed each other jealously, like Montagu and Capulet. The rivalry between the firms was sometimes reflected in the city of Oozemouth; when both firms were submitting tenders for the same contract, Oozemouth was like a city under martial law. To lose a contract to Clydeside, Merseyside or Tyneside would have been a severe blow to Harvey McNichol & Drummond's; but to lose one to Maxwells' was like a mortal wound. Although Dagwood and Ollie had only been in the yard a very short time, they still felt a certain reflected *esprit de corps* for Harvey McNichol & Drummond, enough to be shocked and dismayed when, a few weeks after *Seahorse's* refit began, the news of Maxwells' new contracts broke.

The story was on the front page of the morning paper.

Maxwells' managing director had returned from a sales-promotion trip with orders for a 25,000 ton passenger liner, to be called the *Mombasa Castle,* and for a Dutch tanker of 60,000 tons. Maxwells had obtained the orders by cutting their profits almost to nothing and by promising a firm completion date, covered by a penalty clause in the contracts, which they had achieved by agreeing a two-year strike amnesty with the unions. The two ships would keep Maxwells and their sub-contractors in full employment for at least three years.

'That's wiped their eyes a bit,' said Ollie, when he saw the headlines.

'I wonder how they're taking it?' said Dagwood.

Sam Sollarwood was taking it very hardly. 'I'm not surprised,' he said, bitterly. 'We're living in t'past in this firm. Think of what we've got after that Norwegian tanker is finished. Nowt but two dredgers for Docks and Harbour Board!' Sam's face clouded. 'I remember when they got the order for them. They were that pleased, ye'd think it were two *Queen Marys* we were going to build!'

Dagwood sensed in Sam's manner an atavistic fear of the days of the depression. Sam had been born within sight of Harvey McNichol & Drummond's cranes and had worked in their yard since he was a boy. As a young apprentice he could remember his father lying in bed until midday because there was no work to go to. He could remember the whole family sitting down to bread and tea in the evenings. Sam himself now had a small house, a small car and two children coming up for grammar school but he kept looking over his shoulder at the past as an abyss into which he might one day fall, like his father, at a word from Sir Rollo.

Dagwood could understand Sam Sollarwood's attitude (a firm of the standing of Harvey McNichol & Drummond rejoicing over a contract for two river dredgers was as ludicrous as Rolls Royce celebrating an order for two motor lawnmowers), but he was quite baffled by Mr McGillvray's, when he mentioned the subject of Maxwells' new contract at lunch time. As a senior engineering ship manager and one of Sir Rollo's right-hand men, Mr McGillvray could be expected to take a serious view of their chief rival's success. But, curiously, it was not so.

'Och, *them*,' said Mr McGillvray, derisively. 'They go round touting for business like they were selling stockings, or something.'

'But surely that's not such a bad idea, if it does the trick,' Dagwood pointed out.

'We don't have to tout for business. We have a reputation. This firm was started 1750 and everybody knows about us. Everybody knows about us. Everybody knows we build first-class ships here.'

'They may *know* about them,' said Dagwood, 'but they've stopped *buying* them, haven't they?'

Mr McGillvray went red. 'Look laddie,' he said. 'Just run along and mind your submarine and leave us to mind our shipyard.'

'I'm sorry,' Dagwood muttered.

Mr Burlap, the electrical ship manager, took a more moderate view. When Dagwood reached the door of his office, he was nearly knocked down by a crowd of men who erupted from Mr Burlap's office like reporters rushing to catch the last edition.

'Who were they?' Dagwood asked.

Mr Burlap smiled wearily. 'The shop stewards, believe it or not. They want to know what we're doing about Maxwells' new order. They also want to know what Harvey McNichol & Drummond are doing about building nuclear submarines. I ask you!'

'Why shouldn't Harvey McNichol and Drummond build nuclear submarines?'

Mr Burlap frowned. It appeared to be a new thought for him. 'Well, now I come to think of it, I suppose there really isn't any reason why we shouldn't. I don't think anybody's thought of it, to tell you the truth. It would cost a couple of million at least to tool up the yard for them, but after that . . .'

Mr Burlap's voice trailed away; he appeared to be contemplating a new and wonderful horizon.

'What do *you* think of this Maxwells business?'

Mr Burlap clasped his hands together, blew through them, and then unfolded them in a gesture of futility. 'Nobody minds so much about the tanker. They'll keep everyone in work but they won't make a penny out of it. We build a tanker every eighteen months or so but whoever hears about tankers, unless they happen to blow up or run aground? It's passenger ships, the *Mombasa Castle,* that's the sort of thing we make money and prestige on. We haven't built a passenger ship since the *Empress of Ethiopia* four years ago. I don't know where we're all headed for, I really don't!'

Mr Tybalt, as an almost impartial observer, put the situation in perspective.

'Dagwood,' he said, 'you really must be more tactful. I happened to overhear your conversation with McGillvray at lunch time . . .'

'But, sir . . .'

' . . . I agreed entirely with every word you said . . .'

'Well then . . .'

Mr Tybalt held up his hand. 'But *you're* not the person to say it. As for this Maxwells business, have you ever heard of business games?'

'No sir?'

'They're glorified party games which teach up-and-coming executives how to make mistakes without actually losing the firm any real money. The interesting thing is that they've coined a couple of very neat phrases which exactly define what I'm trying to say. Decision-robust, and decision-sensitive. A decision-*sensitive* business is one where quite a minor decision or a series of minor decisions can have a big effect on profits. Show business, I imagine, is one. A decision-*robust* business is one where you bloody nearly have to burn the whole place down before you have any effect at all. The Navy is a perfect example of a decision-robust business. It's just about the most decision-robust business there is. Nobody's made any effective decisions for years. The last major one was to change from sail to steam. And not everybody agreed with that. The shipbuilding industry is almost as decision-robust as the Navy. It goes on and on for years with nobody bothering very much about it. It's like a very heavy cast-iron wheel trundling along a road, gradually slowing down. It keeps its balance for a long, long time but eventually it falls – and bingo, when it does, that's your lot! For good! It takes some-one with a bit of go and push like Sir Charles Maxwell, to keep his own wheel trundling a bit longer than the others.'

Mr Tybalt gazed pensively out of his window.

'I'll admit this firm are doing what they can. They're spending five and a half million quid on modernisation. Where they got the money from, heaven only knows. They're building that new dock and I've got to hand it to them at the moment it's the biggest damned hole in the road I've ever seen in my life. But it won't be ready for another three years, at the rate they're going. They need it *now*.'

Mr Tybalt carefully traced his initials in the steamed surface of the window.

'*One* of their troubles is demarcation. One man, one job. If you're an electrician, you only do an electrician's job and if you're a shipwright you only do a shipwright's job. And nobody else *but* an electrician or a shipwright can do those jobs. Every time a particular technique is changed, or they try and introduce a new technique, there's a great brouhaha to decide who's going to do it. Every union is making quite sure the other unions don't steal a march on them and they're all quite blind to the fact that in a few years' time they'll all be floating down the river together. What these people need is one union for everybody who builds ships. When you go down into the yard and ask a man what he's doing he should say "I'm building a ship, what the devil d'you think

I'm doing?" If you go down there now and ask a bloke what he's doing he'll tell you he's running these leads or welding up this bracket.'

'Yes, I see that, sir,' said Dagwood.

'Good. But just watch these off-the-cuff remarks of yours. It doesn't matter that you're absolutely right. That only makes it worse. A few remarks like that can ruin years of carefully built up good relations.'

Dagwood walked soberly back to his own office. On his way he passed the slipway where the Norwegian tanker was building. As always, he stopped to look at it. It never failed to amaze Dagwood that ships seemed to be built without any-one actually doing anything to them. (Dagwood had noticed the same phenomenon on building sites – houses rose or fell without anyone apparently laying a finger on them.) The groups of men standing in the slipway were talking amongst themselves. There was a man up in the cab of the crane, but the jib was motionless. Once, while Dagwood was watching, one shower of sparks fell from the bows where a welder was crouched on some scaffolding. More men came and went but they brought nothing and took nothing away. And yet, day by day, the ship was undeniably swelling and taking shape. Dagwood thought of the fairy story of the friendly poltergeist who came during the night and washed up the crockery, shined all the shoes and swept out the house. Perhaps a friendly poltergeist visited Harvey McNichol & Drummond every night and welded up a few seams. But that would not be enough. What Harvey McNichol & Drummond needed was not one, but an amalgamated shipbuilding union of friendly poltergeists.

11

In spare moments at the office Dagwood often amused himself by looking through *Seahorse's* wardroom Visitors' Book. Broody had been enthusiastic about the Visitors' Book, always passing it round when there were guests present. 'If nothing else, it'll give you and Ollie something to read during the refit,' he had said to Dagwood.

The Visitor's Book was, in its own way, as complete a record of the commission as the control-room log. On the first pages were signatures of the visiting dignitaries and shipyard officials who attended the ship's launching and the commissioning cocktail party, followed by the names of the admirals, members of Parliament, scientists and public figures who had visited the Navy's latest submarine. There was even one page containing a Royal signature, but the social tone dropped sharply on the next page in a scrawling, interlocking jumble of pencil signatures which commemorated the party given for the officers of the American nuclear *Samuel P. Peyton.* Then there was page after page of signatures of harbour masters, mayors, governors, naval attachés, members of the chorus, chief constables, burgomasters, wives and girl-friends, and officers from submarines lying in company, all the assorted social flotsam and jetsam of two years' commission, including a dog's footprint in indelible ink and several lip-sticked kiss impressions (a memento of an occasion when one of Gavin Doyles' less inhibited girl friends had had her bare bosom franked with the ship's Personal and Confidential rubber stamp).

One morning, when Dagwood was idly thumbing through

the book, he came across two signatures dating from a visit *Seahorse* had paid to Oozemouth very early in her commission.

'Jane Dodd, Oozemouth 2733, Senior Service Satisfy!' read one entry and 'Hilda Judworth, Oozemouth 3941, Ring me when you're sober!' said the other.

Dagwood could not recall the authoress of either signature but the opportunity was too good to be missed.

'I'm quite sober now, anyway,' he remarked, picking up the telephone.

'If you're trying to get The Bodger, he's gone up to the Admiralty for the day,' said Ollie.

'I'm not trying to get The Bodger, I'm chasing up a couple of these frippets in here.'

'My God, I'd have thought you'd had enough for a bit, after your last fiasco.'

'Oh that,' said Dagwood carelessly. 'I chalk that up to experience.'

'You ought to know better than to go messing about with Admirals' daughters. You can't win. You either have to marry them or stay a two-striper all your life.'

'Oh *that,* you mean!'

'What else could I mean?'

'Nothing.'

Meanwhile, the telephone was being answered by a most mature woman's voice, which could hardly belong to Miss Jane Dodd.

'May I speak to Jane Dodd, please?' Dagwood asked.

'Do you mean Mrs Calder?'

'Oh good heavens I'm terribly sorry, I'd no idea she was married!'

'She's been married nearly two years now. They have a small son and they're living in Singapore at the moment.'

'Oh.'

'I'm Jane's mother. Can I take a message?'

'No, not really, I just didn't know she was married . . .'

'Well . . . Good-bye then?'

'Good-bye.'

'How about that,' said Dagwood viciously. 'She must have been within a month or two of getting married and she puts her telephone number in our Visitors' Book! I give *that* marriage about five years at the outside!'

'Why shouldn't she put her number in the book?' said Ollie. 'After all, she did marry somebody in the Navy.'

'This girl did!' Dagwood was frequently surprised by the accuracy and detail of Ollie's biographical knowledge (not guessing that Ollie's information, like that of most married men, was the result of conscientious staff work by his wife).

'Why do you think she wrote "Senior Service Satisfy"?'

'Well, how about that. I wonder if it's worth me ringing the other one? She's probably a grandmother by now, for all I know.'

But Miss Hilda Judworth was delighted to hear from Dagwood.

' . . . Were you the Navigating Officer?'

'No, I'm Dagwood Jones, the Electrical Officer.'

'Oh.' Hilda sounded puzzled. 'But your boat is in again?'

'Sort of. We're here for a refit.'

'Oh. Well, you must come and see us.'

'I'd love to.'

'Would you like to come to the point-to-point with us on Saturday?'

'That sounds terrific.'

'It's the first of the year. The Beaufortshire Forest. D'you know it?'

'I don't actually.'

'It doesn't matter. We can give you lunch and everything. Have you got a motor-car?'

'Yes.'

'Do you know the "Three Feathers" at King's Monachorum?'

'I know King's Monachorum. That's where Admiral

MacGregor lives.'

'Yes, do you know him? There's only one pub there. In the main street. We'll meet you there at twelve o'clock. O.K.?'

'O.K.'

'Bye.'

'Byee,' trilled Dagwood. 'What an efficient-sounding sort of woman,' he said to Ollie.

'Your telephone bill is going to be interesting at the end of the month,' said the practical Ollie.

Any questions Dagwood had about the Judworth family were answered by The Bodger. 'They're more county than the county people,' said The Bodger. 'Old man Judworth deals with most of the stuff that's eaten or drunk in Oozemouth, from the wholesale angle.'

'He must be loaded, sir.'

'Stinking with the stuff. The chances are that your burgundy and your shush kebab came from Old Man Judworth in the first place.'

'How ever did you hear about that, sir?' Dagwood asked, in astonishment.

'Haven't you ever heard of the Grapevine, Dagwood? You can't beat it. If you're thinking of going to the Forest point-to-point on Saturday, you couldn't be in better hands than La Judworth's.'

Saturday morning found Dagwood in a state of high anticipation but troubled by the question of dress. Dagwood was well aware that this might be his chance to make the acquaintance of quite a large slice of local society. It was, in a sense, a debut, and Dagwood was anxious, at least to start with, to conform.

An ordinary race meeting would have presented no problem. Dagwood would have followed normal submarine practice and dressed in his oldest dog-robbing suit, borrowed a pair of binoculars from the Navigating Officer, taken a fiver from the wardroom wine fund, filled a flask with Red Label, and away. But a point-to-point was different. Dresswise, there were point-to-points, and point-to-points. At some, everyone including the men who parked the cars dressed as though they were waiting to be photographed by The Tatler. At others, though just as fashionable, everyone looked as though they had just sprung, Minerva-like, from the soil itself. Dagwood consulted Molly.

'The Forest?' said Molly. 'They're a scruffy lot.'

'Are they a fashionable hunt?'

'Oh *very* fashionable but they all dress up like navvies. I should wear your oldest things, if I were you. Would you like to borrow a pair of Bill's old gummies? It's normally terribly muddy.'

'If you really don't mind my borrowing them.'

'I'll get them. Would you like to borrow the Land Rover?'

'Well really . . .'

'You can have it with pleasure. It'll be much better than your little car. Last year everybody got stuck.'

'But aren't you going yourselves?'

'No.' Molly grimaced. 'Bill's fallen out with Sir Rollo. They always used to hunt over our farm and we were always invited to the point-to-point but last season Sir Rollo told Bill he was putting too much wire in his fences. Bill told Sir Rollo he'd got a damned nerve to say that and if he ever saw a fox on his land again he'd shoot it!'

'*Did* he?'

'Yes.' Molly giggled. 'Bill didn't mean it really, but he was so wild he told Sir Rollo that if he ever caught him or his horse on our land again he'd give them both a shot up the backside!'

'Did he? Crikey, I wish I'd been there!'

'Yes, it was quite a scene. So we're not invited this year. I'm a bit sorry about it and so is Bill, because Major O'Reilly is a very nice man. He's joint master with Sir Rollo. Sir Rollo's got all the money and Major O'Reilly does all the work. Hold on a minute and I'll get the gummies.'

Dagwood followed Molly's advice to the letter. When he drove out of the farm-yard in the Land Rover he was wearing

113

Bill's most ancient pair of wellington boots, his own maroon corduroy gardening trousers, a submarine sweater which had gone grey with age, and his oldest brown sports coat. Over all he wore his motoring duffle coat and his deerstalker.

The 'Three Feathers' was not hard to find and neither was Hilda Judworth. She was the sort of girl who might have made a magnificent second row forward for Roedean, with the physique of a Percheron mare and excellent child-bearing hips. There was no question of missing her; Dagwood would have had difficulty in getting past her. Her already consider-able bulk was augmented by a sheepskin-lined leather jacket and her height was increased by a pair of seven-league New-market boots. She wore on her head a green silk headscarf embroidered with a picture of every Grand National winner since 1880. Dagwood could see in her the hostess she would one day become, launching herself upon a guest with a gusto which would destroy any confidence he still had left, introduc-ing herself without looking at her guest, announcing his name in such a way that everybody immediately forgot it, if they had ever heard it, and dropping him down in a group of people whom he did not know. Hilda, too, seemed to recognise Dagwood.

'You must be Dagwood Jones,' she said, categorically.

'That's right.'

'I'm Hilda Judworth, how do you do? Come and meet everybody.'

Taking Dagwood by the arm in a proprietary grip, Hilda led him round. 'This is Dagwood, everybody. Dagwood, this is Frieda . . . Colin . . . Freddie . . . Barbara and Tim . . . Cordelia . . .'

Dagwood nodded and smiled endlessly The men gave him a quick glance and then ignored him. But the girls looked at him interrogatively. This was a new face. Where had he sprung from? Dagwood could read their thoughts. Was this Hilda's new one? If so, where did she get him? If not, whose is he? Is he married?

Dagwood took up his pint and assessed the company. It was just as he had expected. This was an agglomeration of first generation Young Farmers, Young Conservatives who were still unmarried, and alumni of the local Pony Clubs. Hilda seemed to have disappeared so Dagwood made desultory conversation about motor cars with a young man in a Paisley scarf and pimples called Digby, trod on the booted foot of a girl called Jacqueline, had half his beer knocked out of his glass by a young man named Jeremy and all at once everybody seemed to be finishing their drinks and pushing outside.

'Oh, have you got a Land Rover?' everybody asked, in surprised voices, as though it were the first reasonable thing they had yet heard about Dagwood. 'We'll come with you then.'

The back of Bill's Land Rover filled up with a further assortment of Paisley scarves, sheepskin jackets and New-market boots, none of whom Dagwood recognised. Hilda reappeared again and filled the front seat next to Dagwood.

'Where do we go now?'

'I'll show you,' said Hilda. 'Straight on over the bridge.'

'Is Sarah riding today, Hilda?' someone asked from the back of the Land Rover.

'Yes, she's riding Hurrymint.'

'Oh,' said someone, sounding impressed.

'Who's Sarah?' Dagwood enquired.

'My sister.'

'Is it true that Major O'Reilly's asked Fulke to ride Nautical Laddie today, Hilda?'

'Yes.'

'*Oh,*' said someone, sounding even more impressed.

'Who's Fulke?' Dagwood enquired.

'My brother.'

'Quite a hard-riding family you seem to have,' Dagwood remarked. 'Do you live on a ranch or something?'

Someone in the back tittered. Hilda frowned. 'Only Sarah

and Fulke ride.'

'And what do you do?'

'I play lacrosse.'

Dagwood sighed very faintly. That figured.

'Left at this fork,' said Hilda. 'Fulke is the best. He does quite a lot of National Hunt riding. He rode a winner at Market Rasen last week. You might have heard of him.'

Dagwood shook his head. 'Can't say I have. I never look at the jockeys, only at the starting prices.'

'He's hoping to get a ride in the National next year. This year, if he can manage it.'

'Sooner him than me,' said Dagwood cheerfully.

'It's a great *honour* to ride in the National,' said a girl's voice from the back.

'Oh I'm sure it is,' Dagwood replied. 'All I'm saying is that I *personally* don't fancy going base over apex on a six foot hunk of hedge and having about three tons of horse land in the small of me back.'

After which piece of descriptive narrative, of which the immortal John Jorrocks himself might not have been ashamed, Dagwood drove on in silence. The others talked amongst themselves, sensing that they had in their midst a Philistine, one of the uncircumcised. As he drove, Dagwood thought of George Bernard Shaw, who always maintained that you could go anywhere in England, where there were natural, wholesome, contented, and really nice English people; and what did you always find? That the stables were the real centre of the household. Dagwood was suddenly irritated by it all. Dammit, horses were things you put money on. From bad, Dagwood plunged determinedly to worse.

'Will everyone be wearing their red coats today?' he asked, deliberately.

Hilda looked at Dagwood with the expression of a wholesome human mother who discovers that her child is a demon changeling. Her protégé was certainly distinguishing himself. Worst of all, every girl in the Land Rover must by now have realised that never, never in a thousand years, could Dagwood be any boy-friend of Hilda's. The back of the Land Rover began to hum with quickening feminine interest. Hilda noticed it.

'I expect the hunt servants will be wearing pink,' she said, with the kindest smile she could manufacture.

'Oh how lovely,' said Dagwood maliciously. 'And will all the *dogs* be there too?'

No more was said until they arrived at the scene of the point-to-point where, directed by Hilda and speeded by the green label she had stuck on the windscreen, Dagwood drove to a vantage point on the course immediately by the last fence. Dagwood wondered at their pride of place until he got out and, looking round him, saw that by borrowing the ·Land Rover he had brought off a coup which was nothing short of a master-stroke. There was only one fashionable vehicle for point-to-points. A man could glide up soundlessly in the gleaming product of generations of craftsmen or he could arrive strapped into the spitting snarling result of three decades of Grand Prix racing, but at any social event involving horses he would have to give precedence to the gentleman in the Land Rover.

Everybody drifted off, leaving Dagwood with one girl by herself. She was very bronzed and her left leg was enclosed in plaster.

'I've no doubt Hilda introduced us,' Dagwood said, 'but I'm afraid I don't know your name.'

'I'm Fiona,' said the girl.

'Well, I'm Dagwood.'

'Oh I know *that!* You know, you're really rather a nasty piece of work, Dagwood.'

'Why?' said Dagwood, rather pleased.

'It wasn't fair to pull Hilda's leg like that. She's a very nice girl and a friend of mine. She's a very kind person, you know.'

'I'm sure she is,' said Dagwood, repentantly. 'I just felt bolshie all of a sudden. How did you do your leg?'

'Skiing, of course.'

'That's why you're so sun-burned.'

'I only got back a week ago.'

'I see everybody's signed their names on your leg. Can I sign mine?'

'*Lunch!*' said Hilda, from the other side of the Land Rover.

It was a very good lunch. They had legs of chicken, sticks of celery, cold sausage, with German mustard out of a tube, hard-boiled eggs, thermos flasks of hot tomato soup, bottles of white wine, and coffee. Standing round the Land Rover or sitting on rugs on the bonnet, they ate lunch and watched the most important part of a point-to-point meeting – the parade.

Like the Mediterranean evening stroll along the main streets, the point-to-point parade was a chance to meet one's friends, exchange gossip, and generally look and see who was there, and with whom. Hilda and Fiona pointed out the local celebrities for Dagwood and made sure he was up to date with the latest scandal.

'Puffing Billy looks a bit mad,' said Hilda.

'Who's he?'

'The Lord Lieutenant.'

'I expect his woman in London is playing him up,' said Fiona.

'Has he got a woman in London?'

'Lord yes, had her for years. He says he's going down to London on business but everyone knows he only goes to the Edgware Road.'

'That's a fair stretch of road,' said Dagwood. 'Any idea how far along it he goes?'

'No idea.'

Dagwood caught sight of Patricia MacGregor amongst the crowd.

'There's Frigid Bridget,' said Hilda. 'Did you know she once had the most *violent* love affair with one of the barmen at the 'Three Feathers'? He was Irish and he had a wife and eight children back in Connemara.'

So the iceberg had been known to melt. Dagwood mentally doffed his cap to the unknown Irishman; he must have possessed rare qualities of charm and persuasion.

'Oh, there's Major O'Reilly. He *is* a doll. That's his third wife, you know.'

'Really? What happened to the other two?'

'He divorced them. But they're all the best of friends. They're all here today.'

'Isn't that a bit embarrassing?'

'Not for the Reilly. He would be hurt if they didn't turn up. Oh do look, there's Sexy Frankie!'

'Ooh where?' said Fiona.

'Outside the yeomanry tent.'

'Who's that with him?'

'His mistress. Her name's Maxine. She's rather glam, isn't she?'

By standing on tiptoe and stretching his neck Dagwood could just see a man in a Cheviot tweed suit quaffing a glass of beer outside the yeomanry tent. Beside him Dagwood could also see a tall auburn-haired girl in a light tweed costume. She was, as Hilda had intimated, rather glamorous. Dagwood relapsed on to his heels again, feeling well rewarded by this gossip. For the first time he was seeing Mr Frank Tybalt, Admiralty Constructor Overseer for Messrs. Harvey McNichol & Drummond (S.&E.) Ltd., in a new light.

'There's that new Admiralty man,' said Hilda.

'He's rather handsome,' said Fiona, 'in a battered-looking sort of way.'

'Where?' asked Dagwood.

'Just walking past the bookmakers.'

The Bodger was making his way along the line of bookmakers, examining their boards closely as he went along. He was accompanied by, in Dagwood's opinion, the two best-looking girls at the point-to-point meeting. One, Dagwood knew, was The Bodger's wife Julia. The other was the girl he had knocked down outside Harvey McNichol & Drummond's offices.

'That must be his wife,' said Hilda.

'Who's the other girl?' Dagwood asked, casually.

'Oh that's Caroline Hennessy-Gilbert.'

Caroline. So that was her name.

12

It was now almost time for the first race. The race card listed twenty runners but only seven horses were parading, rather self-consciously, in the paddock. Dagwood went over to look at the odds. Six of the seven horses were offered at odds ranging from 5-1 to 20-1. The seventh, a strapping bay gelding with black points, called The Whopper, was at even money. Dagwood was standing in front of the board of a Mr Joe Calvin, of Yeovil who, according to his sign, was THE BIGGEST (hearted) BOOKMAKER IN THE WORLD, when he heard The Bodger's voice.

'Hello, young Dagwood.'

'Hello, sir.' Dagwood was disappointed to see that The Bodger was alone; he must have left the women behind while he went to put some money on for them.

'Made up your mind yet?'

'No sir.'

'Let me give you some advice then. Always back the favourite at point-to-points. Those bookies didn't come down in the last shower of rain, y'know.'

'It's only even money, sir. I think I'll have something on Maybe Haiti. Eight to one is more like it.'

'All right, it's your money.'

Dagwood put his modest five shillings in the keeping of Joe Calvin and went back to the others. The start was some way down the course from where the Land Rover was parked and a thin mist made the horses difficult to distinguish, but when Dagwood saw the flag drop, heard the huntsman's horn, and saw the horses spurting into action he knew immediately that the old familiar magic was returning. As always, the sight of horses at a hard gallop brought a lump to Dagwood's throat; whatever he may have said to Hilda, Dagwood's blood always raced when he saw the horses coming. At heart, he knew himself to be an addict.

The seven horses took the first fence in a ragged line. Dagwood heard the crash and rattle as they cleared the fence and watched them thud past him, rise in a flowing curve at the next fence, and gallop out of sight round the bend in the mist. Dagwood blinked, and became aware that his heart had been thumping.

'You're not so blasé about this as you make out, Dagwood,' said Fiona, who had been watching his face.

'Ah, it's always a splendid sight, especially the first race of the season.'

'I didn't think much of the jockey on your selection, though. The boy in the red hoops. Looked as if he was going to come off any minute.'

A tweedy couple, who had been leaning on their shooting sticks nearby, reared as though Fiona had spurred them. The gentleman blew down a large purple nose while the lady gave Fiona a look which would have the Medusa herself run to her mirror for reassurance.

'*Fiona!*' hissed Hilda. 'That was Colonel Sir Eric Glossop and Lady Glossop. That jockey you were talking about was Roger Glossop!'

Fiona was aghast. 'Was it really?' she said, her hand to her mouth.

'You're as tactless as I am, Fiona,' said Dagwood, happily. He remembered some more of The Bodger's advice. 'You must never, never pass loud remarks about a rider at a point-to-point meeting or at show jumping; his mum and dad are sure to be standing right in front of you.'

Fiona blushed. 'Oh, I should have recognised them.'

Only one horse appeared out of the murk after the second circuit of the course. Dagwood noted that it was The

Whopper, being ridden at an easy canter, his jockey looking casually over his shoulder for signs of non-existent danger. As Fiona had prophesied, Maybe Haiti and Roger Glossop had gone the parting of the ways long since.

'Well, that's that,' said Dagwood, philosophically.

'There's my godmother,' said Hilda.

'Hilda, my *darling,* how are you?'

Dagwood had seen a good number of large women that day but The Hon. Mrs Julian Dewberry outstripped them all. Dagwood estimated that she stood six feet in her furry boots which trod the sod as though they owned it. Her hair was a spreading aureole of tightly-rolled grey curls on which rode a minute red lady's Tyrolean hat. Her heavy dark mole-skin coat swung from her shoulders like a medieval tabard and the knees Dagwood could see beneath the hairy McCorquodale tartan skirt would have done credit to a Roman legionary. Her shooting stick, which she handled like a toothpick, was beribboned with innumerable badges for agricultural shows and race meetings. Her face was tanned a deep ruddy apple colour and her sharp blue eyes raked Dagwood searchingly over her god-daughter's shoulder.

'And who's this?' demanded The Hon. Mrs Julian Dewberry. 'We haven't met.'

'This is Lieutenant Dagwood Jones,' Hilda explained. 'He's in the Navy.'

'Then you must know my worthless young nephew, *George* Dewberry.' The Hon. Mrs Julian Dewberry did not so much speak to Dagwood as hail him, warning him to keep a good look-out up there in the watch-tower.

'Oh yes, I know him quite well,' said Dagwood. 'We used to go to the odd jazz concert together in Portsmouth.'

'How is he getting on?'

'Oh very well, I think,' said Dagwood, untruthfully. The last time he had seen George Dewberry, he was being led away by the Hampshire constabulary.

'Stuff,' retorted The Hon. Mrs Julian Dewberry. 'He's

a good-for-nothing drunkard, like his father before him. M'sister's got his liver in a bottle. I saw it last Christmas. Looks like a moth-eaten turd, you've never seen such a thing!'

'Did you back the winner in that race, ma'am?' Dagwood asked.

'Don't call me "ma'am",' said The Hon. Mrs Julian Dewberry, though flattered. 'I never back horses. I only come here to support The Hunt.' She spoke of The Hunt as though it were some savage Aztec fire-god who needed frequent human sacrifices. 'This used to be a place where you could meet yer friends, repay hospitality to the farmers, and so on. Now look at it! Like a circus! All the wrong people can afford to keep hunters these days. I can only just afford Samson.'

'Confound all presents wot eat!' said Dagwood, remembering his Jorrocks.

As a joke, the remark went down flatter than a lead balloon. There was a silence, during which everyone remembered that it must be nearly time for the next race.

The second race, for Adjacent Hunts, went much as the first had done. Seventeen horses were promised in the race card and five paraded in the paddock. Four were offered from 5-1 to 20-1 and the fifth, Legs Eleven, at 2-1 on. Dagwood was tempted but, recalling The Bodger's advice in time, placed ten shillings with Mr Calvin, waited for Legs Eleven (the solitary survivor of the second circuit) to be weighed in and collected his fifteen shillings.

The third race, the Beaufortshire Forest Hunt Cup, provided a little variety on what now seemed to Dagwood the traditional pattern. Exhibition Man, the favourite, fell at the penultimate fence when leading by a distance. The second horse, over-excited by visions of glory, fell at the same fence. The rider of the third horse happened to be Roger Glossop who had already decided to pull up. But on being advised of the position by the crowd and urged to continue, he rallied his horse, completed the remainder of the course with many alarms and excursions, and plodded past the winning post at 100-6, to the great delight of Fiona, whose selection he had been.

The fourth race was the Ladies' Cup. Dagwood disliked ladies' races on principle. They were unfair to male punters. One could hardly shout at a beaten favourite 'Why couldn't yer pick yer feet up, yer lazy lump of 'orse liver, you !' as one would have been perfectly entitled to do had the jockey been masculine. Still, this was the race which included Hilda's redoubtable sister Sarah. Dagwood noticed the family resemblance as Sarah rode past on her way to the post, holding her horse in and looking perfectly collected and competent. Sarah had the same cast of feature as Hilda but in her case they were sharpened and hardened. She looked a horsewoman; Dagwood had no doubt that at some time in the future he would switch on a television set and witness Sarah Judworth being awarded a pair of spurs or a sash at the White City.

The bookmakers evidently shared Dagwood's mistrust of Ladies' races. The betting market was unwilling to open and it was some time before Joe Calvin reluctantly wrote the odds on his board, giving Sarah Judworth's mount Hurrymint odds of 5-4 on and the other two runners which made up the total field of three odds of 2-1 against.

In the absence of any clear lead from the book, Dagwood restrained himself from betting and this proved to be very prudent of him because there were no survivors at all of even the first circuit of the course for the Ladies' Cup. There appeared to be no survivors of even the first few fences because the loudspeaker commentary, which had set off confidently enough with the leader and the order of running, soon tailed off. The crowd, the bookmakers and the line judge waited in an uninformed and lengthening silence.

'Somebody's fallen,' said the loudspeaker guardedly, at last.

'In Australia they guarantee to mention every horse every

furlong,' said Dagwood.

'One normally *knows* all the horses here,' said Hilda.

'There's somebody else fallen,' said the loudspeaker, still refusing to commit itself.

'Perhaps they're going the long way round,' Dagwood suggested.

'Oh *really* Dagwood, do shut up!' Hilda burst out. 'Can't you see I'm worried about Sarah?'

'I think they've all fallen,' said the loudspeaker.

At last, a mud-spattered figure appeared out of the mist, on foot, and leading her horse. It was Sarah. Hilda rushed to the rope rail.

'Sarah, what *happened?*'

Sarah turned and looked blindly into the crowd through her tears.

'The bugger threw me,' she said, calmly.

'*Sarah!*'

Sarah led her horse sadly away, to appreciative cheers from the bookmakers who, because no horse had properly completed the course, had had a skinner on the race. 'Never mind, lass,' said a stentorian voice from their ranks, 'at least you must have bounced!'

The last race of the day, the Open Race, had attracted the comparatively enormous field of eleven runners. This large number had its effect on the betting market which was much more open than for any previous race. Favourite at 2-1 was Nautical Laddie, to be ridden by Fulke Judworth, with a mare named Sweet Fanny Adams, the property of Sir Rollo, second favourite at 9-2. The Beaufortshire Forest Hunt was blessed with a particularly conscientious parade ring official (the Chief Constable in private life) who insisted that all horses parade in race card order and prevented the more bashful contestants from executing a token circuit of the paddock and then mounting and escaping the critical eyes of the crowd. The conduct of the Beaufortshire Forest parade ring was probably more orderly than that at many meetings under Rules. Dagwood, however, was not so interested in the horses as in the crowd. At last, he caught sight of The Bodger, with Julia and Caroline, on the other side of the paddock. He sidled round towards them.

'How are you doing, Dagwood?' The Bodger greeted him.

'Not so well, sir, I'm afraid.'

'You should take my advice. Julia, have you met Dagwood here?'

'Yes darling, we met at *Seahorse's* commissioning party. How are you, Dagwood?'

'Very well, though I could do with a winner at a decent price!'

'So could we all!'

Julia was just the sort of wife Dagwood would have expected The Bodger to marry. Although she had been married to a naval officer for some time she had not acquired that weather-beaten appearance characteristic of so many officers' wives. She looked as fresh and as gay as the day she was married. She had cheerfully packed and followed her husband, making a new home after every move. She looked as though she had had almost as much amusement from her husband's career as The Bodger had had himself.

'Caroline,' said Julia, 'you haven't met Dagwood Jones.'

'How do you do,' said Caroline, in a neutral voice.

'How do you do,' Dagwood said, politely.

She was wearing calf-length boots, blue woollen stockings, a tweed skirt and a light blue duffle coat with the hood folded back. She had a white skiing band round her hair and she looked at Dagwood as she might have looked at one of the paddock posts.

'We have met before, actually,' Dagwood ventured. 'I'm afraid I was the clumsy fellow who knocked you down the other day.'

'Oh, that was you, was it,' said Caroline, closing the subject.

Dagwood cleared his throat. 'What do you suggest for this

race, sir?' he asked The Bodger.

'That horse looks in good nick.' The Bodger nodded towards Nautical Laddie, a big chestnut with a white star which was being held by a man in a tan polo jacket. Major O'Reilly and Fulke Judworth were in deep conversation near by.

Fulke, too, had the family face but he looked much younger than his sisters and very nervous. He kept licking his lips and blowing out his cheeks and fiddling with his padded jockey's skull cap.

'I don't blame you, son,' thought Dagwood. 'If I had to ride that great brute I'd be nervous too.'

'They do say that one ought to back the horse that's come the longest distance in Open Races,' said The Bodger. 'That's that bay over there. Speedy Gonzales. He's come all the way from Shropshire.'

Speedy Gonzales was a handsome half-bred gelding, by Bois Roussel out of a hunter mare. His groom had obviously taken a great deal of trouble over his appearance. He was fully clipped out, his mane carefully plaited and his hooves polished. He was standing stock-still with his head up and his ears pricked, looking fit to jump out of his skin. A well-known amateur jockey under National Hunt Rules had travelled up specially to ride him and in the circumstances it seemed curiously brave of the book to oppose him with odds as generous as 6-1 against.

'I'm going to put all my winnings on that one,' said The Bodger.

'I think I'll do the same, sir. He looks fit enough to jump over the moon.'

The Open Race promised to be the best race of the day. Roger Glossop went straight into a ten lengths lead, fighting to hold in a black horse called Lucky Alphonse which seemed so determined to treat the race as a six furlong sprint that the crowd were divided as to whether Roger Glossop or Lucky Alphonse had the upper hand.

'He won't last,' said The Bodger, laconically.

Nevertheless, Roger Glossop led the field for the first time round, Lucky Alphonse plunging and pecking at each obstacle, with Nautical Laddie and Speedy Gonzales taking close order behind.

When they passed the winning post for the first time Roger Glossop was still leading but came off precipitately at the next fence. Fulke Judworth and the National Hunt jockey were left to go on together, the rest of the field now trailing them by thirty or forty lengths.

At this point Caroline was distracted by the arrival of a young man who announced himself by coming up to Caroline and giving a little pirouette and a sort of hiccough.

'Nigel!' said Caroline, in surprise. 'How are you? Are you on leave?'

'Yes, my darling, how lovely to see you!'

'The boy-friend,' Julia murmured to Dagwood. 'His father's in shipping.'

Dagwood hated Nigel on sight. He hated his suit, he hated his small hat which was tilted forward so obliquely as to cover his eyes, he hated his glassily-polished shoes, his cane, his binoculars, his race card, his slack lower lip, and his nervous habit of tossing his head. It was an irrational hatred because Dagwood knew very well that Nigel's ensemble was the product of much time and money, that it was nothing less than the approved appearance of young Guardees attending any race meeting between Goodwood at the end of July and Guineas Week at Newmarket in April.

Nigel fastened his attention on Dagwood. 'Are you a farmer?' he asked, without waiting for Caroline to introduce them.

'No.'

'What do you do then?'

'I'm in shipping.'

'Good God, what line?'

'Grey Funnel Line. The underwater branch of it.' Dagwood saw that he had not been understood. 'I'm a submariner. I go to sea in a submarine,' he explained, labouring the point.

'Good God.' The nostrils flared and the lower lip curled in another maltreated catenary. 'Didn't know we still made that sort of thing.'

'Indeed yes, we still have them,' said Dagwood pleasantly. 'And what do you do, if you don't mind my asking?'

The head tossed and the nostrils twitched. 'I'm in the Brigade, actually.'

Dagwood pounced. '*Really?*' he said, with interest. 'Which one – Fire, Boys', or St John's Ambulance?'

Nigel's shocked expression was so exquisitely frozen, so cinematically perfect, that everyone who saw it laughed out loud. Even Caroline could not help smiling. Also, Dagwood fancied that he caught in her eyes a look of awareness, of awakening interest.

'Fulke's down!'

It was a cry of pain from Hilda. Fulke had been riding extremely well, matching the gentleman N.H. jockey jump for jump. But at the open ditch on the far side of the course Nautical Laddie put in one step too many. The horse crashed through the fence and dumped Fulke on the ground. The N.H. jockey was left with the race at his mercy and proceeded to reel off the remaining fences as though at riding school. The nearest runner was now Sir Rollo's mare Sweet Fanny Adams, a full three hundred yards behind.

With a fatherly eye The Bodger watched the sum of thirty pounds which he stood to win jumping calmly and confidently towards him round the rest of the course.

But at the last fence, in front of The Bodger's eyes, the situation suddenly changed. Either through tiredness or over-confidence, Speedy Gonzales made no attempt to rise for the fence but took it by the roots, wallowed and writhed on its crest, and recoiled back towards the take-off side. The jockey toppled from the saddle and lay on the ground, holding his right wrist with an expression of agony on his face.

'Can't you get up?' roared The Bodger. 'Hell's teeth, I've

got thirty quid on this!'

The jockey made no reply, neither did he protest when The Bodger leaped the rope rail, seized his skull cap off his head and snatched his whip from the ground.

Speedy Gonzales was an animal of equable temperament and showed no sign of surprise when The Bodger flicked the reins over his head and struggled up into the saddle. Once more possessed of a rider, Speedy Gonzales trotted towards the fence again, but being also an animal of some discretion, headed towards the gap torn in the fence by his previous attempt. The fence came nearer. The Bodger gritted his teeth. '*Giddap!*' roared the crowd, in unison. The Bodger tapped with his whip. Speedy Gonzales hopped neatly and delicately through the gap.

The Bodger, coming down, met the saddle, coming up, in good order and began to scrub the horse for home like a veteran flat-race jockey. A purist might have pointed out The Bodger was riding a good deal faster than his horse was coming, but the crowd were in no mood for such niceties and The Bodger was cheered as though he were first over the line in the Derby.

In the general hubbub in the unsaddling enclosure Speedy Gonzales's owner so far forgot herself as to rush forward and offer The Bodger assistance in removing his tack.

'Stand *back,* madam,' commanded The Bodger sternly. 'I don't want to be disqualified after all that trouble!'

Acknowledging congratulations on every side by touching his cap with his whip, The Bodger passed into the Weighing Tent. There, he slapped his whip on the table, sat on the scales and held his saddle on his lap as to the manner born. The Clerk of the Scales gaped at him.

'What weight?'

The Bodger was non-plussed. 'Half a minute, let me get my race card out and I'll tell you.'

A voice spoke in The Bodger's ear. 'The Stewards wish to see you at *once.*'

'I've no doubt they do!' replied The Bodger.

Meanwhile, on the course, the loudspeakers had announced that the Stewards had objected to the winner. The book-makers were offering as much as 7-1 against Speedy Gonzales keeping the race. Dagwood, who knew The Bodger better than did the bookies, borrowed all the money he could and backed The Bodger heavily with the eager Joe Calvin. After twenty minutes of sensation such as few point-to-point meetings have ever provided, Dagwood had his reward.

'Objection over-ruled,' said the loudspeaker, flatly. 'Weighed in.'

13

There was, understandably, a considerable crowd waiting for The Bodger when he emerged from the Stewards' Tent.

'How's that jockey who fell off?' The Bodger asked.

'I think he's sprained his wrist,' said Speedy Gonzales's owner. 'May even have broken it. They've whisked him away for an X-ray.'

'Darling, what did the *Stewards* say?' Julia could not restrain her impatience a moment longer.

The Bodger looked thoughtful. 'Well,' he said, 'there's no doubt I should have been disqualified . . .'

'But why *weren't* you, darling?'

'Because there's nothing in the book of words that covers it! Believe me, they went through the National Hunt Rules and the Appendix with a fine tooth-comb and they couldn't find anything which actually *says* you can't change horses in midstream, so to speak . . .'

'What about the weight?' said Speedy Gonzales's owner.

'I was only two pounds overweight, even with all that clobber I had. You can't be disqualified for that. I was wearing an approved pattern of skull cap, the horse completed the proper course. I don't even have to be a licensed jockey to ride in a point-to-point. The only thing they could get me for was not riding in the proper colours. They could fine me one sovereign for that. Which they did!'

'But what about Sir Rollo?' asked Speedy Gonzales's owner.

'He couldn't take part in the enquiry. His horse was second so he was an interested party. It was a straight fight between

Admiral MacGregor and some Major General fellow . . .'

Speedy Gonzales's owner nodded significantly. The crowd pressed closer to listen.

' . . . Rob Roy said he thought it was a splendid effort and if he'd been thirty years younger and stood to win thirty pounds he'd have done the same! The Major General knew a bit more about racing and he said he'd never heard anything like it in all his life. He said he was going to report it to the National Hunt Committee . . .'

'You'll be warned off,' said Speedy Gonzales's owner gloomily.

'You can't be warned off for things that happen in a point-to-point,' said a pundit in the crowd.

'Can't you just!' retorted Speedy Gonzales's owner, with unladylike heat. 'A fat lot you know about it!'

The pundit in the crowd stepped back a pace, crushed.

'Never mind,' said The Bodger. 'The main thing is, I can collect me thirty quid. Minus one sovereign for expenses, that's not a bad reward for half a jump and less than a furlong's riding!'

The Bodger had the crowd behind him. He had done something which almost every man and woman present had longed to do at one time or another, given the necessary nerve. Whatever the National Hunt Committee might say in the future, the crowd dispersed feeling that justice had been done, and been seen to be done. It was perhaps just as well that the Open Race was the last of the day; after The Bodger's pyrotechnics, anything else would have come as an anticlimax. The general attitude was summed up by a man in a pork-pie hat and H.A.C. tie outside the yeomanry tent. 'I take off my hat to him,' said that gentleman. 'I often wished I had the courage to do something like that myself.' The final compliment was paid by the jockeys, who offered The Bodger the use of the cold water ablutionary pail in their tent, an offer which The Bodger gladly accepted, feeling that he was washing his hands with demi-gods.

Back at the Land Rover, Dagwood said: 'Where to now, Hilda?'

'You're coming to our house. We're giving a party.'

'I can't come like this. I've got to change first.'

Hilda looked at Dagwood's wellington boots, corduroys and duffle coat. 'Perhaps you'd better,' she said. 'You go home and change and then come on. I'll go back with Sarah.'

By the time Dagwood had reached the farm, returned the Land Rover, satisfied Molly's curiosity with gossip about the point-to-point, bathed and changed, and found the Judworths' house, the party was in full swing.

It was too dark to see much of the house but Dagwood could tell that it was big. Inside, there was an atmosphere which vaguely disturbed Dagwood. He found it hard to put a name to it. Bogus was too strong a word; contrived was nearer. The Judworths' house had been built as a country house but it was too like a country house to be believable. The grey stones in the hall fireplace were too accurately cut, the Grand National prints round the walls were too obviously an exact set and the wood panelling too meticulously stained with age. It all looked as though it had been built by a man who had studied photographs of country houses until he had learnt the type by heart and then gone away and built the house from memory.

The party was in progress in a beautifully-proportioned drawing-room (here the architect had recalled the photograph perfectly). Music was provided by a radiogram longer than Dagwood's car, the carpets had been rolled up and removed, and the lighting depressed to a mellow glow. The whole of the 'Three Feathers' set were in attendance and as many more arrived after closing time.

Dagwood circulated assiduously. Sarah Judworth danced as neatly and precisely as a horse progressing through the steps of a dressage championship.

'I'm surprised you can dance at all after your efforts to-day,' Dagwood remarked.

'I hardly did anything.' For a girl with such a hard face, Sarah's voice was unexpectedly soft and feminine. 'That was the trouble. We only got half way round the first time. I hadn't time to get tired.'

'It was jolly misty and we couldn't see. What did happen to you all?'

'It was all my fault. I was leading and I fell off. That seemed to upset the other two because they fell as well. Virginia Bristol was *furious*. She'd backed herself for an awful lot of money.'

'Serve her right,' said Dagwood callously. 'Teach her not to back horses, particularly ones she rides herself.'

Virginia Bristol was a tall girl with hollowed cheeks and shadows under her dark eyes. She had a disconcerting habit of tossing her hair back without warning. She danced jerkily, as though her reflexes were taking time to pass messages from her brain to her legs; Dagwood was terrified that one of her jerks would topple them both on to the floor. Worst of all, Dagwood discovered, too late, that she was a 'Do you know so-and-so?' conversationalist of exhaustive acquaintanceship and great endurance.

'Do you know Paul Vincent?'

'No,' said Dagwood.

'I thought you said you were at Dartmouth.'

'I was, but I didn't know anyone called that there. Why do you ask?'

'Oh nothing, he married a friend of mine in London. Do you know Gavin Doyle?'

'The name's familiar,' said Dagwood, grimly. 'Why?'

'He was a submariner. I used to know him in London. Do you know Tim Castlewood?'

When Virginia Bristol looked as though she was about to go through the Navy List from A to Z, Dagwood broke in. 'I know quite a lot of people in the Navy,' he said defensively, 'but I don't know everybody.'

'I just thought you might know them. A lot of people do.'

At last a mutual acquaintance was discovered in The Hon. Mrs Julian Dewberry's nephew George and they discussed him minutely until Dagwood was able to make good his escape.

Hilda Judworth's hips were round and spongy – Dagwood had the sensation that he could have taken a handful out of her if he had gripped tightly. She danced a simple step, rocking from side to side, the movement of a full back trying to prevent a forward dribbling a hockey ball past her. She danced with the abstracted air of the conscientious hostess, with one eye constantly cocked to see how the other guests were doing.

'Fiona's leg doesn't seem to be holding her back,' she said to Dagwood.

Fiona's leg was indeed such a success she might have planned it. The men deserted fully mobile girls, who might have wished to be entertained or to dance, to cluster round Fiona. She had more attention than she would have done had she competed in the open market. Several girls began to wish they had broken their ankles skiing.

Dagwood himself was talking to Fiona when Caroline came in, with Nigel. Dagwood could hear his voice. 'Sorry we're late, Hilda. We've been having Chinese chow.' Nigel's eye roamed the room and rested on Dagwood. 'Oh good God, there's that *frightful* underwater butler again!'

Dagwood grinned. The epithet had certainly not been intended as a compliment but it had a significance which Nigel could not have appreciated. 'Underwater butler' had been one of the nicknames given to the wardroom steward in *Seahorse*. Hearing it again gave Dagwood an unexpected twinge of nostalgia.

'I don't think that chap likes me very much,' he said to Fiona.

'Who, Nigel? Oh, don't worry about him! That remark of yours this afternoon was simply splendid. He'll never live it down. He's been asking for somebody to say something like that ever since the Guards took him on. Somebody had to say it, and you did!'

Caroline caught Dagwood's eye, and to his stupefaction, smiled at him. Unable to resist that small thrill of pleasure he felt whenever he saw her, Dagwood got up, said 'Excuse me' to Fiona, brushed past Nigel, collected Caroline, and began to dance. If there is a tide in the affairs of men then Dagwood's was in full spate.

Fiona looked after Dagwood through narrowed eyes. The pricking of her thumbs told her something was up.

'Well,' said Dagwood.

'Well?' said Caroline.

'I'm afraid I was very rude to Nigel this afternoon.'

Caroline shrugged. 'He's quite capable of looking after himself.'

Her lack of concern for Nigel filled Dagwood with a wild surge of exultation and power. The victory could be his, if he pursued it. He felt like some bearded barbarian, crouched in the hills, gloating over the peaceful valley below, knowing that soon the women would be his to ravish, the cattle his to drive away and the houses his to burn if he wished.

Something of this feeling must have glowed in his eyes, because Caroline said: 'Do you always leer at girls like that?'

'Always.'

'Well I don't like it!'

'I'm sorry.' The top of Caroline's head was on a level with Dagwood's eyes. Her hair smelled of fresh grass, and wild thyme, and violets.

'That's a nice little bottom over there,' he said, inconsequentially. He nodded towards a girl in a tight black terylene skirt, who was joggling violently while she danced.

Caroline looked. 'It's engaged.'

'To the chap it's dancing with?'

'Yes.'

Just then, Nigel tapped Dagwood on the shoulder.

'What do you want?' Dagwood demanded belligerently.

138

Nigel smirked. 'I thought I'd let you know, old boy, I've decided to make this one a Gentlemen's "Excuse me".'

'Well, you're excused then,' said Dagwood coldly.

Caroline stopped dancing and let out a long peal of laughter. Nigel retired, discomfited and muttering. Dagwood bared his teeth in a grin of savage triumph. The bearded barbarians had crept down the hill-side and put the first outposts to the sword.

'How long are you staying in Oozemouth, Dagwood?'

'Don't know. Depends on how long your father and his merry men, with all due respect, take to refit us.'

'Have you got digs?'

'No, I've got a flat.'

'Have you?' Caroline was interested. 'That's very enterprising of you.'

'You must come and have dinner with me and see it.'

'I'd like very much to.'

'How about next Wednesday?'

'Oh, I'm sorry I can't . . .'

'Why not?'

'I'm going to Switzerland on Monday.'

'Skiing?'

'Yes, we're all going in a party. Nigel and Virginia and a whole lot more.'

'For how long?'

'Three weeks.'

'Oh,' said Dagwood despondently. Three weeks together in Switzerland. He could hardly compete with that. The barbarians were on their way back into the hills, their tails between their legs; the fat plainsmen had summoned reinforcements from an unexpected direction.

'Who does the cooking in your flat, Dagwood?'

'I do. Who else?'

'Are you any good at it?'

'As I say, you must come and try it. I graduated to roast chicken the other night.'

139

'That was very clever of you.'

'It wasn't very difficult. I just slapped it in the oven, poured fat over it now and again, kept prodding it and when it went soft I took it out and ate it.'

Dagwood was not minimising his own cooking. That was exactly how he had cooked the chicken. Chubb the moocher, who had supplied the chicken from a source Dagwood did not enquire into, had come round later to see how Dagwood was progressing. He had arrived just as the chicken was being served and he and Dagwood had finished it off between them, together with slices of brown bread and butter and a jar of cider Chubb happened to have with him.

Dagwood was suddenly disappointed with this conversation. It was too polite and commonplace. His blood yearned for more intimate matters. The barbarians had not struggled across the mountain range just to sip afternoon tea and nibble at scones.

Whatever plans Dagwood might have formulated for becoming more intimate were hampered by the curiosity his interest in Caroline was arousing. The boys, those of them who noticed anything, were amused at the prospect of Nigel's nose being sharply yanked out of joint. Few of them had any idea who Dagwood was but they wished him the best of British luck. Everyone had always assumed that Nigel would marry Caroline, once the time, the hormones and the respective parents' marriage settlements were ripe; but this new chap, whoever he was, seemed to be about to put quite a different complexion on matters. If nothing else he would teach Nigel not to take anything in life, least of all a woman, for granted. The girls, led by Fiona, watched with a far closer, almost professional interest. Caroline was playing a new fish, and playing it cool. The girls were all agog to see which way it would leap.

There was therefore a feeling of anti-climax when Caroline announced that she had a sore throat and wished to go home.

'Can I take you home then?' Dagwood asked eagerly.

'If you'd like to,' said Caroline.

'I'd like to very much.' The bearded barbarian was bounding down the hill-side once more. 'Tell you what, would you like to come back to my place? I can give you some hot punch and an aspirin.'

'That's sweet of you Dagwood, but I don't think . . .'

'Come on, it's not very far. You can see my flat at the same time. It's not a flat really, it's a Tithe Barn.'

'A *Tithe Barn!*'

'Converted. All mod cons. You needn't be afraid it's terribly primitive.'

Caroline made up her mind. 'All right. Let me get my coat.'

It was a clear, frosty night. A half moon threw a glistening light on the trees and houses sliding by outside the car. The white lines sped towards the bonnet, illuminated one by one in the headlights. The car was a warm, comfortable box, lit by the glow from the dashboard instruments. Dagwood was well aware of the aphrodisiac effect of motor-cars. Perhaps, he thought, that accounted for his present desire to stop the car and seize Caroline.

Then Caroline changed her mind.

'I don't think I want to go back to your flat after all, Dagwood,' she said. 'I really think I should just go home.'

Dagwood was astounded. 'Why, what's made you change your mind?'

Caroline tossed her head. 'Need I have a reason? Surely it's a girl's privilege to change her mind if she wants to?'

'Yes but . . .' Dagwood paused. The Dagwood of only a few hours before would have made some sharp retort. But Dagwood was trying hard to learn to be circumspect. 'There must be *some* reason for you to change your mind! If you think there's going to be some . . .'

'Some what?'

'Well, funny business, you're mistaken.'

'It never entered my head there would be any *funny*

business, as you call it. I just want to go home now. Are you disappointed?'

'Of *course* I'm disappointed . . .'

'Don't *shout* Dagwood, I can hear you all right . . .'

'One minute you say you'd love to come to my place and the next you say you want to go home. Which do you want?'

'I want to go home.'

'All right, I'll take you. You'll have to show me the way because I don't know where you live,' Dagwood added, ungraciously.

'It's almost next door to Hilda's.'

'Oh Good God,' said Dagwood, in exasperation.

'There's no need to be so rude. I don't *have* to come to your place.'

'All *right*. You don't.'

Caroline said nothing more except to give Dagwood curt directions, which he acknowledged with grunts. They passed the Judworths'. The cars were still parked outside. The lights were still blazing. Dagwood thought bitterly of his own exit from the party in such gleeful triumph, only a few minutes before.

When the car stopped, Caroline jumped out quickly and slammed the door.

'Mind that door!' Dagwood bellowed. 'You'll have it off its hinges!'

Caroline bent to the window. 'Oh you *stupid* man,' she hissed, and marched up the steps to her front door.

Dagwood raised his eyebrows, opened his mouth to retaliate and then shrugged and drove off towards the farm. The whole thing was much too difficult.

14

'He's met her,' said The Bodger, significantly.

'At the point-to-point, you mean,' said Mr Tybalt, speaking in a low voice out of the side of his mouth.

'I introduced them myself.'

'How did it go?'

'Bit cool at first but they all shot off to a party afterwards. I've great hopes.'

'That's good,' said Mr Tybalt huskily.

'Why do you keep talking like Guy Fawkes, Frank? Anyone would think we were plotting something.'

'Well, aren't we? I feel kind of guilty about all this, Bodger. We can't just marry the wretched fellow off for political reasons.'

'Why not?'

'It all seems a bit like white-slaving or something,' said Mr Tybalt, uneasily.

The Bodger looked sternly at Mr Tybalt; so might Guy Fawkes have looked at a conspirator who pleaded to be excused on the critical night. '*Anything* that gives *Seahorse* a chuck-up is worth doing, isn't it? She needs it, doesn't she?'

'That's true,' Mr Tybalt admitted, unwillingly.

'Well then. I shouldn't let it worry your conscience too much, Frank. We can't really influence these things. All we can do is throw the raw materials together and hope they'll gell.'

'How did *you* come to know the wench, anyway? At the last showing you and Sir Rollo were not exactly *en rapport.*'

'We're not now, but Julia is on some women's committee

or other with Lady H-G. She hates racing and Sir Rollo was
going to be tied up with being Joint Master and Steward and
Lord High Everything Else and the regular boy friend hadn't
turned up so Lady H-G asked us to take Caroline. You should
pay attention to these women's committees, Frank. Julia tells
me they're an eye-opener. Julia says she can't imagine why
the press bother to turn up to council meetings and that sort
of thing. If they really want to know what's cooking she says
they ought to hide under the sofa when the Lady Mayoress
is entertaining the other wives to tea and scandal. And that
reminds me, I've got a committee meeting myself this afternoon so I'd better not have any more of this stuff. I don't
want to go to sleep in the middle of it.'

'What sort of committee meeting?'

'Civil Defence.'

'How did you come to be lumbered with that?'

'My predecessor left it to me.'

'To tell you the truth, Bodger, I didn't know there was
any Civil Defence in Oozemouth.'

'That's just it. Nobody knows and nobody could care less.
Everyone says if the bomb goes off we'll all be fried up anyway so why worry?'

'It's a point, you must admit.'

'It's absolute balls. There's a hell of a lot you can do. If
you can survive the first few days you might survive for good.
It's every citizen's duty to survive!' The Bodger's voice rose
in a sonorous rumble which made Guv look up anxiously
from his stance at the other end of the bar.

'Seriously Frank, this is a vital question which affects
everyone. When I was in Singapore a few years ago I met
an old Johnnie of an Engineer Captain who told me, between sobs, that one of his jobs was to organise Civil Defence
in Singapore and in two years' hard bashing his head against
brick walls he had achieved exactly nil. Everybody patted
him on the head, said There there, don't worry about it old
son, if anything happens we won't be here, we'll be miles

away out of it all. They seemed to forget that last time anything happened most of them were still there and that in any case the fall of Singapore would affect them wherever they were. It's the same in this town. Civil Defence-Wise, Oozemouth runs Singapore a close second.'

Mr Tybalt sympathised with The Bodger's problem but the whole subject was immediately driven out of his head by an event which eclipsed everything else in Oozemouth. The boilermakers and the shipwrights in Harvey McNichol & Drummond went on strike.

The strike arrived like a thunderbolt out of a clear blue sky. Neither Ollie nor Dagwood knew anything about it until they arrived at the office after lunch and the Chief Stoker broke the news.

'Heard about the strike, sir?'

'What strike?' said Dagwood and Ollie together.

'Boilermakers and shipwrights are all on strike, sir.'

'Since when?'

'Noon today, sir.'

'How did you come to know about it, Chief Stoker?'

'My cousin told me, sir. Her brother-in-law's a fitter in Maxwells and he came home to lunch full of it.'

'What are they striking about, do you know?'

The Chief Stoker shook his head. 'Couldn't tell you that, sir.'

'Doesn't your cousin know?'

'No sir. Her brother-in-law says the strike's the thing. It doesn't matter what it's about.'

'I must try and find out what this is all about,' Dagwood said.

Dagwood could excuse the Chief Stoker's cousin's ignorance of the cause of the latest industrial unrest at Harvey McNichol & Drummond, but he was surprised to find that this ignorance was general. Nobody knew why the men were on strike. Furthermore, nobody cared.

' . . . Does it matter what they're out for?' said Mr

McGillvray, bitterly.

'. . . It's the time of year for it,' said Happy Day.

'. . . Probably the full moon,' said Sid Burlap.

'. . . I expect they just want to dig their gardens,' said Sam Sollarwood.

It was Mr Tybalt, as usual, who had all the details.

'Come here,' he said to Dagwood. 'Come and look out of this window.'

Once more Dagwood looked out of Mr Tybalt's window at the gloomy ravine through which Christian must surely have trudged on his perilous path to Castle Despair.

'. . . Can you see that round man-hole cover down there, underneath that water tap, just by where that jet of steam's coming out?'

'Yes, I can see it.'

'Can you see four holes drilled in it?'

'I can't say I can, sir.'

'Just take my word for it, there are four inch holes drilled in that man-hole cover.'

Mr Tybalt paused.

'Well?' said Dagwood.

'Well, those holes are what this strike's all about.'

Dagwood searched Mr Tybalt's face, expecting to see the tell-tale sign of a practical joke. 'You're pulling my leg, sir.'

'My dear Dagwood,' Mr Tybalt exploded, 'I was never more serious in all my bloody life! It's like this. Every man-hole cover fitted in this yard for the last two hundred years has been made by a little foundry firm just down the road from here. They're the same firm that replaces the iron knobs as they fall off the Great Iron Bridge. I'm told that those are their only two contracts so you can imagine they're a pretty go-ahead, progressive sort of firm. Every man-hole cover is made of cast iron and comes here undrilled, that's to say with no holes in it. But there's a local by-law or something which lays down that every man-hole cover in the urban district of Oozemouth must have four or more holes or

146

apertures in them. You may then ask, as I did when I first heard about it, why don't the foundry drill the holes in the man-hole covers before they send them here? Ah, but that's not the way they do things here. Whenever a new man-hole cover arrives in this yard the holes are, or were, drilled by Old Vic.'

'Old Vic? He sounds like some sort of impresario.'

'He's only called Old Vic to distinguish him from his son Young Vic, the present foreman of slingers here. Old Vic was a very responsible official. He was no less a person than sole man-hole cover hole-driller for Harvey McNichol & Drummond's. Mind you, they only had a new man-hole cover about once every twenty years so he didn't exactly break his back doing the job. In between man-hole covers he was head plate-shop sweeper. But just lately, what with the new dock and everything, they've had dozens of new man-holes put in. I guess the strain must have been too much for Old Vic because he retired last Friday and the jackpot question now is, who's going to take over from him?'

'But anyone can drill four holes. I'd do it myself for five bob an hour and my keep.'

'Dagwood,' Mr Tybalt said patiently, 'your naïvety continues to astound me. Don't you understand, this whole *strike* is about who should drill man-hole covers. It's our old friend demarcation again. Way back in 1929 Old Vic must have had a sudden brainstorm because he joined the Boilermakers' Union. He soon sobered up because he never paid his subscription, never attended any meetings and he doesn't seem to have had anything more to do with them. But technically he's still a boilermaker and boilermakers are like Red Indians. Blood brothers. Once an Apache, always an Apache. Once a boilermaker, always a boilermaker. Now that Old Vic's gone, the boilermakers insist that he be replaced by another boilermaker. The shipwrights say it's a clear case for a shipwright. So there we are.'

'But they *can't* be striking about who should drill holes in *man-hole* covers!'

'This won't be the first time whole shipyards have struck over who should drill holes in things, Dagwood, and it won't be the last. I could tell you even more fantastic stories . . . But I won't. Just believe me when I say that in about six weeks' time this mighty yard will be at a complete standstill and all because of Old Vic.'

Mr Tybalt made a gesture of irritation. 'Devil take the man, if I'd only known he was going to retire I might have slipped him a fiver or two to keep going for another few weeks, at least until they'd finished stripping out your submarine.'

'I still can't quite believe it,' said Dagwood, shaking his head.

'I had the Director of Dockyards himself on the telephone just before you came in and if he believes it I don't see why you shouldn't. Now push off Dagwood, and leave me to me dark thoughts. I've got to try and recast your programme in the light of all this. And if you pass a man-hole cover on your way . . .'

'Yes sir?'

'*Spit* on it, will you?'

The next time Dagwood went to 'The Smokers' for his usual pint and gossip with Daphne, he saw a new aspect of the strike. There were two strangers at the bar, both burly men in heavy overcoats and bowler hats. They both had florid heavy-jowled faces and were drinking double Scotches. They were talking so loudly that Dagwood could not help over-hearing their conversation.

'Well, Bob,' said the one nearer to Dagwood, raising his glass, 'here's to Old Vic.'

'Aye, Fred,' said the other, 'sent from heaven, were Old Vic.'

'Or t'other place,' Fred said, with a laugh which reminded Dagwood vividly of doubtful jokes, told in low voices. 'I reckon we did a nice job there, eh?'

Bob shrugged his shoulders casually. 'Fair,' he said. 'Not as good as t'power station last Christmas.'

'Ah.' Fred sighed, as though granted a glimpse of paradise. 'That were perfect. A whole power station shut down over the Christmas peak period and for why? One lad comin' to work wearin' an earring! Old Ted would ha' been pleased wi' that, God rest him.'

'Aye, do you remember the way old Ted did that waxworks job? That's going back a bit now, though.'

Fred threw back his head and laughed so violently that whisky slopped from his glass and splashed Dagwood's foot. 'Sorry brother,' he said. Turning back to Bob, he said : 'Shall I ever forget that waxworks? They'd never 'ad a strike for a hundred years and then Ted has them all out over the colour of . . . what was it?'

'Ramsay Macdonald's eyebrows!'

'Aye that was it! Ramsay Macdonald's eyebrows! Ah, old Ted knew how to play on 'em, all right. Like a ruddy violinist, he was.'

Bob raised his eyes reverently towards the ceiling. 'We'll not see his like again, Fred.'

'That we won't. But that were not a bad job tha did thaself, with the buses. Timed it for August Bank Holiday, too. That were a chip off the old block.'

Bob accepted the compliment gracefully. 'You should talk. I'm thinking of your business with electric light bulb factory.'

Fred grinned. 'It were only lasses though. They thought they were striking for love money! Loss of matrimonial prospects through working in t'bulb factory! *Love money,* I ask you !'

'It's a good job folk are a bit mad, Fred, or we'd be out of a job, wouldn't we?'

'Aye, that's true enough. Having another, Bob?'

'No, I've got train to catch. I'll see you . . . what was it old Ted always used to say?'

'We meet at Philippi.'

'Aye, that's it. We meet at Philippi.'

Fred stayed for a little while after Bob left, smirking to himself and winking at Daphne. Then he drank up his whisky and nodded to Daphne, who returned the nod coldly, hitched his shoulders inside his coat, patted his bowler hat on the crown, and left.

'Who were they, Daphne?' Dagwood asked, at once.

Daphne grimaced. 'I don't know who they are, love. They're always here when there's a strike on. I think they must go round startin' them up, you know. They're as pleased as punch about it all. It's a shame to take their filthy money, I say. But Guv says a bob's a bob no matter who spends it. I suppose he's right, really.'

Dagwood did not know quite what he expected to happen during a strike. He had thought that at least the yard would be deserted, as though Bob and Fred had walked through it fluting like the Pied Piper. Dagwood was somewhat disappointed when there appeared to be no immediate change in the yard at all. There were still plenty of workmen about whenever he visited the submarine, the cranes still swung, the trains still trundled and the crowd pouring through the gates at noon and evening seemed undiminished.

But the activity Dagwood had noted was misleading. The strike was a creeping paralysis rather than a sudden stroke. The yard carried on, just as a tree will continue to flower after its roots are cut, but the heart and sap had gone out of it. Men who belonged to unions who were not on strike carried on with their work until they reached a stage where they required the assistance of a boilermaker or a shipwright. There the work had to stop. Another job would be started, progressed to the same point, and then that job too had to stop. The tide of work slackened, thinned, and finally dried up.

Dagwood's own immediate concern, the electricians, were least affected and were still in employment after the rest of the yard was idle. But as the strike continued they too ran out of profitable work. The day came when not only was there nothing fresh for Dagwood and Ollie to see when they went down to *Seahorse,* but they were physically prevented from going on board. Interpol, the watchman at the gangway, refused them permission, pass or no pass, informing them that the firm's security officers had locked up the submarine and nobody except a security officer was allowed on board.

On the same day, the refitting ship's company lined up outside Ollie's office and announced that they had nothing to do. This was an event quite outside either Dagwood's or Ollie's previous experience.

'They won't let us down the boat, sir,' said the Chief E.R.A., 'and there's damn all going on in the yard so there's no point in going round the workshops. We've mustered all the spare gear and put in demands for what's missing. Every book's been amended up to date, we've all done the tank, we've all been X-rayed and we're not due for any more leave until August. Half of us are making tea for the other half, sir.'

'Very well put, Chief E.R.A.' observed Ollie. '*Well . . .*' he looked helplessly at Dagwood.

'This is a new problem, I must say,' Dagwood said. 'Come back after stand-easy Chief, and we'll think of something by then.'

'It's one long stand-easy, sir.'

'Aren't you lucky?'

The sailors outside all sucked their teeth and made what Dagwood called 'Rhubarb rhubarb' noises.

'It's an interesting psychological phenomenon, isn't it?' he said to Ollie, when the sailors had withdrawn. 'Ask any sailor in a running submarine what he would think of a job in refit where he turns to between nine and four, never wears a uniform, no duties and nothing, *absolutely* nothing, to do all day. It sounds like Jolly John's idea of the promised land, doesn't it? And now they've got it, they're fed up with it!'

'In the meantime,' said Ollie, 'we've got to find them something to do.'

'I wonder if The Bodger's got any ideas? Let's give him a ring.'

As might have been expected, The Bodger had an immediate solution at his fingertips. 'Whenever you've got quantities of gash sailors, Dagwood, the standard service procedure is to send them all on courses.'

'What sort of courses, sir?'

'*Any* sort of courses!·For goodness sake it doesn't matter what the course is *about!* All courses are the same in the Navy anyway. You ought to know that, Dagwood!'

'How shall I allocate them sir?'

'Dagwood, you *are* being solid this morning! Out of a *hat* of course!'

'Thank you very much, sir.'

Dagwood took down two large tomes of Admiralty Fleet Orders (which in the matter of courses corresponded to the Sibylline Books) and went to work. Dagwood had always suspected that the Navy offered a wide variety of courses but he had never realised their scope. It seemed that there was nothing, from nuclear technology to wall-papering, on which the Navy were not prepared to run courses. Dagwood summoned the ship's company.

'I've got a lot of courses here,' he said, 'which you're going to do as long as the strike lasts. Just so there's no dripping about who goes on what course, we're going to draw for them. I've written them all on a slip of paper and put them in my hat. I want you to draw in turn. You first, Chief E.R.A.'

There were enough courses for at least two each, and more to come if necessary. The Chief E.R.A. drew 'Guided Weapons Acquaintance Course' and 'Basketball Coaching.' The Chief Stoker was rewarded by 'Survival at Sea' and 'Boot Repairing and Leatherwork.' The Electrical Artificer's selection was equally catholic: 'Boiler-brick Fastening' and

'Helicopter Direction.' The others drew from the hat in succession, Leading Seaman Gorbles a course where he volunteered for immersion in icy water, and an Outward Bound up Ben Nevis; Leading Stoker Drew, 'Mine Counter-Measures' and 'Hockey Umpiring,' and Leading Seaman Miles, the torpedoman, 'Paint Application' and 'Moral Leadership.' The most junior ratings had by no means drawn the most elementary courses. Ferguson, the Chief Stoker's storekeeper, faced 'Jam Testing' and an Arabic interpreter's course. Stoker Gotobed looked forward to 'Instructional Technique' and 'Gyro-Compass Maintenance,' while Able Seaman Quickly's programme was 'Oxy-Acetylene Welding and 'Meat-telling.'

'What do I tell it?' he asked.

'Very very funny, Quickly,' said Ollie. 'Let me tell you the meat-telling course is normally reserved for very senior supply officers. Nothing less than Commanders or Captains. But you've been specially chosen from a host of applicants so you'd better like it.'

Able Seaman Quickly retired, making what Dagwood called mutinous 'Rhubarb rhubarb' noises.

15

However, Dagwood's miscellaneous selection of courses proved to be only a partial solution. Many courses only lasted a few days, some had waiting lists, and others were not due to begin for some weeks. Dagwood and Ollie were still left with a pool of spare sailors on their hands. Ollie might, as a last resort, have asked for them to be returned to spare crew but once there they might never return and besides the strike might end at any time and the subsequent upheaval would have caused more trouble than ever. As time went by, and sailors began to return from courses, Dagwood and Ollie began to have the most widely read, broadly instructed, variously talented, but still the most idle ship's company in the Submarine Service. It was Mr Tybalt who proposed another solution.

'Why don't you have a look and see how the other half lives?' he said. 'You've got a city of more than half a million people here. Why don't you and your sailors take the opportunity to find out how they make their livings? I know a few people who run businesses here and one or two local blokes like the Chief Constable. Shall I see if I can fix up a few visits for you?'

'That sounds a splendid idea, sir,' said Dagwood.

'I'll see what I can do. I'll check with The Bodger but I expect you'll have to go in uniform. There's the recruiting angle to think of. You never know, there might be some Oozemothians soft-headed enough to be thinking of joining the Navy. You and your merry men might just tip the balance. Though which *way*, I wouldn't care to forecast.'

Dagwood broached the idea to Ollie.

'I don't think I'll join in,' Ollie said. 'I'm going to dig my garden.'

'How did you find that little house, Ollie, I've always meant to ask you.'

'I didn't find it. Daphne told me about it. I mentioned that I was looking for somewhere and she told me about this place. Alice and I went to look at it and it was just the job.'

'There can't be much going on in this town that Daphne doesn't know about.'

While Ollie dug his garden, Dagwood and the sailors embarked upon a comprehensive tour of Oozemouth, sponsored by Mr Tybalt, which probably gave them a more intimate knowledge of the city than many of its citizens possessed. They visited breweries, sewage farms, steel-rolling mills, leather tanneries, textile mills and power stations. They were shown round the printing presses of the 'Oozemouth Echo,' the totalisator at Oozemouth race course, the operations room at AA headquarters and the finger-print department of the local C.I.D. Dagwood was surprised and touched by the warmth of their reception everywhere.

'I must say people just couldn't be kinder,' he told The Bodger and Mr Tybalt. 'They fall over backwards to give the sailors a good time. Did you know that the 'Echo' took the sailors out to that road-house on the bypass last week and bought them beer and sandwiches all night? They had quite a run ashore, judging by reports.'

'It's not very surprising,' said The Bodger. 'For some reason, the people of this country are very fond of their Navy. It must be a case where ignorance is bliss but they get all sentimental about it. They *like* to see sailors about the place. It reminds them they've got a Navy. They see a sailor and it bucks them up. They square their shoulders and go on their way rejoicing, singing snatches of "Hearts of Oak." Some of them even try and grow beards.'

'There is also a sordid, commercial aspect to it,' said Mr

Tybalt, 'particularly where you personally are concerned, Dagwood. Why do you think you're welcomed everywhere, or nearly everywhere? Have you ever stopped to think why nine-tenths of the managing directors in this country will roll out the red carpet for *any* naval officer, no matter how junior? It's not because of your frank, boyish good looks, your clear blue eyes, or your casual charming manner, let me hasten to disillusion you. It's not who you are, laddie, it's who you might become. They don't know who you're going to be when you grow up. You might be a pleasant, fairly nondescript sort of chap now but one day· you might be in a position to place a very valuable Admiralty contract and from what I know of him the average naval officer is more than likely to place a socking great Admiralty contract with one particular firm just because they gave him a slap-up dinner and floorshow when he was a sub-lieutenant!'

'You're a cynical bastard, Frank,' said The Bodger.

'Cynical nothing! It's time you fellows learned the facts of life! You'll find the small minority of firms who won't roll out the red carpet for you are those who have all the Admiralty contracts they need already. By the way, how are you getting on with the local talent, Dagwood?'

Dagwood looked pensive, while The Bodger and Mr Tybalt watched his face closely. 'Oh so-so,' he said, off-handedly.

'When's your visit to the ball-bearing factory?'

'Tomorrow.'

'Mind how you go there. Always stay in the middle of the room. Don't let them lure you into corners.'

'This sounds interesting, Frank,' said The Bodger.

'Interesting isn't the word. I went there once and it was what I would call a traumatic experience. I reckon it's left me psychologically scarred for life.'

'Do you mind if I come with you tomorrow, Dagwood?' said The Bodger.

'Don't say I didn't warn you,' said Mr Tybalt.

In spite of Mr Tybalt's warning, the visit to the ball-bearing factory began quietly enough. The Bodger, Dagwood and the small party of sailors were shown the raw material for the balls – coils of steel wire – being chopped into small cylinders. They watched the rough wire cylinders being forge-stamped, ground, smoothed and polished into shining round balls. They saw the balls being graded for size and truth. It all seemed innocent enough.

It was not until they reached double green doors marked 'Inspection' that Mr Tybalt's words assumed their true meaning. Their guide opened one of the green doors, pushed them in, and stepped smartly back.

The Bodger and his party stood in the doorway, appalled.

The Inspection Department consisted of only one room but it was roughly half the size of a main-line railway terminus. The room contained nearly a thousand girls and its atmosphere was as steamy as a hot-house, with an odour compounded of nearly a thousand sources of perfume, talcum powder and deodorant. The noise level was at such a pitch as to make a perceptible physical impact upon The Bodger's unaccustomed eardrums. There was the yammering of conversations, the rattling of trolleys, the tapping of feet and above everything else the relentless pounding of a rock-and-roll record being relayed at full volume through loudspeakers set in the roof.

The Bodger's party were observed at once. Every conversation stopped in mid-syllable. Every trolley-wheel stopped in mid-revolution. Every tapping foot poised. The rock-and-roll record broke off in mid-beat.

For a few moments, there was silence. Then simultaneously the loudspeakers burst into 'All The Nice Girls Love a Sailor,' again played at full volume, and there arose from the girls a piercing wailing ululation, more blood-chilling than the howling of wolves, more penetrating than a police siren, gaining in power and intensity, swelling and growing until it reverberated from the air, from the walls, from the ground and from inside The Bodger's very skull.

The Bodger, looking back afterwards, decided that stepping forward from that door into 'Inspection' at the ball-bearing factory was the bravest single act of his whole life. He shuffled forward, encouraged by the stout voice of the Chief Stoker behind him, saying 'Pack together, men!'

Cautiously, almost back to back, like a wagonload of settlers moving through howling Sioux country, the party from *Seahorse* edged further into the room.

A petite, dark-haired girl in a blue nylon overall took charge of them. She had 'Supervisor' on a badge in her lapel and her name was Doris. She looked about twenty-five years old and she seemed to be in sole command. The Bodger found himself wondering humbly at a discipline which could single-handedly control a number of females corresponding to the ship's company of a heavy cruiser.

They began to walk round, pursued by giggles, sidelong glances and crescendoes of sudden idiot laughter. Every sailor in turn, including Dagwood, received a hundred signalled invitations. All were invited, except The Bodger. As far as the girls were concerned, The Bodger might not have existed. The Bodger felt piqued.

The basic operation of 'Inspection' was very simple. The girls sat at long tables, fifty or sixty girls to a side, each girl having her own stall. Every stall had a small tray fitted with a sliding bottom and, above it, a bright light. Bags of ball-bearings were tipped into trays and the girls moved the tray bottoms so that the balls rolled over and their surfaces could be examined for flaws by the light of the lamps. Doris laid on a demonstration.

'Here you are, Nessie,' she said to one woman of about fifty. 'Show the gentlemen what you can do. We call her Nessie,' she added to The Bodger, 'because of the monster, y'see.'

Every girl in ear-shot gave a shrill cackle. Nessie, who did not appear to The Bodger to be at all a bad-looking woman, smiled amiably.

Doris took a ball-bearing from her overall pocket and showed it to The Bodger. 'It's a flawed one,' she said.

The Bodger examined the ball closely. He could just see, if he looked hard, a tiny chip in the surface.

Doris took the ball, dropped it into a bag and poured the contents of the bag into Nessie's tray.

With a speed that baffled the eye Nessie pulled down her lamp, nudged her tray and deftly poured the shining flow of balls sideways into a shute. One ball remained on her tray. Nessie handed it up to The Bodger. The tiny chip on it was unmistakable.

'Well I'll be damned!' said The Bodger, in astonishment. The whole performance had been as slickly executed as a conjuring trick. The Bodger acknowledged that he could never do Nessie's job, not if he practised for a year. The Bodger had no doubt that if he were forced to work in this room he would be under the care of a psychiatrist inside a week.

The Bodger noticed that one stall was decorated with greetings cards, flowers, coloured streamers, and an old shoe.

'What's that mean?' he asked Doris.

'She's getting married Saturday.'

Here and there, other stalls were appropriately decorated. Every major event in a girl's life was commemorated. The Bodger could see several 'Happy Birthday' signs, one or two golden keys, and a scattering of significant storks. Almost every stall had a piece of red cord in the partition netting.

'What's the cord for?'

'It means she's had her first man,' Doris explained.

The ball-bearing factory was patently more than a mere place of employment for the girls who worked there. It was an important part of their lives. They came to it from school, carried on after marriage and left only to have a baby. When their children were grown up they returned, like Nessie, to work until they were too old.

The Bodger had been so absorbed in his tour that he had failed to notice that his party had gradually been dwindling. He awoke just in time to see the Chief Stoker's hat disappearing through a side door. Even Dagwood was trapped on the other side of the room, surrounded by a crowd of girls. The Bodger was isolated in 'Inspection,' with Doris. He intercepted a look flashed between Doris and another girl and it dawned upon him why he had received no welcoming signals. Doris was reserving him for herself. Without a word being spoken, the jungle drums had passed their message; like a banner being carried through the room, the word had been passed: 'This one's *mine*.'

Panic-stricken, The Bodger tapped the nearest girl on the shoulder.

'Let me have a go at that.'

The girl got up readily. The Bodger sat down and Doris poured a bag of ball bearings into the tray. The Bodger pulled down the light and began to concentrate upon the balls as though his life depended on it. Every girl round about stopped work to watch him.

The Bodger had no doubt that the inspection was almost a formality. The odds against an imperfect ball reaching this stage of production must be several thousands to one. Nevertheless, it would be a triumph if he could find one. The Bodger moved his tray in and out for some time, without noticing anything. Then something caught his eye. It was no more than a suspicion, a reflection which was not quite true. Perhaps it was a minute speck of dust on that ball. The Bodger blew at it. It was still there. Feeling his pulse rate beginning to accelerate, The Bodger manipulated the tray again. Now, he was almost sure. One more roll, and he was certain.

'There's a flaw in it!'

The Bodger's cry of glee was apparently the funniest sound he had ever uttered in his life. The girls slapped their thighs, doubled up, and hooted. Some of them staggered about, crying and coughing into their handkerchiefs, and supporting themselves on the table.

'I tell you there's a flaw in it!' cried The Bodger again. 'Just look! A flaw!'

Doris received the news calmly. 'It's a special visitors' bag you got there,' she said. 'They're all flawed.'

16

Dagwood kept in touch with the latest strike situation through Mr Tybalt's grapevine. There seemed to be no other source of information; the yard itself was virtually shut down, Bob and Fred never visited 'The Smokers' again, and the newspapers had relegated the 'Old Vic' or 'Plug-hole' strike as they called it, to a small middle page paragraph once a fortnight. Only Mr Tybalt seemed always to have the latest gossip.

'I was hoping to have some good news about the strike today,' he told Dagwood, one brilliant May morning. 'Last week the yard did the sensible thing and arranged with the foundry to have the bloody covers drilled before they get here. That was fine, but it meant that the foundry had to take on a driller and as they've never employed a driller before their men objected. So now *they're* on strike and we're back to square one again. It's a case of Go straight to the Doghouse, Do not pass Go, Do not collect Two Hundred pounds. Maddening, isn't it?'

'Yes sir,' Dagwood agreed. He could never have admitted it to Mr Tybalt but Dagwood was secretly enjoying the strike and would be sorry when it ended. Apart from the unexpected holiday it was giving him, it also had other, unforeseen, advantages. For instance the conquest of Barbara, the girl who worked in the Norwegian shipping firm's office next door to Dagwood.

Dagwood had heard of girls being swept off their feet. He had heard of them succumbing to a cunning, waiting game. (One could, according to the best authorities, either play the part of a mixture of Young Lochinvar and the Sheik of

Araby, or a sort of amatory Quintus Fabius Maximus Cunctator.) But Dagwood would never have believed that a girl would drop into his arms, like a ripe plum, out of sheer boredom. Dagwood had never succeeded in getting on more intimate terms with Barbara than saying good morning and occasional sugar borrowing. From time to time the basin in Barbara's office was blocked and Dagwood sent in his shock troops, Gotobed and Quickly, to clear it and possibly prepare the way for a closer relationship. But Barbara had hitherto remained aloof.

The strike changed everything. The Norwegian tanker had been within a fortnight of her launch date when the strike began, but when work on her was stopped the firm's marine superintendent and his assistant, who were Barbara's immediate employers, both vanished. Barbara was left with nothing to do for days on end but withstand the steady pressure of willpower exerted by Dagwood, lurking next door. Sometimes Barbara's telephone rang, she would make a note, and occupy herself for an hour or two in searching through her files, typing and dispatching letters. The rest of the time she painted her nails, looked out of the window, and read 'Woman's Own.' Next door, Dagwood watched and waited.

His preoccupation was so intense that even Ollie noticed it.

'Dagwood, you baffle me,' he said. 'For a bloke who says he doesn't want to get married you're acting in a bloody strange manner. You're like a man who says he's terrified of catching pneumonia and then spends all his time cavorting about in the snow in the nude.'

'Who said anything about marriage? I didn't say I was in love with the girl. A roll in the snow wouldn't be such a bad idea, now you come to mention it.'

'You don't have to love a girl to marry her, in any case.'

'Ollie, you cynical old devil.'

'Good heavens, half the married couples you meet don't *love* each other. Not any more, anyway. They *like* each other and that's a hell of a lot more important, believe me. After

163

all, it's only comparatively recently that any idea of love entered into marriage.'

'Do you love Alice, as well as liking her, if you don't mind my asking?'

'I think so. I think I'm very lucky. The important thing is not to expect too much.'

'How did you meet her?'

'She was a Wren steward. I first noticed her when she let a plate of soup slip on top of the Commander and I heard the Chief Wren giving her hell afterwards. I just thought "Poor kid".'

'Oh *Ollie,* that's the oldest trick in the book!'

Ollie reddened. 'Maybe. I fell for it, if that's what you mean. And I've never regretted it.'

'What do you mean by love, Ollie?'

'What do *I* mean by love? I don't mean anything by love. Life just seems simply splendid, that's all. You bounce around like a two-year-old. You feel all tense before you ring her up. You want to know all about her, who she met, what she did, what she thought about things, before she met you. You want to give her things. You're always pleased when you compare notes and find that she must have been in the same town as you were before she met you. You're surprised at the amount she eats when you take her out to dinner.' Ollie suddenly blushed a vivid carmine colour. 'Anyway, I don't know why I'm telling *you*. Judging by your past record and present performance you ought to be telling me.'

'No no, that was very interesting, Ollie.' Dagwood had indeed been deeply interested and respectful; he had not expected such words from the pragmatical, down-to-earth Ollie. He recognised in them the authentic ring of personal experience. He was ashamed to think that he had served with Ollie for eighteen months without noticing that he was a romantic at heart.

There was a tapping of heels down the corridor.

'Here she comes now.'

164

Dagwood sprang up to look through the glass window partition.

'Hush you now, the fair Ophelia,' he whispered. 'She smiles! My lady she smiles at me! Oh frabjous day, calloo callay!'

Barbara reached her office door and smiled once more at Dagwood before going in.

'Boy,' said Dagwood thoughtfully. 'I go for that woman. That bosom. Positively Byzantine! She's like one of those girls you see doing the belly dance in Turkish night clubs. You know, lovely black hair, creamy complexion and a body like chewing gum! Licensed for Levantine lust!'

'A rag, a bone and a hank of hair,' said Ollie, disparagingly.

'Give me that bone!'

'You'd better get cracking then. Strike while the iron's hot, as they say. She may not smile again for another fortnight.'

'Right!' Picking up his heels, Dagwood scudded along the corridor like a March hare, paused while he put on his best would-you-like-to-dance expression, and knocked on Barbara's door.

'May I come in?'

Barbara looked up from the do-it-yourself carpentry kit spread over her desk, with which she was paring her nails. (Those eyes, thought Dagwood, those eyes must surely have seen their first light by the Golden Horn. They were the eyes that welcomed Leander when he rose dripping from the Hellespont, the eyes which shed tears over Icarus dead).

'If you'd like to.' Barbara held out one forefinger and cocked her head appraisingly at the finger-nail upon it.

Dagwood slipped inside and shut the door. 'I thought you looked rather lonely these last few weeks.'

Barbara shrugged, so that her bosom rose and fell. (Those breasts, shaped like mosques, each tipped with a rose of Macedonia.) 'Not particularly,' she said.

'Been a bit quiet since the strike started, hasn't it?'

'So so.'

'Our office has been like a graveyard.'

'Has it?' said Barbara noncommittally. She pouted. 'Poor you.'

(Those lips, Curved, red and ripe, like the apple promised by the Prophet.)

'I wondered if you might like to come out this evening somewhere?'

'Where to?' Barbara wriggled on her chair. (Those buttocks, spread so engagingly on the chair; which suleiman was it who said that heaven is the shape of a woman's buttocks? The Great, probably.)

'Oh, anywhere. We might go and eat somewhere, go and see a movie, anywhere you like . . .'

'All right.'

'Splendid, shall I pick you up at home?'

'No, I'll meet you at the "Black Cat." Do you know where that is?'

'No, but I can easily find out. What time?'

'About seven.'

'I'll be there.'

Humming like a contented suleiman, Dagwood skipped back to his own office.

'The Black Cat?' said Ollie. 'I think I've heard of that. It's where all the Oozemouth University types go and drink coffee and tell each other what a lousy world it all is. Our sixteen year old babysitter goes there. For kicks, she says. It doesn't sound like your sort of run ashore, Dagwood.'

'Never mind,' Dagwood said, loftily. 'You won't find a hunter complaining if his quarry leads him over difficult country.'

'Well, I suppose you know what you're doing,' said Ollie.

Nevertheless, as Dagwood mounted the wooden steps to the former tea warehouse under the western end of the Great Iron Bridge which was now the 'Black Cat,' he could not entirely suppress an uneasy reluctance to go on. Dagwood had never been enthusiastic about parties where there was very little to drink, where the only light came from the pilot bulb of the record-player, and where people lay on the floor stroking each other, stimulated by West Coast jazz. Whenever a party showed signs of tipping from the vertical to the horizontal Dagwood always felt a strong urge to turn up the lights and call for his hat and coat. From what Ollie had told him and from the 'Yugga-dug-dug' music he could hear coming from the top of the steps, the 'Black Cat' had all the signs of being a spawning ground for horizontal party-givers.

There was a figure leaning against the doorpost at the top. He was smoking a cigarette and tapping his foot in time to the music. Dagwood recognised him as Digby, one of Hilda's friends at the point-to-point.

'Evening, squire,' said Digby.

A voice was now making itself heard above the music. ' . . . Luh-luh-*love* yer bub-bayeebeeyah . . .' it was saying.

Dagwood nodded towards the door. 'Do you know if there's a girl called Barbara in there?'

'Lovely body.'

'That's her.'

'*Lovely* body. God, you get around a bit, don't you?'

'Do I? I could hardly have missed Barbara, could I now?'

'True, squire. That's a whole lot of woman.'

The music had changed. It was backed now by another, woman's, voice stringing rhymes together. Dagwood could hear them more clearly as he went through the door. ' . . . Blue . . . because of you . . . said you'd be true . . . like you're steeped in glue . . .'

The 'Black Cat' was, and still looked like a former tea warehouse which had been fitted with a juke box, a coffee machine a soft drink bar, rows of hard wooden benches and some tables. There were no windows, the only lighting being provided by half a dozen naked light-bulbs hanging from the ceiling. A small fan set in one wall was struggling against the smoke and heat rising to the roof. The juke box provided a great pulsing heart for the tumult of conversation.

The place was crowded and it took Dagwood some time to find Barbara and when he did he hardly recognised her as the girl who sat every day in the office next door. Gone were the plain skirt and blouse. The hair which was carefully brushed and set in the day-time was now hanging loose to her shoulders. She was wearing skin-tight black pants, a tight black sweater and a short waistcoat of leopard or ocelot skin. Six or seven heavy metal bangles hung on each wrist and she seemed to be stooping forward under the weight of a necklace of colossal red beads. Dagwood goggled at her for he knew that in spite of her Middle Eastern appearance she was a local girl; Mr Tybalt (who of course knew all about her) had told Dagwood that her father was actually a senior draughtsman in Harvey McNichol & Drummond's, and they lived in a semi-detached on one of the new estates Dagwood passed on his way from the farm to work.

Dagwood need not have been so astonished. Barbara was merely wearing the dress *du pays,* the protective colouring being worn by almost every other girl present. Barbara was conforming strictly to the 'Black Cat' code. It was Dagwood, in his office-going suit and his submariner's tie, who was incongruous.

Barbara caught Dagwood's eye and waved him over to the table where she was sitting with some friends.

'Come and sit on my knee, Dagwood,' she said.

'Ah no, actually I don't think I will,' Dagwood said uncomfortably. He perched himself on the edge of the table next to Barbara.

'Who's the business tycoon, Barbara? What's he doing here, slumming?'

'Oh Humphrey,' said Barbara.

Before Dagwood could think of a suitable retort or even properly identify his opponent, another voice asked eagerly: 'I say squire, did you go to the University of Western Australia? They *are* swans, aren't they?'

Dagwood squinted down at his tie. 'No, they're dolphins. It's a submariner's tie.'

'*Submariner!*'

Dagwood was startled by the apparently percussive effect of the word. A shudder seemed to run right round the table. A couple who had been crouched over a chess board at the other end of the table, absorbed in their game, straightened up. Slowly, their heads swivelled enough to enable them to gaze reproachfully at Dagwood. Next to them, a young man who had been idly plucking a guitar crashed a hideous chord with the knuckles of his right hand. His hand carried on with its swing and remained frozen at the end of the sweep. Meanwhile, he kept his eyes fixed on his guitar, as though he were unwilling to look into Dagwood's eyes for fear of what he might read in them.

'*Not* one of the nuclear boys?'

'Unfortunately not,' said Dagwood carelessly. 'I haven't been selected. I probably wasn't intelligent enough. The competition's pretty stiff, you know.'

' . . . *Unfortunately!*'

' . . . Not *intelligent* enough !'

' . . . Competition's pretty stiff,' echoed Humphrey. 'It chills one's blood, this does.'

The guitarist took another sideswipe at his instrument, but still didn't dare to meet Dagwood's eyes.

It was already plain that in coming to the 'Black Cat' wearing a submariner's tie Dagwood had committed a major social gaffe; he might just as well have burst into an anti-blood-sport meeting waving a fox's bloody mask.

'Would you go to sea in a nuclear submarine if you *were* selected?' Humphrey asked. Dagwood marked him as the leader of the wolf pack. He was a lanky individual with straight black hair and a long nose. He looked intellectual, but down-at-heel. His thoughts might have been lofty but his brown wind-cheater was faded and stained, his shirt was torn at the collar and, having no buttons left on it, hung open

169

to reveal a greyish vest.

'Would I go to sea in a nuclear? Of course I would. Apart from anything else, I'm paid to do it.'

'Even if it had nuclear warheads on board?'

'Certainly.'

'And would you press the button when the time came?'

'Undoubtedly,' said Dagwood cheerfully. 'It would be a pleasure. I only hope to God it works.'

There was a hissing intake of breath all round the table and murmurings of 'Hired mercenary,' 'Murderer,' and 'Cold-blooded, I call it.'

Dagwood was perplexed by their attitude. They were menacing, yet respectful. They wanted to attack him, while yet keeping their distance. They were behaving like mountain peasants who, having lived for years in terror of a certain notorious bandit, had now captured one of his lieutenants, with blood still on his hands and proud of it.

Dagwood concentrated upon Humphrey. 'You seem to know an awful lot about submarines. What do you do for a living?'

'I'm an artist. Something you wouldn't understand.'

'You mean you paint?'

'No, I etch.'

'Then why the devil don't you scratch?' Dagwood retorted viciously.

A girl in a white wool polo-necked sweater who was sitting next to Humphrey gave a cry of anguish. 'How dare you! It's not *fair,* a murderer like you saying things like that to Humphrey! At least he doesn't go round killing people and saying he likes it. He *creates* things, not destroys them!'

The girl's eyes flashed venom and contempt at Dagwood. Dagwood was intrigued by her. She was really rather a pretty girl. Her pointed chin, pale complexion, green eyes and ash blonde hair cut in a low fringe gave her, when she was not angry, a wistful elfin expression. Dagwood transferred his attention to her.

'I don't know why *you're* getting so heated about sub-marines,' he said. 'That's a submariner's sweater you've got on, if ever I saw one!'

The girl gave a gasp and put her hand to her mouth. The others looked at her sweater as though it were a badge of shame.

'Vera,' said Humphrey, in a pained voice.

'Humphrey darling, I'd no *idea*. In the shop it said they were ex-Air Force.'

'They've got *far* more nuclear weapons than we have!' Dagwood said cruelly, following up his advantage. 'Look, before we go any further, I might point out that we're only employees. We don't decide when and where to use these weapons, or any weapons in fact. The politicians do that. If I could be impartial about it, which of course I can't, I would have said that the stronger armed forces you had the less likely you were to get blown up. In time of peace prepare for war sort of thing.'

The last was an unfortunate remark. It was exactly what Dagwood's audience had expected him to say; it was a key phrase which touched off an even more violent chain reaction of protest and mutterings of 'Gun-boat politics,' 'Jingoism,' and 'Throwback to Kitchener.'

The attack was taken up by another young man who was almost a replica of Humphrey. They were so alike they might have been brothers. Their opinions were also similar. His name was Donald and Dagwood soon found in him a more dangerous opponent than Humphrey.

'That argument is plain nonsense,' said Donald, categorically. 'For two reasons. First, neither the Navy nor any of the armed services are capable of protecting this country at the moment in any sort of war, global or limited. Even our deterrent is not really a deterrent. It's more of a detergent. The Navy in particular is the biggest confidence trick played on the nation since Horatio Bottomley went to jail. When I look at the number of ships we've got and what they're armed with, it makes me wonder how you've got the nerve to collect your pay at the end of the week . . .'

'Here, just a *minute* . . .' Dagwood protested indignantly.

' . . . Second,' Donald went on, as though Dagwood had never spoken, 'even a deterrent is no deterrent against irresponsibility. 'We've got to live with this bomb, for years and years . . .'

'Oh we're talking about the bomb now, are we?'

' . . . As the years go by we'll get used to it, we'll get careless with it, more and more small countries will get hold of it and one day, some time, somewhere, one of them will use it to settle some private parochial squabble of their own. And then, before you can say 'Megadeath' we'll all go up together. If you honestly believe that *no* politician *anywhere* will *ever* use this bomb, from now until Doomsday, then all I can say is you've got a pretty naïve idea of human nature. One of them is *bound* to. It may not be for five years, ten, maybe fifty years, but it'll come . . .'

'All right,' said Dagwood, swiftly changing his stance, 'supposing it does come. There will be a period afterwards, what we call the 'broken-back' stage, where the Navy . . .'

'And what makes you think the *Navy* won't have its back broken as well, along with the rest of us lesser mortals?'

It was a good point. Dagwood made a mental note to put it to the next staff officer he met.

'Yes,' said Humphrey, 'what makes you think you're all demi-gods?'

Dagwood was astonished by the heat these people had managed to generate on frothy coffee. They had achieved a height of argumentative fervour which would only have been reached in a wardroom after many, many whiskies late into the night.

'Anyway,' he said placatingly, 'as long as they keep on calling each other names in the newspapers and over conference tables, I reckon we're safe. It's when all the shouting and tumult *stops* and there's a deathly hush, *that's* when

I shall take to the hills.'

'No you see, that's just where you're wrong. That's exactly the attitude they want you to have. You've been brainwashed . . .'

It was a girl whom Dagwood immediately recognised as one of those who would worry deeply about the Meaning of Life, the Future of Mankind, the Place of the Citizen in a Power-Mad World, and other abstracts. Her face was round, her nose was snubbed and her spectacles were large and horn-rimmed. Her hair was done in two thick plaits and she was wearing a square-necked jersey which looked as though it had been knitted in some form of coarse dark rope. With her nicotine-stained fingers and her quick nervous gestures, Dagwood was convinced that she was the type to take matters to heart and put her whole life and soul into a project where her conscience or her compassion were touched; Dagwood forecast that she would die an old maid, honoured by an obituary in the local newspaper warmly commending her life-long struggles for the sick parrots of her neighbourhood.

' . . . Don't you see, they caught you at an early age and now you're content to look on at things. You're a perfect example of what I call the *New Spectator*. You don't take part in life, you observe it, like a bird-watcher. You're like forty million people in this country. *You* wouldn't think of cheering the Queen as she drove by, no more than you would think of cheering her if you saw her driving by on TV. You're not even looking, you're *viewing!*'

'Well *said* Agatha !'

Humphrey, Donald and Vera pounded the table approvingly and then, abruptly, got up and left, taking Agatha with them.

'Blimey, that was a bit sudden,' said Dagwood.

'Probably time to go and picket the local T.A.,' said the guitarist, still picking at his instrument.

'Do you play that in a band or anything?' Dagwood asked, anxious to make friends with someone.

'No. Do you think I should?'

'Not at all.'

'Solo guitar is the purest music existing. Have you ever heard Segovia?'

'Only on records.'

'He makes the sort of music the angels hear every day.'

'I quite agree. Still . . .'

'Still what?' demanded the guitarist pugnaciously.

'I was just thinking, if they heard it every day all day they might get a bit bored with it.'

'You needn't try and insult me like you did Humphrey!'

Oh God, thought Dagwood, here we go again. 'I'm not trying to insult you, I assure you. I just feel that solo guitar sometimes needs a little support.'

'The more instruments the better?'

'Well no, within limits of course . . .'

'I suppose you're the sort of person who thinks Mahler's Sixth Symphony is the finest music ever written?'

'I didn't say that,' Dagwood defended himself, having barely heard of Mahler at all.

'Do you know how many instruments that's scored for?'

'I'll make a guess . . .'

'Sixteen first violins, sixteen second violins, twelve violas, twelve cellos, twelve basses, four flutes, four oboes, one clarinet in E flat, three clarinets in B flat . . .'

'Yes, but . . . .'

' . . . One bass clarinet in B flat, three bassoons, one double bassoon, eight horns, four trumpets, three trombones, one bass tuba, two harps, celesta, timpani, cymbals and a tambourine!'

'What, no guitar!'

'Would you like some more coffee, Dagwood?'

It was Barbara. Dagwood had quite forgotten about her. She had made no contribution to the previous conversations, probably, Dagwood suspected, because she could think of nothing to say. Barbara was a delectable body and not much

174

else. She was accepted in 'Black Cat' circles because of her decorative appearance, being the sort of girl a man needed to feast his eyes on after sixty days at sea (what effect she might have had in such circumstances upon as volatile a personality as Gavin, *Seahorse's* late Navigating Officer, Dagwood could hardly bring himself to contemplate).

On the other hand, there was another way of looking at it. Barbara may have been a handicap in a dialectical discussion but she was just the sort of girl for a cosy cuddle on a sofa. Which reminded Dagwood.

'Come on, Barbara, let's go and get something to eat.'

Dagwood had taken the precaution of laying in some raw materials for shush kebab and some burgundy before he went out and within ninety minutes he and Barbara had eaten and drunk and taken up their positions on the sofa.

The evening had all the makings of a satisfactory consummation for Dagwood, but he could not rid himself of one small disturbance. Whenever he bent to murmur in Barbara's ear (those ears, each like a lotus nestling on the banks of the Euphrates) he could hear an extraordinary ringing echo of his own words.

'Kissing your lips is like taking a long cool drink of water,' he whispered to Barbara.

' . . . Drinka water,' said the echo.

Dagwood blinked. He lay back and studied the moon shining on the skylight in the Tithe Barn roof.

'Had we but world enough, and time,' he began.

' . . . And time,' came the tinkling spectral echo.

'This coyness lady were no crime.'

' . . . No crime.'

'We would sit down and think which way . . .'

'Whichaway . . .'

' . . . To walk and spend our long love's *day*.'

'Love's *day*.'

It was a full minute before the solution occurred to Dagwood. He had frequently read descriptions of the physical phenomena associated with falling in love; if the descriptions were to be believed, the collision of two people irresistibly attracted to one another was clinically similar to the symptoms of severe concussion. Dizziness, ringing in the ears, the music of celestial choirs, flashes and stars exploding in front of the eyes, a sudden apparent drop in stomach level – the symptoms were fully documented and Dagwood was quite familiar with them. But this was the first time he had experienced such a manifestation himself. This must be love, Dagwood told himself, I'm hearing double.

He looked tenderly down at Barbara. There was no denying the evidence of one's own sensory organs. Dagwood resolved never to sneer at women's magazines again; clearly they were reporting scientific facts.

Dagwood was so elated by his discovery and so buoyed up by the thought that he had been granted what amounted to a sign from heaven, where all good marriages are made, that his sense of deprivation and shock was all the sharper when he later came across the hearing aid, neatly concealed in Barbara's Byzantine bosom.

17

'I don't like the look of this at all, Frank,' said The Bodger.

'I know. He seems to have dropped the girl altogether.'

'Not only that, he seems to have gone overboard with every other girl within a radius of fifty miles. You remember you put me up for the Conservative Club when I first got here?'

'Yes. It's a good way of keeping your finger on the·pulse.'

'Exactly. Well, there isn't a member there with a daughter of marriageable age who hasn't told me at some time or other that his daughter was being taken out by young Dagwood! That *barn* of his seems to have a fatal attraction.'

'For every girl except the one who matters.'

'What's more, none of them seem to have any objection to becoming Dagwood's father-in-law. I should have thought that the last thing any man wanted was a son-in-law in the Navy but some of them seem to be all for it.'

'All except the father-in-law who matters.'

'I may be mistaken, but I got the impression that Dagwood was quite attracted to the wench, you know. And she didn't seem to be exactly repelled by him, either.'

'What are we going to do about it then?'

'What can we do? I've introduced them once. I can't keep bouncing them together like billiard balls. I shall just have to give the thing a bit more thought. I'll think of something, never fear.'

Meanwhile, Dagwood was quite unaware that his social life had been causing The Bodger and Mr Tybalt concern. As Daphne had said, when he told her he had taken the Tithe Barn, he was having the time of his life. For the first time since he became a submariner, he could appreciate the changing seasons on the land. Often while he was in a running submarine he had noticed very little more of the approach of summer than that the weather was getting warmer and the nights shorter. On the Watsons' farm Dagwood was living in a society where the cycle of the seasons and the weather were not merely subjects of conversation but vital facets of existence. Long after he had left the farm Dagwood remembered small happenings of that spring and summer : the two hares which played in the ten acre field behind the barn, fleeting over the grass in the early morning sun like two wisps of brown smoke; Shep, obeying the instinct of his breed, herding ducklings through the farm gate; the hawthorn hedge outside the back door exploding almost overnight into star-bursts of white blossom; the day Chubb took him out to a clump of pines to see the hobby's nest and they waited in a ditch for four hours to see a flash of red plumage as the bird arrived at the nest; and Bill's haymaking, when Dagwood and such sailors as were not on courses worked ten hours a day for half a crown an hour and free cider.

Dagwood did not attend any courses himself. He did not have the time. Instead he took Sarah Judworth to Oozemouth Races on Gold Cup Day, Hilda Judworth to the beach, and Fiona to an open air performance of 'A Midsummer's Night's Dream.' He had supper occasionally with Ollie and Alice and he spent many happy hours, hat tipped over his eyes, watching the cricket at the County Ground. Sometimes a sailor would drift back from a course. Dagwood shook up the slips in his cap and sent him off again.

Sometimes, while he sat watching cricket or lay sun-bathing on the beach, Dagwood thought guiltily of his friends daily going down to the sea in their submarines and being paid less for it. But such thoughts were short-lasting and Dagwood's conscience was appeased by the knowledge that his friends, had they been given the chance, would have done exactly the same and would probably not even have spared him a thought while they were doing it.

Like the people of many northern cities, the people of Oozemouth were kindly but hard-headed. They had a great respect for money and for those who possessed or wielded it. Some Oozemouth families had known each other for three generations or longer. They visited each other regularly, almost religiously, and their children were permitted to grow up in a state of social stability. It was not so important that a family were rich or poor; it only mattered that they had lived in Oozemouth a long time. Families did not arrive, allow their children to grow half-roots, and move on again – like Dame's neighbours in Buckinghamshire, who changed every five years. At home, Dagwood witnessed a social ebb and flow, a rising and falling in the world, a continual household migration caused by the irresistible centripetal force of London. By contrast, Oozemouth had remained almost untouched, one of the last bastions of the unperturbed middle class. The boys joined the professions or went to work in their family businesses; a few joined the Army, a few went to London, but almost all returned to Oozemouth and their families and friends to settle down. The girls were lured by the prospect of a flat in London and independence but they too, with a few exceptions, came home eventually. Dagwood often told himself that he ought to write down his impressions of Oozemouth, that he ought to record this way of life, lest he return one day and, like Macaulay's traveller from New Zealand, stand on a broken arch of the Great Iron Bridge to sketch the ruins of the people who built and paid for it.

Dagwood had grown accustomed to the sensation that he was regarded as unusual and even exotic – particularly by the girls. He was not only a new face, he was unique. It was nothing new for young men from other parts of the country to spend a year living in digs in Oozemouth; the city was on the established circuit of provincial posts to which large firms sent their trainees to gain experience. But someone in the

Navy, living on his own in a Tithe Barn, cooking his own meals – nothing could be richer nor stranger. Dagwood's little dinners, tête-à-tête, became well known. The girls who had thus been entertained exchanged experiences. The word was passed round. Dagwood was known by many more girls than he knew. They went out of their way to meet him. The shush kebab and the burgundy became status symbols. Dagwood's guests expected them and when Dagwood himself tired of them and made a change by roasting one of Chubb's chickens and washing it down with some hock he caught such looks of disappointment that he felt morally driven to return to his traditional recipes.

Dagwood also possessed another advantage in that he was a Londoner. Anyone from London automatically assumed a sort of vicarious glamour in Oozemouth. Oozemouth displayed a disdainful curiosity about London which almost amounted to an inferiority complex. No stage play which did not contain famous names could hope to draw an audience in Oozemouth until it had been judged a success in London, whereupon it returned to Oozemouth and played to packed houses. Oozemouth United F.C.'s biggest home gates were always taken at matches against teams from London. Dagwood never gave greater pleasure to his listeners than when he said (with partial truth) that he preferred living in Oozemouth to London and never gave greater offence than when he stated that London was the undisputed hub of the universe.

The shush kebab and the burgundy were not Dagwood's only properties. The tape-recorded music and recitations at the Tithe Barn skylight played an increasingly important part. The skylight became so important that Dagwood took the trouble to borrow a ladder from Molly and climb up and clean it.

Though the shush kebab and the burgundy were invariable, Dagwood varied the rest of his programme to suit his guest. For Barbara, Dagwood had recited Marvell and afterwards played Brahms's Fourth Symphony. For Vera, Dagwood's 'Black Cat' opponent, once she had conquered her scruples and descended to breaking bread with a hired assassin, Dagwood chose Mozart piano concertos and recited 'In such a night did Thisbe fearfully o'ertrip the dew.' For Olga, who was Mr McGillvray's secretary, Dagwood chose Brubeck, declaimed 'Now more than ever seems it rich to die, to cease upon the midnight with no pain,' and was rewarded by Olga's bursting into floods of tender tears. For Doris, the ball-bearing supervisor, Dagwood took a less sophisticated line: 'The Gold and Silver Waltz' and 'The Owl and the Pussycat.' And for Sheila, who worked in the Royal Ooze-mouth Mercantile & Far Eastern Bank, Stravinsky and 'How sweet the moonlight sleeps upon this bank' – a pun·which passed wholly unnoticed.

Dagwood's only serious crisis was caused by Stella, his partner in the Oozemouth Tennis Club mixed doubles. She was a frilly little thing, though possessing a most mature backhand, who evidently thought that dining alone with Dagwood in his barn was morally equivalent to a life of easy virtue. Protesting that she had never known what it was to be intoxicated, she drank two half-glasses of Dagwood's burgundy and promptly crumpled up on the hearth-rug. Wild visions of newspaper headlines racing through his mind, Dagwood worked frantically to revive her and talked persuasively for a while longer to convince her that he had made no assault upon her chastity (at which she seemed perversely disappointed). However, such moments of unintentional drama were rare; Dagwood steadily improved as a home entertainer.

'I've got it down to a fine art now,' he told Ollie. 'If we haven't had food, drinks and a quick best of three on the sofa inside two hours I reckon I'm losing me grip.'

'How about your landlady?' Ollie asked realistically. 'How does she react to all this?'

'No trouble at all.'

Molly was indeed the ideal landlady. She never complained, no matter how late the lights burned in the barn nor how early in the morning Dagwood's car started in the yard. But she could hardly avoid noticing the stream of Oozemouth feminine society visiting her barn and she could barely conceal her curiosity about Dagwood's social life. At last, she could not resist asking him.

'How do you get them to *come* to the flat, Dagwood?'

'Oh, just ask them,' Dagwood said, airily.

'And they just come?'

'Oh yes. They'd do the cooking too, if I let them.'

'But you don't?'

'Of course not. I do it myself. There's nothing to it, really. I can't think why people make such a fuss about cooking. Mind you, when *I* say *cooking,* I mean making sure the stuff's not actually *raw.* There's more to cooking than that, of course.'

'Oh yes?' Molly said, in a small voice. This was obviously a new Dagwood, Dagwood resurgent. Molly remembered the initial Dagwood: Dagwood and the coal, Dagwood and the milk, Dagwood and the electricity man. Molly appreciated something which Dagwood probably did not suspect himself; that he was, in his own way, very attractive to women.

But Dagwood's path was not always smooth. He had grossly oversimplified the true state of affairs to Ollie. He met stumbling blocks, psychological impedances whose existence he had never suspected until he encountered them. There was Drusilla, the secretary of the tennis club. She was one of the most useful acquaintances Dagwood made in Oozemouth. She was a bouncing, buxom, rosy-cheeked, healthy girl who knew everybody. She was excellent company, ready to make up a party and go anywhere, no matter how short the notice. She was almost always available when Dagwood called her and he often accepted invitations for functions where he needed a partner knowing that, if all else failed, Drusilla would be available. Dagwood came to know her so well that he found it impossible to associate any suggestion of sex with her. The essential feminine mystery had been dispelled by too frequent, hearty contact. Dagwood discovered that he was too friendly with Drusilla even to think of her as a woman.

Conversely, there was Sonia, who was quite the most beautiful girl Dagwood met while he was in Oozemouth. She very rarely came home, being a model in London, and on the only occasion she came to dinner with Dagwood the evening was an utter failure. Acting on his own private theory (that the more glamorous the girl, the more like a tramp she should be treated), Dagwood suggested strip poker-dice whereupon Sonia obediently, and in due course, stripped to the skin and sat in her chair waiting expectantly for Dagwood. Her disrobing was performed so unemotionally that Dagwood was dumbfounded. His purpose was sapped. Paradoxically, now that the only possible outcome of the game had actually come about, Dagwood could do nothing except recommend that Sonia dress again and he would drive her home.

Fiona, once she had discarded her plaster leg, proved to be almost as difficult. The better Dagwood came to know her, the clearer it became that she was more than a match for a thousand Dagwoods. She was so perfectly constructed and assembled and instructed that she might have been the prototype for the perfect Modern Partner. She was the sort of property fulsomely described by estate agents. Dagwood could even imagine the advertisement: 'Desirable Modern Partner. All mod. cons. Runs h. & c. Easy reach. Immed. poss. Freehold (or catch as catch can). Spacious dog house (suit antisocial dwarf). Many other attract. features. $38 \times 19 \times 36$. Offers.' She moved into a clinch as competently as a Cumberland wrestler and she left Dagwood in no doubt that he could go as far along his chosen path as he wished, provided always that journey's end was the altar.

Drusilla, Sonia and Fiona happened to come in quick

succession after each other. Dagwood's confidence **was** undermined.

'I don't know what's wrong with me,' he complained to Ollie. 'Three times I've reached the moment critique and three times I've shied off like a scalded cat.'

'Whatever happened to the food and drink and best of three on the sofa and all that jazz?' Ollie asked cynically.

'It's not as simple as all that.'

'I wondered when you were going to find that out. What seems to be the trouble?'

'It's different each time. There was a girl called Drusilla. I couldn't go on because it would have been like seducing a chum. Then there was a girl called Sonia. That time I was stymied because it would have been like seducing one of those photographs they stick up outside strip clubs. Last time it was Fiona. It would have been like seducing a slot machine . . .'

'A unique experience, I imagine . . .'

' . . . You put a penny in and the right answer comes out each time. I hate to admit it, but it looks as though the women's magazines have got something. It's got to be not only the right time and place but also the right person.'

'It's an idealistic view,' said Ollie, 'but you're beginning to get the right idea.'

18

Weekends were occasionally a problem for Dagwood. Whenever his social engagement diary happened to be blank he faced the prospect of entertaining, and feeding, himself from Friday evening to Monday morning. Dagwood was therefore pleased and relieved when The Bodger rang up on Friday morning with a suggestion.

'What are you doing with yourself this weekend, Dagwood?'

'Nothing much, sir.'

'Then how would you like to come sailing?'

'That sounds a very good idea, sir.'

'My wife and I are taking a boat down the coast tomorrow and we need an extra deckhand to haul on things and make the tea and so on. Are you fit?'

'Of course, sir.'

'Good. Nine o'clock tomorrow morning at the yacht club basin.'

'What's the boat called, sir? How will I know it?'

'It's got one mast and a blue hull and it's called *Fancy That*. It's a pretty soft sort of name but it's not our boat. We're only borrowing it. Tomorrow morning then.'

'Aye aye, sir!'

'And you'd better bring a couple of blankets. We'll be sleeping on board tomorrow night.'

'Right sir.'

Carrying his blankets and an old oilskin over his arm, Dagwood arrived at the yacht club, where *Fancy That* was tied up to the mole, at five minutes to nine. The first person he saw was Caroline. She was wearing sandals, blue jeans, a yellow anarak over a light blue sweater and she had a flower-patterned silk scarf round her throat. Her curly black hair was loose and Dagwood noticed a band of freckles over her nose. Dagwood's heart executed a quick entrechat and returned, quivering, to earth again.

'Hello Caroline, what are you doing here?'

'I'm a deckhand,' Caroline said, simply.

'How extraordinary, so am I! Have you done it before?'

'Oh yes, I've done a lot of sailing already this summer.'

'I didn't know.'

'No, you wouldn't.'

Dagwood felt a twinge of pain. He had been so unreasonably annoyed with Caroline on the night of Hilda's party that he had made up his mind there and then to forget all about her. He had found the decision easier to make than to carry out.

The Bodger's head popped up from the sail locker hatch in the forepeak.

'There you are, Dagwood. Come and give me a hand to get some sails up.'

Fancy That had originally been built in Germany and there was still a reminiscently Prussian look about her stiff flat bow and squarely chopped-off stern. Her owner, a stockbroker whom The Bodger had met in the Conservative Club, was obviously house-proud about her. Her standing rigging was new, her decks were freshly varnished and her running gear in mint condition. She also had a good sail outfit. The Bodger passed up a couple of foresails, a workmanlike green genoa and a stout brown canvas stormsail. Then he reached a brand new sail, candy-striped in red and white nylon.

'What sort of sail is that?' Caroline asked.

'A spinnaker,' said The Bodger. 'If the wind stays as it is we should get a chance to use it as soon as we're outside. The genoa will get us out to the entrance. Hop down and start the engine, Dagwood.'

The engine was just by the galley where Julia was experimenting with the primus stove.

'Hello, Dagwood,' she said. 'Have you come to give me a hand?'

'Not yet, I'm afraid. I've come to start the engine, if I can find it.'

'It's just under my feet here. I'll move.'

The engine and its auxiliaries were much more sophisticated than Dagwood had hoped for. Dagwood was not expected to swing starting handles and wrestle with decompression levers. The engine was a four-cylinder diesel fitted with a battery-operated starter. Dagwood primed the fuel pump and pressed the starter button. The engine turned, fired for a few revolutions, and then stopped. Dagwood tried several ·times. The engine fired and stopped. Dagwood swore in frustration. As a technical officer, his professional reputation depended on this engine.

'Having trouble?' said The Bodger, from above.

'It probably hasn't been started for a bit, sir. It'll go once the injectors are all properly primed.'

Dagwood tried again. This time there was only a click from the starter.

'That sounds bad,' said Julia.

Every time Dagwood tried the starter he heard the same maddening click.

'What's the trouble, Dagwood?'

'Have you got a screwdriver, sir?'

'There's a marling spike up here.'

'That'll do.'

Dagwood slid aside a small plate in the flywheel cover, inserted the marling spike and levered the flywheel round a little way. When he tried the starter once more the engine went away with a roar, spurting out a plume of blue smoke and, a little later, a trickle of circulating water.

'The flywheel had stopped in a position where the starter couldn't engage,' Dagwood explained. 'I had to shift the flywheel round a few teeth.'

'That's very clever of you, Dagwood,' Caroline said, admiringly.

Dagwood shrugged casually. 'I'm not just a pretty face, you know.'

'Just as well we had a technical officer on board,' said The Bodger. 'Now that we're mobile, let's go.'

With The Bodger sitting like Ulysses at the tiller, Dagwood keeping a careful eye on the engine and Julia and Caroline both trying to look like hardened sea-dogs, *Fancy That* threaded through the yachts in the basin and out into the river where they stopped the engine, ran up the mainsail and hoisted the genoa. It was a soldier's wind and they went down river on a full reach. As they left the city behind a dull opaque filter seemed to lift off the river and the sky. The sun came out and the water colour changed from brown to blue. The air was keen and clear, smelling of the sea. At the fairway buoy The Bodger bore away to bring the wind almost astern.

'Now's the time for that spinnaker,' he said. 'Julia darling, you steer while Dagwood and I hoist it.'

Julia was appalled. 'But where shall I steer?'

'Anywhere, so long as you keep the wind just over your left shoulder.'

The Bodger and Dagwood bent on the spinnaker, slung the boom and led the sheets. Dagwood and Caroline hoisted when The Bodger gave the word. The giant sail flapped, half-filled, flapped again, and bellied out in a glorious balloon in front of the boat.

'Oooh *doesn't* that look lovely!' cried Caroline.

The Bodger looked critically along the curve of the spinnaker. 'It's filling nicely,' he admitted.

Dagwood had been impressed by The Bodger's handling of the sail and the gear. Although it must have been the first time he had ever sailed in the boat he had arranged the sheets and organised the operation as smoothly as though he had designed the boat. It was plain that The Bodger knew more about sailing than he ever admitted.

The Bodger took over the tiller again. The girls went below to change into bathing costumes, Julia in deep midnight blue and Caroline in a rich plum red.

'Wowee!' The Bodger whistled. 'I haven't seen that one before!'

'I got it at the sales last January,' Julia said. 'It's the best time to buy a bathing costume.'

'Well I'm damned.' Once again The Bodger could only wonder at the feminine instinct for a bargain, which could buy a bathing costume in January.

It was the first time that Dagwood had had an opportunity properly to admire Caroline's figure and he now saw that his original speculations about her at *Seahorse's* refit conference had been absolutely correct.

'Did you get yours at the sales, Caroline?' he asked.

'No, this is two years old, I'm afraid.'

'I must say it still looks very nice.'

'Thank you, Dagwood.'

The Bodger, overhearing this piece of dialogue, smiled cunningly to himself.

Julia and Caroline together mastered the galley equipment sufficiently to produce a lunch of stew, peas, potatoes, and tinned peaches and cream. Afterwards they all stretched themselves out to sunbathe, taking it in turns to steer. The brisk wind lasted until teatime when, with a miraculous concord, wind and sea fell quiet all at once. The Bodger struck down the spinnaker before it collapsed and hoisted the large genoa. For a time The Bodger tacked to and fro, pursuing the darker wind smudges on the sea but the wind had died almost completely. The sea calmed and they drifted for a while under a sun which blazed down from a sky cleared of cloud. Towards evening The Bodger was rewarded by a light wind which sprang up off the land, carrying with it a fragrant smell of corn, warm earth, heather and honeysuckle.

'That's it,' said The Bodger. 'I can smell it. Beer!'

Just before supper they arrived at the entrance to a small harbour about fifteen miles along the coast from Oozemouth. Dagwood started the engine while The Bodger took out a chart.

'It's a pretty narrow opening this one,' he said. 'It's got a dog-leg in the middle. There should be two leading marks to start with and a church spire once we get round the corner.'

'Are those them?' Julia said, pointing at two red posts set in the nearer hillside.

'That's them. You must have good eyesight, Julia. I can only just see them and I know what to look for.'

'I'm not just a pretty face, you know,' said Julia.

'Ah, I asked for that,' said The Bodger, grinning.

The shelter of the hills blanketed the wind and the harbour was so still that they could hear the sound of the engine echoing clearly off the hill-sides and the sucking of their wake against the rocks on the shore. The setting sun flooded the harbour in a luminous golden glow. The water was a shining mass of gold except where the wake split it into coins and pools of light.

'What a heavenly place,' said Julia.

'We're not the only ones who think so,' said The Bodger.

The Bodger nodded ahead at the yacht anchorage which was an unbroken armada of hulls with a bristling crop of masts.

The Bodger anchored where he could, finding the bare amount of swinging room next to an elegant green yawl whose only crew was a black and grey clumber spaniel barking from the top of the cabin.

'Julia and I are inviting ourselves to dinner with some people we know up on the hill there,' The Bodger said. 'Do you two think you can entertain yourselves for the evening?'

Dagwood and Caroline looked at each other.

'I think so,' said Dagwood.

Dagwood ferried The Bodger and Julia ashore in the dinghy and came back for Caroline.

'Let's see what this place has to offer,' he said.

The village did not have much to offer. It consisted of a church, a few dozen houses set on the hill, two shops and the 'Skylark.'

The landlord of the 'Skylark' had evidently exerted himself to attract the custom of yachtsmen. The saloon bar was furnished like a very superior bosun's store; it looked like a Fortnum & Mason's among ship-chandlers. The walls were decorated with burgees, knots mounted on varnished boards, and paintings of sailing ships. The room was lit by ships' steaming lanterns converted from oil to electricity. A port and starboard bow light burned at each end of the bar and above it hung a notice: 'Do not leave your seats while the bar is in motion.' In one corner a green parrot (addressed by the landlord as 'Admiral') sat in a cage and morosely cracked nuts. An anemometer on the wall by the door registered a wind speed of half a knot, direction variable. Near it hung a polished spoked steering wheel, a ship's telegraph counter, and a binnacle. The bar was filled with young men in grubby polo-necked sweaters, canvas trousers, gym-shoes and two days' growth of beard, all talking loudly about reefing, gybing, luffing and other nautical matters to subdued-looking girls in blue anaraks and untidy hair styles sitting on upturned barrels.

Dagwood was well aware that he was seeing only the summertime aspect of these young men. In winter, they would be inhabiting other bars and talking just as loudly and knowledgeably about slaloms, snowploughs and telemarks. Nevertheless the nautical jargon, hammered into his ears at such close range, slowly began to make Dagwood feel uncomfortable. Although he was probably the only person present who could possible be described as a professional seaman, these people were beginning to make him feel like a landlubber.

Caroline looked at the 'Skylark's' clientele and then at Dagwood's face.

'Do be tactful,' she whispered.

'Tactful!' cried Dagwood. 'I'm always tactful.'

'Oh no you're not. You're so prickly. Whenever anyone says anything you don't agree with you . . .'

'Well?'

' . . . Well, you sort of *whip* round on them and run them through the heart.'

'Never fear, I'm in no mood for an argument tonight. Let's go outside.'

They found a quiet place on the harbour wall.

'Those people in there quite frighten me, Caroline. I can't understand what they're talking about half the time. Once when I was a cadet I sailed about two hundred miles from Barbados to Trinidad in an open boat and I've done quite a lot of sailing on and off, but I hadn't any idea it was so complicated!'

'They were just showing off. I was afraid you were going to pick an argument with one of them.'

'*Me?*'

'Yes *you!*'

'By the way, what's happened to Nigel these days? I don't see him around the bazaars any more.'

'He's been posted to Germany with his regiment.'

'Ah,' said Dagwood, smugly. So Nigel had been posted abroad. It was reassuring to hear of the Army suffering a fate normally reserved for the Navy.

'He's not really my boy-friend, you know. It's just that we've known each other a long time. Daddy doesn't really like him.'

'Doesn't he?'

Caroline glanced at Dagwood accusingly. 'You mustn't get the wrong idea about my father, Dagwood. He's really very shy. He always puts on a big act when he goes into the yard. He always looks in the mirror before he goes out in the mornings. My mother says he's practising his "Shipyard Face." He hates it.'

'Then why does he do it?'

'He's the only one left. It was my Uncle Bertie who used to run it. He loved it. But he died just after the war so Daddy had to leave the Army and take over.'

'Is is true your father hates the Navy?'

Caroline considered the question. 'He doesn't like them much,' she admitted. 'He doesn't like *any* ships much. He thinks the Navy has too much glamour and doesn't do enough hard work.'

'He's got a point there! Does he know you're spending the weekend on a yacht?'

'Not exactly,' said Caroline, guiltily. 'I sort of glossed over it when he asked me what I was doing.'

'Did you know I was coming on this trip?'

'Of course.'

Dagwood was stunned into silence by the implications of that answer.

At closing time the saloon bar admirals emerged, still conversing of shoals, foul water and wreck buoys. Caroline put a restraining hand on Dagwood's arm, but she need not have worried; Dagwood was thinking of other matters. 'What would you say to going back on board and having something to eat?'

They rowed out to *Fancy That* in an intimate silence. In the cabin Caroline said: 'I'm sorry I changed my mind the other night.'

'I'm sorry I was so annoyed about it.'

'I just felt . . . That I wasn't ready somehow. I didn't want to plunge in too far all at once. I lost my nerve, I suppose.'

Dagwood nodded. 'I should have realised it. In fact I meant to ring you up. Somehow I just didn't. I wish I had, now.'

Caroline looked carefully at the cabin deck. 'I wish you had, too.'

Dagwood pulled her towards him. He was surprised at the warmth of her response. It was as though she had waited for him to make up his mind ever since they first met. Their kiss now seemed so inevitable that Dagwood wondered what they had been doing to avert it all this time.

'Caroline . . .'

'Yes!'

'*Dagwood!*' A voice roared from the shore.

'Crikey, what's that?'

'*Dagwood!* Ahoy there, Dagwood! Dagwood!'

'Oh God, that's The Bodger. He wants the dinghy. Damn and *blast* him!'

It was ironical that The Bodger himself should frustrate the very consummation he so devoutly wished. It was possible that he guessed at the emotional storm which had just taken place, but he only said : 'Let's hope we get a proper wind tomorrow. That wasn't real sailing today.'

In the event, The Bodger's wish was completely fulfilled, his cup pressed down and running over. The next morning grey clouds were scudding overhead, a swell surged up the estuary from the open sea and the array of masts bobbed wildly on either side. The Bodger immediately took in a large reef in the mainsail and exchanged the genoa for a much smaller foresail.

These precautions were well taken. As soon as *Fancy That* had crept out from the shelter of the headland, a stiff northerly wind laid her on her side and poured a torrent of water over the cockpit. Julia and Caroline hurriedly scrambled below.

After half an hour, while the yacht drew further and further from the coastline, it became obvious that even the smaller foresail was going to be too much for the boat and Dagwood spent a wet ten minutes in the pulpit above the bows changing the foresail for the storm sail.

Meanwhile, the wind had increased and Dagwood looked longingly back at the harbour they had just left. If it had been his decision they would have turned back, but The Bodger sat with his feet braced against the side of the cockpit, both

194

hands gripping the bucking tiller, his yellow sou'wester hat tilted on the back of his head, singing exultant songs at the top of his voice, apparently welcoming the thought of a hard fifteen-mile beat back to Oozemouth dead in the eye of a strengthening wind. The sea roared and tumbled along the lee gunwale, smashed against the weather side and foamed over into the cockpit. The boat heeled until Dagwood, crouching on his seat, could look straight into the water without raising his eyes. Whenever Dagwood looked up he could see nothing but a dark livid sky, lightened by a white band on the horizon, and rows of advancing waves, their metal-grey flanks streaked with wind spume, the sure sign of a hard blow. Dagwood cowered on the deck boards, fully occupied in pumping out the cockpit and in handling the sheets when The Bodger went about. Julia did not reappear but about lunch time Caroline pushed open the cabin door, and balancing herself with her elbows, held out two cups of cocoa. Dagwood tipped his hat to her; he could only imagine what that cocoa had cost Caroline, down in the galley.

Just as they were about to take the cocoa a larger wave creamed along the deck, over the cabin and into the cockpit. Caroline's cocoa was heavily diluted with sea water.

'Never mind!' thundered The Bodger above the wind. 'It gives it that certain *je ne sais quoi!*' He downed his cocoa in two colossal swallows.

Dagwood had also observed Caroline's look of disappointment when the wave engulfed her cocoa and, steeling himself, drank his. It tasted like no other beverage Dagwood had ever sampled but, miraculously, he felt much better for it.

'Ready about!' sang The Bodger.

It was the last long tack before the fairway buoy. Dagwood sprang to the sheets. *Fancy That* came through the wind and, when Dagwood should have let go one sheet and hauled in on the other, the weather sheet jammed in the winch.

'Get that sheet in!' bellowed The Bodger.

With the storm sail acting as an awkward wind cup, *Fancy*

That slowly lost steerage way and laboriously paid off down wind.

'Get that bloody sheet in!'

'It's jammed sir!'

Wind and sea were pounding *Fancy That* flat on her side. The cockpit deck was almost vertical. Water was flooding into the cockpit so that Dagwood was standing thigh-deep as he struggled with the jammed sheet.

'For God's sake get that sheet away, Dagwood, we *must* get some way on!'

Dagwood braced himself against the side of the cockpit and wrenched with all his strength. The sheet gave way. Dagwood flew backwards and would have vanished overboard had Caroline not grasped one of his ankles and hung on to it.

For a moment there was a small tableau of The Bodger coaxing the boat under way again, Dagwood hanging head and shoulders in the sea. Caroline holding his leg in both hands, and Julia's wan face in the cabin door, while up forward the loosened stormsail methodically set to work to flap itself to shreds.

Dagwood emerged, dripping, from the sea. 'Many thanks,' he said breathlessly, to Caroline. 'Just as well you were there.'

'I'm not just a pretty face, you know.'

'Yes you are. Very pretty.'

'Dagwood,' said The Bodger, remorselessly, 'do you mind taking up on that sheet?'

Dagwood sheeted in the thundering storm sail and the boat began to move properly through the water again.

'How much longer is this going on?' complained Julia.

'Not much longer, darling. Just till we reach the buoy.'

When they reached the fairway buoy, The Bodger turned to bring the wind on the beam and ordered Dagwood to change the stormsail for a bigger foresail. At the same time he let out the main sheets until the mainsail bellied in a full rich curve. It was the fastest point of sailing and it gave *Fancy*

That a chance to show her paces. Stern down, bucking and throbbing under power, the boat fled up the river. She was still under full sail when she passed through the yacht club basin entrance travelling, Dagwood estimated, at over eight knots. Dry-mouthed Dagwood watched the mole rushing towards them. A man in a blue sweater carrying a bucket along the jetty stopped to watch them and remained paralysed, like a man in the path of an avalanche, as they swept down on him.

Just as Dagwood was about to advise Caroline to lie flat on the deck so as not to be catapulted off when they hit, The Bodger heaved on the tiller and ducked to let the boom pass over.

'Down with that foresail!'

Dagwood needed no second order. The foresail rattled down. The boat headed into the wind, hung for a moment and then gently paid off, grazing along the jetty with about the force required to crack an egg-shell.

Dagwood swallowed.

'Sorry about that,' said The Bodger apologetically. 'I was showing off. I've been showing off all day. There was a bloke at dinner last night who pounded my ear all night long about *yachting,* as he called it. That annoyed me.'

'It all turned out all right in the end, sir,' said Dagwood loyally.

The Bodger grinned malevolently. 'I'm not just a pretty face, you know,' he said.

19

After the weekend in *Fancy That* Dagwood began to make up for lost time. It was a period of enchantment, a sort of temporary insanity where all his perceptions were lifted on to another plane. Never before had such a sun shone on the world. Never before had the most casual smile held such meaning. Never before had the wind so wonderfully moved the trees so that Dagwood walked lightly with his head cocked to catch the echoes of the flutes and horns of fairy land, heard on a summer evening far away. At the farm, Molly wondered at the abrupt halt in Dagwood's promiscuous entertaining and his concentration on one girl. In the office, Ollie complained that Dagwood could not be trusted even to open the morning's mail without falling into a day-dream. In 'The Smokers', The Bodger and Mr Tybalt gleefully rubbed their hands together and summoned Daphne for more pints of best bitter.

'It's working, Frank,' gloated The Bodger. 'It's working!'

'It seems so. I often wonder where he takes her. We never see him during the afternoons.'

'I don't care where he takes her, provided he conducts himself in a seamanlike manner.'

'That remark is what I would call a *double entendre,* Bodger.'

The Bodger and Mr Tybalt would both have been surprised if they could have seen Dagwood rowing Caroline in a small boat along the Oozemouth Union Canal. For no reason at all, the Union Canal had become one of Dagwood and Caroline's favourite spots. In its heyday the Union had been part of a network of canals connecting Oozemouth by water to Manchester, Birmingham and London but it had long since ceased to carry traffic and was now used only by people like Dagwood who had the leisure to hire a boat and row for a few hours up the canal as far as the first disused lock. There, by the derelict lock-keeper's cottage, was an inn called the 'Barleystorm.' It was a dark and rather smelly little pub but Dagwood remembered it with affection. There seemed no logical reason for a public house at that spot. The clientele for whom it had been built had gone and the only approach to it on land was by a rough lane which stopped at the front door. There were no houses, not even a farm, within three miles. The landlord seemed to be aware of his isolation and his superfluity and made no attempt to encourage business. He served Dagwood grudgingly, barely waiting to take Dagwood's money before returning to the television set in his parlour. The only programmes Dagwood ever overheard from the parlour were westerns and in time the crash of gunfire, the whine of ricocheting bullets and the clatter of galloping hooves became for Dagwood as much part of the background of the 'Barleystorm' as the marshes and the poplar trees which surrounded it.

There was a wooden seat placed by the tow-path, facing the canal, and beyond it were the marshes, a line of poplar trees, and on the far side, meadows bordered by a tall beechwood. Dagwood and Caroline often sat there on fine evenings, listening to the gabble of ducks in the canal, the song of a skylark high overhead and somewhere the lonely cry of the marsh birds while behind them the interminable western reached a routine climax.

'. . . Looks like he's telling the truth, Marshal . . .'

'Ya gotta believe me, Marshal, ya gotta . . .'

Dagwood picked up a stone and tossed it among the ducks, who were temporarily ruffled, looked at Dagwood reproachfully, and then ignored him.

'Say something, Dagwood.'

'What shall I say? You're so easy to talk to? Do you come here often? All men are little boys at heart? London can be a very lonely place? You look lovely when you're angry? I don't want to talk clichés with you. I keep those for people like Fiona. I wonder if there's such a thing as duck etiquette?'

'What do you mean?'

'I was just looking at those ducks. Some of them seem to be taking precedence over each other. I expect the drakes have an order of precedence and the ducks take the same place as their drakes. Quite right and proper too. What a wonderful life, to be a duck. No worries, no cares, all you have to do is paddle along and look for grub. Sometimes you won't even have to do that. If you hang around long enough people will throw it to you.'

Dagwood drained his tankard and stood up. 'I'll just go and see if old Rawhide in there will serve us the other half.'

When he came back, Dagwood said: 'I interrupted at a critical time. I reckon the only way to get service in that place is to go in and fire a six-shooter through the roof. It's the only frequency that man operates on.'

'Did you go into the office this morning, Dagwood?'

'I looked in to see the mail and then phoned you. It's a funny thing, I look forward to telephoning you. I get all keyed up inside, I don't mind telling you.'

'Gracious, should I feel flattered?'

'I don't know. Are you?'

'No.'

'Good.'

'Dagwood, you're the *meanest* man I know. Just as I think you're going to say something nice you go and pour cold water all over it.'

'Oh, she doth teach the torches to burn bright. It seems she hangs upon the cheek of night like a rich jewel in an Ethiop's ear. How's that?'

On which note, they sat in companionable silence for a

time. From the parlour window a hoarse voice whispered 'You work around to that rock, Jess. I'll cover you from here.'

'Why did you join the Navy, Dagwood?'

'Blessed if I know. They asked me that when I joined and it seemed a reasonable question at the time but damned if I could think of a sensible answer. Why do you ask?'

'You're just not the sort of person I would have imagined being in the Navy, that's all.'

'I'm very sorry my dear, but I've shaved off my beard and I've left the binoculars and "Don't give up the ship" expression at home.'

'That's what I mean. You seem to treat the whole thing as the biggest joke you ever heard.'

'So it is. As someone was telling me the other night, it's nothing more than the biggest confidence trick ever played on the nation. That's the only way to treat it. If you take yourself seriously you have one of two futures. Either you become an admiral or you wind up in a nut-house. And as there are many more beds in the nut-house than there are vacancies for admirals you can see which is the more likely. The chances are they'll come for you in a plain van long before they make you a Sir. That happened to a friend of mine.'

'They *didn't* make him an admiral!'

'No, they came for him in a plain van. He was as crazy as a warthog. He was quite convinced he was a 'Confidential' stamp. Whenever he saw papers lying about he would leap up and do a sort of highland schottische all over them.'

'He *didn't!*'

'That wasn't the end of it. After a time he upgraded himself to 'Top Secret,' locked himself safely up in a steel cupboard, and it took a whole team of men with hacksaws and burning gear half a day to get him out. After that there was nothing for it but to wheel him away. You get like that after you've been in the Navy for a little while.'

'How long have you been in the Navy, Dagwood?'

'About seven or eight years. Nearly eight years, actually. What were you doing eight years ago, Caroline?'

'I was still at school. A girls' boarding school called Forest House.'

'Where was that?'

'Gloucestershire.'

'Forest House,' said Dagwood, pensively. 'Was a Miss O'Malley there when you were there?'

'Miss O'Malley! Of course! She used to teach us scripture and free movement. How on earth do you know her?'

'I don't actually know her. I know of her. She's an old crony of my mother's. My mother goes and has tea with her when she comes to London.'

'She used to make us sit with our palms flat down on our desks and recite. She used to say 'In unison, ladies, in unison' and we would all chant 'Genesis, Exodus, Leviticus, *Numbers,* Deuteronomy, Joshua, Judges, *Ruth,*' and so on through the Bible. I've forgotten all the books of the Bible but I still remember her.'

'Where were you during the war, Caroline?'

'We were all over the place. Daddy was almost always away. We went to Scotland and then down to Cornwall and then to Ipswich and everywhere. I *loathed* the war.'

'I loved it. I thought the whole thing the greatest fun in the world.'

'You would. I was terrified during the air-raids. I remember one early in the war, during the blitz. I remember it vividly. Mummy and I were in London, I can't remember why. It was a lovely day and we were standing in front of D. H. Evans and suddenly the sirens went and a man said to me "That is not yours. The next one will be yours." I don't know what he meant but I felt cold all over.'

'Do you know, that's a very funny thing. *I* remember going up to D. H. Evans one day. There was a rumour that I might be evacuated to America and my mother and I went up to London to buy me some underpants. I remember my mother saying they didn't have proper underpants in America. It was a lovely day, too. I *wonder* if it could have been the same day? How about that?'

'Well, did you notice a little girl with blue shoes and a dress with cornflowers on it and a small hat?'

'Did *you* notice a small boy in a red school blazer and a red school cap and grey shorts on? And I had a black eye! Do you remember that?'

'I'm afraid I don't remember it, Dagwood.'

'Never mind. It would have been too much of a coincidence. But I bet it was the same day!'

'Oh, I meant to tell you, I met a friend of yours at a party in London a few weeks ago.'

'What was his name?'

'Gavin something or other. He said he knew you.'

'I should think he does know me! That must have been Gavin Doyle. He's just served with me for two years. What did you think of him?'

'He wasn't a bit like you. He was smooth.'

'Thank you very much.'

'Oh, I didn't mean anything disrespectful. He was *too* smooth. He got me in a corner . . .'

'*Did* he?'

' . . . And told me all about women.'

'And did he know all about women?'

'He knew a bit.'

'He should. He's had enough experience.'

'I rather gathered that. He looked me up and down and to'd me I'd make an excellent naval wife. I didn't know how to . . . Why are you laughing?'

'I . . . I was just thinking of Gavin talking about naval wives! Did you know he's the *Arch*-bachelor? He's the President of the Bachelors' and Grass Widowers' Mutual Protection Society!'

'Strikes me he's the sort of man who takes lots of pretty girls out and then marries some very nice, plain girl with a face like a taxi. I don't expect he's ever been in love in his life.'

'But you don't have to *love* a woman to marry her! It's far more important to like her than love her.'

'Why Dagwood, what a very profound thing to say! It's either very profound or very cynical, I don't know which.'

'It's neither, but it's true all the same.'

'Well, I'm not sure . . .'

'Of course it is! It's only very recently that any idea of love has entered into marriage at all.'

'*Dagwood!* This is not like *you* at all. Who've you been talking to about this?'

'Nobody.'

'Bet you have. You'd never have thought of that on your own.'

'All right then. But you can't blame me for not knowing much about it, because the Navy doesn't agree with its officers getting married. They'd stop it if they could. There used to be a saying about marriage. Lieutenants should not marry, Lieutenant-Commanders may, Commanders should, and Captains must. You see the idea? You can only marry when you've reached a stage where you need a hostess.'

'What a dreadfully cynical outlook!'

Dagwood's mind went off at a tangent. 'You know, Caroline, it seems funny to think of you eating three square meals a day . . .'

20

On the first day of July the strike ended and Mr McGillvray resigned his position with Harvey McNichol & Drummond's. The first event Ollie and Dagwood received with a mixture of surprise and relief; the second they found quite incredible.

'Your cousin must have got the names mixed up, Chief Stoker,' said Ollie. 'McGillvray was one of Sir Rollo's blue-eyed boys.'

'It's true enough, sir. There was a bit about it in the local rag last night.'

'Did it give any reason?' Dagwood asked.

'Ill-health, sir.'

'Ill-health!' Ollie snorted. 'He was in "The Smokers" with me last Friday lunchtime and there was nothing wrong with him then. Nothing wrong with his drinking arm, anyway.'

'Perhaps he went sick when he heard the news, sir?'

'I'll bet,' said Dagwood. 'He's got the sack, that's what it is. How about that, Ollie. A chap who'd be equivalent to a four-ring captain in our racket gets his cards on a Friday night just like any other hired help. I wonder what *really* happened?'

Dagwood did not waste any time casting around for opinions on the end of the strike or McGillvray's dismissal but went straight to get the inside story.

'As it happens I can answer both your questions,' said Mr Tybalt. 'The strike was ended by Lady Drummond herself.'

'*What!*'

'Yes, she arrived at the yard after packing-up time on Friday. Drove up in her Rolls, pavilioned in splendour and girded with praise, and demanded to see the Board of Directors and all the Union leaders. There was a great coming and going while they hauled various people out of pubs and telephoned their homes and stopped all their weekends. The old girl sat in the boardroom for over an hour, drumming her fingers on the table and no doubt rehearsing a few choice remarks, while they got the lads together. Unfortunately I wasn't there myself, I would have given a month's pay to have been a fly on the wall, but Happy Day told me the meeting only lasted about four minutes by the clock and old Lady Drummond did all the talking after which she swept out and away. Sir Rollo and the union boys appeared a bit later, all looking a bit green, and announced that the strike was over and the men would go back to work, pending negotiations.'

'It must have been like a visit from Mount Olympus,' said Dagwood. 'When was the last time the old girl visited the firm?'

'1926, I think, during the General Strike.'

'So the strike's finally over.'

'Yes. The original dispute's not settled of course, but if you ask me there's another reason why they wanted to come back. They've got their eyes on their summer holidays. They've suddenly woken up to the fact that unless they pull their fingers out and turn to pretty dead sharpish they won't have enough money to take their wives and kiddies to the seaside. I expect some of them will be a bit skint by now in any case.'

'But if the whole strike was on a matter of principle then holidays shouldn't matter.'

'Dagwood,' said Mr Tybalt wearily, 'I've warned you about this naïvety before.'

'But *surely* sir, if the whole thing's as irresponsible as that, isn't there anything the firm can do? This strike must have cost them thousands! There must be *somebody* they can get for it, somebody they can serve a writ on? I should have thought they could have got them on a charge of conspiracy or something.'

'No they can't.'

'Why not? I would have said they had a cast-iron case . . .'

'You might, but they haven't. There's a little thing called Section Four of the Trades Disputes Act, 1906. The whole thing is a lot of legal Japanese to me but briefly it all boils down to the fact that you can't nail a man for anything he does in the name of or on behalf of a trade union. It's very complicated but that's what it comes down to. You just *can't* nail these buggers. Or at least it's not easy. And they know it.'

'So that's that.'

'So that's that. As for poor old McGillvray, the reason he was sacked . . .'

'So he *was* sacked?'

'Oh yes, he got the sack all right and the reason he did dates back to about six thousand years B.C. The Greeks and Romans used to do it. The ancient Britons used to do it. The Aztecs did it. All primitive peoples, including politicians and the ship-building industry, still do it.'

'Do what, sir?'

'Choose a scapegoat. Blame everything on one man, pour shit and derision on his head and kick him out. Then everyone else miraculously feels better for it and they all go on their way singing a gipsy song. You're living in the dark ages here, Dagwood. Once you get past that policeman at the gate you're back in the Stone Age.'

'Poor old McGillvray.'

'Oh, there's nothing personal about it! The lot just fell on him. Last time it was the Foreman of Glass-cutters, a more inoffensive man you could never hope to meet! I think Sir Rollo picks the names out of a hat. One day I expect he'll pick me or old Swales. Well, now the strike's over, we can all get back to work, can't we? You'll have to cut down on the gay life a bit, won't you?'

'Gay life, sir?' Dagwood's face clouded. Talking of the 'gay life' had reminded him of a private problem which had been troubling his mind for some days and which would soon need a solution.

'Don't try and kid me,' said Mr Tybalt. 'I see you flashing here, flashing there. Now push off a moment and let me have another bash at your programme.'

Dagwood went back to his own office to think his problem over.

Mr Tybalt was allowed no time to work upon *Seahorse's* programme. His next visitor was The Bodger, accompanied by a short, ginger-haired man who bounced into the room as though on rubber heels.

'Morning, Frank. How do we find you this morning?'

'Oh you know how it is, Bodger. Little drops of water, little bits of sand, make a mighty ocean and send you round the bend.'

'Frank, I've brought someone to see you. An old friend of mine, Commander Jerry Leanover, from the Admiralty. This is Frank Tybalt, Jerry, the Chief Constructor here.'

Mr Tybalt and Commander Leanover shook hands.

'Didn't I see a letter about you the other day?' said Mr Tybalt. 'A fact-finding tour, or something?'

Commander Leanover guffawed. 'I suppose you could call it that!' He crossed to Mr Tybalt's window and looked out. 'God, what a prospect! I thought the Admiralty was bad enough but that's positively beautiful compared with this!'

'It's not very breath-taking,' Mr Tybalt conceded. 'What sort of facts are you looking for, Jerry?'

Commander Leanover turned from the window. 'I'm not sure myself, old boy,' he said. 'It's all a bit vague. Somebody in the Controller's Department rang me up a month or so ago, gave me a list of firms and told me to find out which, if any of them, are capable of building whole or parts of nuclear submarines.'

'I *see*,' said Mr Tybalt.

'It was stupid asking *me*, in any case. I don't know anything about nuclear submarines. I wouldn't know one if it got up and bit me in the backside. I don't even know anything about *ordinary* submarines! I was only ever in one once, when I was a midshipman. It was cold and it was wet and it was draughty and it hurt my ears. Never again, I told myself. But the call went out 'Leanover to look at submarines,' so Leanover goes.'

'But I suppose you have a team of advisers?'

'*Advisers?*' Commander Leanover's china-blue eyes popped. He looked quite shocked by the suggestion. 'The more advisers you have the less facts you get. I don't need advisers. I go by the managing director's secretary and the lunch they give me.'

Mr Tybalt and The Bodger exchanged glances.

' . . . If the gel's got good legs and the lunch is good then there can't be much wrong with that firm, eh? I was at Maxwells last week, that firm across the way there. D'you know them?'

'Yes, we know them,' said Mr Tybalt.

'First class firm! Sir Charles gave me the lunch of a lifetime and that secretary of his must have stepped straight out of a Hollywood line-up! What's this fellow over here like? Sir Rollo Whatshisname?'

'He's a very good chap,' said The Bodger, mendaciously.

'That's not what I heard across the river, Bodger. Sir Charles put me in the picture. He said, "You'll like old Rollo. You always know where you stand with him. Beneath that cold exterior there beats a heart of stone." '

The Bodger concealed a grin. 'You should be all right, Jerry, with your well-known charm of manner.'

Commander Leanover ducked his head modestly. 'But you've got to watch some of these people. They'll pull a fast one over you as soon as look at you. Did I tell you about that ball-bearing factory I visited? Don't ask me why I went there, it was on me list. Fascinating place. You been there?'

'Yes,' said Mr Tybalt and The Bodger together.

'That room full of girls! Where they test the balls or something! Incredible! They asked me if I'd like a go at it and you know what? The cheeky monkeys, they tried to palm me off with a batch of duff balls!'

Mr Tybalt caught the shrewd twinkle in Jerry Leanover's eye and found himself regarding him with a growing respect; it occurred to Mr Tybalt that underneath the flippant manner and the casual assertions of ignorance there was more to Commander Leanover than met the eye.

'I don't think anyone will try and pull a fast one over you here, Jerry,' he said.

'I hear strange things about this firm. Don't they strike over nothing at all?'

'Don't worry about that,' said The Bodger. 'It won't happen again. We've found the right approach now.'

'Still,' Commander Leanover said, doubtfully, 'it's one of the things we have to consider . . .'

'Just a minute,' Mr Tybalt broke in. 'What was that you said about the strike, Bodger?'

'Nothing, I merely said we'd found the right approach.'

Mr Tybalt leaned back in his chair with a flabbergasted expression on his face. The Bodger could see realisation rising in him like a perceptible fluid level.

'I might have guessed it,' said Mr Tybalt. 'I should have recognised that fine Greek hand behind it all. How did you do it, Bodger?'

The Bodger grinned. 'Do you remember me telling you about my Civil Defence Committee? Did you know that old Lady Drummond was the patroness of Civil Defence in Oozemouth?'

Mr Tybalt shook his head. 'No, I didn't.'

'Neither did I until I saw her name at the top of the official writing paper. I wrote to her and asked if she'd like to turn up at one of the committee meetings one day. I told you you should pay more attention to these committee meetings, Frank.'

'And did she come?'

'Of course she did. The old girl was flattered to death.

I don't think she even knew she was the patroness or if she did she'd forgotten it. While she was there, I just happened to mention that the men were on strike, which she knew, and why they were on strike, which she didn't know, and she stormed off at once to see about it. I gather that everybody at the yard was searching for an excuse to come back without losing face and the old lady provided it. It's what I always say, if you want something you must not only ask for it you must pick your time to ask for it.'

Commander Leanover was intrigued. 'Is this sort of thing normal, Bodger?' he asked. 'All these *machinations* behind the scenes?'

'Not always, Jerry. Now, I'm going to leave you with Frank for a minute. When he's finished behaving like a goldfish out of water he'll give you a few more facts about this firm. I'm just going to pop down and see young Dagwood.'

The Bodger found Dagwood staring glumly at the office bulkhead, grappling with his private problem.

'Cheer up, Dagwood! You look as though you're just about to go over the top!'

'That's a very good description, sir. That's exactly how I do feel.'

'What's the trouble?'

Dagwood hesitated; he appeared to be groping for words. 'Well, sir . . . Well . . . It's about Caroline and me . . .'

'Sir Rollo's daughter, you mean?'

'Yes, sir.'

'What about her?'

'I don't suppose you've noticed that I've been taking her out quite a bit, sir?'

'I hadn't noticed particularly, no,' lied The Bodger, 'but so what? What's so strange about it? From the little I've seen of her she struck me as being a very nice girl . . .'

'Oh she is, sir,' said Dagwood, warmly. 'The fact is . . . We want to get married, sir !'

'Splendid, Dagwood! Congratulations!'

Dagwood went beetroot red. 'Thank you very much, sir,' he said, awkwardly. 'But it's not quite as simple as that. You know what Sir Rollo's like about the Navy. He's got a thing about naval officers. The idea of having a naval son-in-law is going to take a bit of selling and I'm just sitting here wondering what's the best way of going about it.'

'There are other ways,' The Bodger suggested, tentatively. Inwardly, he was administering to himself a severe reprimand; this was a snag he should have foreseen. 'Other ways like . . . Special licence? . . . Gretna Green?'

Dagwood shook his head emphatically. 'That's right out, sir. Caroline says she wants a white wedding and be given away by her old man with all her chums and relatives there and all the trimmings. It's that or nothing as far as she's concerned.'

'I don't blame her,' said The Bodger. 'Women set a lot of store by these things. Now look, Dagwood, what I always say is, you've not only got to ask for what you want, you've also got to choose the right time to ask for it. What I suggest we do is *this . . .*'

21

'Ollie, have you seen the paper this morning!'

Ollie was accustomed to being woken from a deep sleep by a wife who was bubbling over with news; normally it meant that some girl Ollie could barely remember had just had a third baby.

'How could I have seen it when you've got it?' he said grumpily. 'Has somebody been blowing up Harvey McNichol and Drummond's without telling me?' Ollie sat up in bed and glared at the front page. 'Hell's teeth! I see what you mean! They've made it! *Three* nuclears! That'll be one in the eye for Maxwells! I wonder . . .'

'Not the front page, stupid,' Alice retorted, taking the paper from him and folding it. 'The engagement page. There!'

'Blow me down! So Dagwood's taken the great plunge after all! He's a quiet bastard, you know. He never mentioned a word . . .'

'He didn't need to. It's been written all over his face for weeks.'

'I would have said that Dagwood was the least likely man I know to get married.'

'Darling Ollie, how can you be so *stupid!* He's been *dying* to get married!'

'All right dear, if you say so.'

In his office later that morning Mr Tybalt read his morning paper with a mixture of wonder and excitement. Furthermore, Mr Tybalt had on his desk a copy of a personal directive to all yard managers, signed by Sir Rollo himself, which referred in particular to the refit of H.M.S. *Seahorse* and ended with the significant words 'the great resources of this great shipyard must be fully utilised to give this Sovereign's ship a fresh start in life.' Mr Tybalt read the concluding phrases over and over again, tasting the words on his tongue.

Mr Tybalt needed no prompting at all to discern once more the fine Greek hand of The Bodger. He reached for his telephone.

'Bodger . . .'

'Morning, Frank! All parts taking an even strain down there! It's not every day : . .'

'How did you do it?'

'*I* didn't do anything, Frank. It was Jerry. He said there was nothing to it. Sir Rollo may have his faults but even he could see what a nuclear contract would do for his yard. Jerry told me that after he'd dropped a few references as to the possibility of a nuclear *fleet,* and the possibility that *Maxwells* would get the contracts, he had Sir Rollo more or less eating out of his hand. Then Jerry said that of course any future work would depend naturally on the success of the present refit of H.M.S. *Seahorse. Naturally.* I must admit that was a refinement I suggested to Jerry. That settled Sir Rollo. Our next problem was Jerry. As you know, he didn't have a very good opinion of your yard so we had to do something about that. Ivy, Sir Rollo's secretary, well, she's got a heart of gold but she's no oil painting so we simply substituted Caroline while Jerry was around . . .'

'Good God!'

' . . . Sir Rollo always does himself well in the lunch line anyway, and he rather took to Jerry and pushed the boat out for him in a big way. Jerry eventually tottered off about four o'clock breathing brandy fumes and benevolence over everybody . . .'

'Good God!'

' . . . As for the engagement, that was too easy. If you were

Sir Rollo and you had the chance of a contract from the Navy which would put your yard on its feet again and then immediately afterwards a naval officer appears with your daughter and asks for her hand in marriage, what would you say?'

'Good God.'

'Not in so many words, you wouldn't. You'd say "Blessings on you, my children, for warming a father's tired old heart." Or words to that effect. I wasn't actually present, of course, but I imagine it would be something on those lines. Is that all you wanted to know, Frank?'

'Yes,' said Mr Tybalt, weakly. 'I suppose that's what I wanted to know.'

'Good . . .'

'I just can't help thinking that I slipped up in my education somewhere, Bodger. I was taught how to build ships and how to repair them. Nobody ever told me about all this behind-the-scenes stuff.'

'Why struggle to shift a bloody great weight when a word at the right time will get the bloke who put it there to shift it for you gladly?'

'I guess you're right, Bodger.'

Dagwood and Caroline decided to throw an engagement party almost immediately, in the Tithe Barn (although Caroline had a few misgivings about the number of girls present who would have private memories of the place). After some discussion about whom they should invite they decided to make a clean sweep and invite everybody. Caroline's invitations were easily given; she merely went through her address book. Dagwood's were more complicated. He had no address book so turned out his pockets and discovered telephone numbers written on scraps of paper, old theatre programmes, laundry and shopping lists. There were a couple scribbled in eye-shadow pencil inside his cigarette case and several more on his desk blotter.

When Ollie saw the list of guests he said: 'Where are you

planning to have you party, Dagwood?'

'In the Tithe Barn, of course.'

'By the size of that list I should say you ought to hire the Town Hall.'

Dagwood frowned. 'It does seem a lot, now you mention it.' Dagwood ran his finger down the list. 'A hundred and twenty three!'

'I'm surprised it's so few. You haven't been exactly hiding your light under a bushel while you've been here, have you? Are you going to invite them all?'

'I don't see why not. I doubt if they'll all be able to come.'

But in spite of the short notice, Dagwood and Caroline seemed to have picked a night when nobody had anything else planned. The ticks on the invitation lists multiplied. It looked as though the Tithe Barn was destined for a big night. 'Now you've invited all these people,' Ollie said, 'what are you going to give them to drink?'

There was only one place to take such a problem.

'You take my advice, love,' said Daphne, 'and don't mess about wi' *cocktails*. People like to know what they're drinking and besides, you'll spend the whole night mixing'em. You give them straight drinks and you won't go far wrong.'

Guv offered to supply spirits, minerals and a firkin of best bitter at wholesale prices and deliver them free of charge. Daphne offered to lend twelve dozen assorted glasses. Dagwood was so touched by their gesture that he invited them both to come to the party, after closing time.

'I'm sorry, love,' Daphne said, 'but we can't come. I know Guv don't like parties, for one thing. When you watch people drinking every day of your life you don't feel like doing it in your spare time.'

'How about you coming then, Daphne?'

'Ah, I'd *love* to come but it wouldn't be right. I'm a barmaid and it wouldn't be right for me to be seen at your party.'

'Daphne, what utter *nonsense!* You've got more right to

come to my party than anyone else in this town!'

'It's kind of you to say that and I know *you* wouldn't mind but there's folks who would. Never you mind. Guv and I'll drink a glass to you both here. Now love, stop chewing the fat, we've got work to do . . .'

The logistical arrangements for the party went very smoothly. Guv arrived in his van at five o'clock with the liquor and the firkin. Gotobed and Quickly, who had volunteered their services as barmen, helped Guv and Dagwood unload the stores. The main living-room in the Tithe Barn had been cleared of all furniture except the table, which was placed in front of the long orchard window. The firkin was set up and broached in the kitchen. The rest of the liquor and the glasses were laid out on the table and on the window-sill for Able Seaman Quickly to dispense – leaving Gotobed to act as tray-carrier and freelance agent provocateur. Dagwood and Caroline had considered providing food for the party but had decided that the arrangements would be too complicated. They settled for two capacious Victorian chamber pots, loaned by Molly, which Caroline filled to the brim, one with potato crisps and the other with peanuts. Music was provided by the guitarist from the 'Black Cat' and two of his friends who took their places behind Dagwood's bedroom rail, thus converting the bedroom into a minstrels' gallery. Everything was ready.

'Isn't this heaven?'

'Here we go!' exulted Dagwood, seizing Caroline by the waist and doing a makeshift polka round the room.

If the village had not already guessed that something unusual was happening at the Watsons' farm that evening, all doubts were dispelled by the cavalcade of motor cars which began to arrive from half past six onwards. They filled the farmyard first, then the lane, then the minor road at the end of the lane, and by seven o'clock were lining the main road for a hundred yards either side of the minor road junction. The small boys of the village, who seldom had the opportunity to spot strange number plates, had an enchanted evening, capturing a variety of motor cars, from Sir Rollo's Rolls, through Mr Tybalt's Riley, to the shipyard managers' small Austins and Sarah Judworth's bubble car.

Chubb was the first guest to arrive. He came on his bicycle which he parked outside the Tithe Barn front door and he arrived very early (while the musicians were experimentally picking out the first chords of 'La Malagueña' and Dagwood, Caroline and the two barmen were having one all round to fortify themselves). He brought with him half a dozen trout which Dagwood hurriedly hid under the bath where Sir Rollo (whose property Dagwood had no doubt they were) would be unlikely to see them.

Chubb asked for whisky, received his glass, and drained it in one swallow.

'Arrh,' he said, blowing out his cheeks. 'That's got the right sort o' taste, Mister Dagwood, thank ye.'

'Have another, Chubb.'

'I will that.'

Chubb took his second glass. 'Here's the best o'luck to ye both, Miss Caroline.'

'Thank you, Chubb, and the same to you,' said Caroline, who was well acquainted with her father's arch-poacher.

Chubb squinted at the diamond on Caroline's finger for which Dagwood had mortgaged two months' pay. He winked at Caroline. 'He get that out of a cracker, did he?'

'*Chubb!*'

Chubb cackled. 'If your young man had stayed with me for another five years I coulda taught him something. Give me a lad at the age o'ten, make him work ten hours a day for ten years and he could be a man o'leisure like me for the rest of his days.'

'I wish I could, Chubb. Excuse us a minute.'

The guests were beginning to flood through the front door. Mr Tybalt arrived, in his best drinking suit, with Maxine, in skin-tight black velvet. Behind them were Mr and Mrs

Swales and the other Admiralty Overseers and their wives, the Overseers looking less harassed than Dagwood was used to seeing them and their wives looking like the wives of Admiralty Overseers. Happy Day and Mrs Day followed, with the other shipyard managers and their wives, the shipyard managers looking less pessimistic than usual and their wives looking like the wives of shipyard managers. Then came a miniature cross-section of Oozemouth society – some family friends of Sir Rollo's who were mostly members of the Conservative Club; Sarah and Hilda Judworth with the point-to-point, Young Conservative, Young Farmer and Pony Club set; Vera, Barbara, Humphrey and a team from the 'Black Cat'; Drusilla, Stella and the 1st, 2nd and 3rd VIs from the tennis club; Ollie and Alice; The Hon. Mrs Julian Dewberry; the Reverend Godfrey and Mrs Potter; Admiral and Patricia MacGregor; Sir Rollo and Lady Hennessy-Gilbert; Bill and Molly Watson; and The Bodger and Julia. Fiona came with her newly-captured fiancé, a rather bemused young man called Robin who was reading history at Cambridge. Doris also came with her young man – an inoffensive-looking boy called Norman; plainly the officer-like qualities which could control the Inspection Department at the ball-bearing factory were not likely to be tested by Norman. The girls all clustered round Caroline to inspect her ring. The men commiserated with Dagwood.

'Cheers, Dagwood,' said Mr Tybalt. 'And many congratulations.'

'Thank you, sir.'

'Looking around me, I can see that you haven't been letting the grass grow under your feet while you've been here!'

'That splendid strike helped.'

'Yes, you looked as though you had mixed feelings about it when it ended! At least you haven't done what a lot of naval officers do when they're standing by ships up here. They get themselves some gloomy digs and sit gloomily in them every night and tell themselves what a horrible hole Oozemouth is. If you do that, of course it will be a horrible hole. But so would anywhere else.'

Maxine was looking about her with interest. 'So this is the famous Tithe Barn,' she said. 'I've heard a lot about it but I was never invited!'

Dagwood looked at Mr Tybalt. 'I could hardly do that,' he said.

Mr Tybalt laughed. 'It wouldn't have been your sort of evening, Maxie. From what I hear it was life in the raw. Raw meat, raw wine and lying on the sofa in the raw!'

Maxine looked wistful. Dagwood blushed. 'Not so loud, sir,' he said cautioningly. 'It's good-bye to all that now!'

Gotobed and Quickly were dispensing drinks like men possessed – working on the old sailing-ship principle of one hand for the ship and one hand for themselves, which they interpreted as meaning one drink for themselves for every drink dispensed. They had already reached a state of fine careless rapture and were making it their business to see that everyone else followed suit. The noise level rose. The musicians in the gallery began to accompany their own renderings with full-blooded shouts. Cigarette smoke swirled up towards the skylight. Ollie, on whom alcohol always had a dramatic effect, had to shout to make himself intelligible to Lady Hennessy-Gilbert.

'Have I told you the one about the Chief Stoker and the Yellow-and-Black Striped Bandit Kreit?'

'No!' shrieked Lady Hennessy-Gilbert. 'You haven't!'

It was a long story and several times during the telling Ollie was swept away by the crowd and had to continue the narrative by bellowing over a row of intervening heads but Lady Hennessy-Gilbert listened attentively and then screeched: 'Not bad! Have you heard the one about the Honeymoon Couple and the Parrot?'

'Which one do you mean?'

'*Listen!*'

Agatha, the Student of Life from the 'Black Cat,' had

Happy Day wedged in the angle of the bedroom stairs, Happy Day was looking unhappier than Dagwood had ever seen him.

'You're a perfect example of what I mean by the *New Tyrant*,' Agatha was saying. 'I can see the day coming when there will be a *blood-bath* in every shipyard in the country . . .'

Sid Burlap was also trapped in another corner, by the kitchen door. 'Of course,' boomed The Hon. Mrs Julian Dewberry, 'I introduced them. It was at the Forest point-to-point. It was love at first sight . . .'

Sid Burlap nodded wordlessly.

Cyril Swales had had four quick, Quickly-sized gins and was now wearing what his friends of his younger days would have called his Drinking Grin; it spread almost from ear to ear and made him look like a mandarin sated with good living. Furthermore, he was displaying more courage than Dagwood would ever have believed of him. Under the eye of Mrs Swales he was gradually isolating Barbara from the rest of the throng. Being a short man he was achieving his object by fitting his head under Barbara's splendid Byzantine bosom and rhythmically rising and falling on his toes. Barbara, who showed no surprise at this manoeuvre, was slowly being cut out of the crowd like a cow at a round-up.

Once Sir Rollo had recovered from the shock of seeing Chubb grinning demoniacally at him from the top of the stairs, he began to enjoy himself.

'You're the point-to-point fellow, aren't you?' he said to The Bodger. 'Never laughed so much in all my life! Privately.'

'I'm relieved to hear it, Sir Rollo,' The Bodger said, smoothly.

'Don't go making a habit of it, not at our point-to-point. We got a stiff letter from the National Hunt Committee and we were damned lucky not to be warned off, the whole lot of us!'

The Bodger made apologetic noises.

'You and your wife must come up and see us some time. Muriel and I will be glad to see you. Come to dinner some time, eh?'

'We shall be very pleased, Sir Rollo.'

'That fellow Leanover was telling me about you. Why don't you stay on in Oozemouth and take a job in the yard? We're always on the look-out for new talent.'

'I couldn't do that, Sir Rollo. The Navy's very much a full time job.'

'Well, resign your commission, man!'

'You just can't do that.'

'What, can't you just send in yer papers?' Sir Rollo looked perplexed.

'No, I'm afraid not.'

'What a bloody funny outfit the Navy must be, if a man can't retire when he wants to!'

Dagwood circulated diligently amongst the guests, followed closely by Gotobed who made sure that Dagwood's glass was never empty. No matter how quickly Dagwood drank, the level in his glass seemed never to falter. By nine o'clock Gotobed's handiwork was having its effect. From that point onwards Dagwood's memories of his engagement party became disjointed. He had a recollection of the Reverend Godfrey Potter and Admiral MacGregor wringing his hand and giving him messages to pass on to Admiral Submarines when he next saw him. He could remember wishing Humphrey, from the 'Black Cat,' the best of luck with Patricia MacGregor and Fulke Judworth the best of luck in the Derby. He could dimly recall Major O'Reilly singing 'The Sash Me Father Wore, it was old but it was beautiful' in the vernacular.

By ten o'clock Dagwood had achieved that state of intoxication where he was possessed by an urgent desire to be hospitable to the whole world; his heart overflowed with good wishes; he wanted to go out into the highways and by-ways and compel them to come in. Dagwood went out into the yard and came upon a small tableau; Bill and Molly Watson were watching Gotobed demonstrate how to get a bucket of clear water from the old well.

The next morning The Bodger was sitting in his office trying to concentrate upon his work when the telephone rang. It was Mr Tybalt.

'Frank, must you make so much noise with that telephone! That bell went straight through my head!'

Mr Tybalt sounded panic-stricken. 'Bodger,' he whispered, 'I've got a little man outside who says he's looking for Her Majesty's Dockyard, Oozemouth.'

'He must be a lunatic.'

'No, that's what I thought at first, but he's got an Admiralty letter addressed to the Admiralty Overseer, H.M. Dockyard, Oozemouth! It's all about that nuclear contract.'

'Tell him he's got his knickers twisted in a knot.'

'I have, but he insists. The letter looks genuine enough.'

'Wait a minute, Frank! H.M. Dockyard . . . H.M.D . . . Frank, have you ever thought what Harvey McNichol and Drummond's initials are?'

There was silence while Mr Tybalt chewed over the awful possibilities of The Bodger's suggestion 'It *can't* be!' he whispered, at last.

'Bet you it is! You remember we were all so staggered when *Seahorse* first came up here straight out of the blue? I bet I know what happened. Someone in the front office saw initials H.M.D. somewhere, thought there was a Royal Yard here and packed *Seahorse* off.'

'You mean that *Seahorse* coming here in the first place was all a mistake?'

'I shouldn't be surprised.'

'But that's *fantastic*, Bodger! That *can't* be right!'

'I don't know why you should act so surprised, Frank. You ought to know by now that this is exactly the way things *do* happen in this man's Navy!'